P9-CUK-898

Walk Like a Man

Walk Like a Man

Sue Swift

Five Star • Waterville, Maine

This novel is a work of fiction. Names, characters, places and incidents are either the product of the author's imagination, or, if real, used fictitiously.

First Edition
First Printing: March 2006

Published in 2006 in conjunction with Tekno Books and Ed Gorman.

Set in 11 pt. Plantin by Christina S. Huff.

Printed in the United States on permanent paper.

Library of Congress Cataloging-in-Publication Data

Swift, Sue, 1955–
Walk like a man / by Sue Swift.—1st ed.
p. cm.
ISBN 1-59414-434-6 (hc : alk. paper)
1. Women physical therapists—Fiction. 2. Quarterbacks (Football)—Fiction. 3. Medical personnel—Malpractice—Fiction. 4. Napa Valley (Calif.)—Fiction. I. Title.
PS3619.W546W35 2006
813′.6—dc22 2005029760

For
Blondie
(the original Jolly)
1992–2005

Acknowledgments

Many people helped in the writing and production of this book, and the author would like to acknowledge the help of Cheri Norman, Judy Myers, Sara Myers (no relation to Judy), Brenda Novak, Susan Grant, and especially Caroline Cummings. Alice Duncan, and John Helfers of Tekno Books have been marvelous to work with, and I thank them.

Chapter One

"Mr. Wellman, you're not concentrating."

Jim glared at his physical therapist. He was concentrating so hard the top of his head was gonna blow off. Didn't she get it?

His life was on the line. He had to walk again, because he'd lose everything if he couldn't. His legs had shattered eight months ago at the Pro Bowl in front of a TV audience of millions. His career as an NFL quarterback had shattered with them.

Jim searched for her nametag, but couldn't see it through the sweat dripping into his eyes during this first painful therapy session at the rehab center. He leaned against the parallel metal bars and rubbed his forehead dry with his wrist, then peered down at his therapist.

A small woman, his brunette taskmaster had a cute pointy chin and greenish eyes. Her nametag, pinned over her left breast, drew his glance; the breast, small but perky, spiked his hormones. "Miss, er, Marti, I'm trying very hard." His glance shifted to her ringless left hand.

"Staring at my hand won't help."

She'd caught him. Embarrassment made him hotter and sweatier. He couldn't help his habit. Whenever he met a pretty woman, he automatically looked at her left hand to find out if she was free. "Just checking for a ring." Concluding that Marti was available, he grinned at her and waited for her to smile back.

"I'm not available," she snapped. "Mr. Wellman, if you don't want to focus on your recovery, it's nothing to me."

Jim gaped.

She turned and pointed at his wheelchair. "You can sit there like a fat, useless blob for the rest of your days for all I care. In the meantime, I have other patients. Patients who care." Pivoting, she walked to the door, her steps decisive.

He recovered, managing a laugh. "Good try, but you're as transparent as glass. What happens now? Does Katrin pat me on the back and play the good cop?" He glanced at the other therapist, a pretty blonde with a big, square rock on her ring finger.

Marti returned and gave a little shrug. "Well, it was worth trying."

"Yes," Jim said. "Very entertaining."

"Now that the banter is over, can we get back to work? I want you to focus, Mr. Wellman. Focus on the muscles of your legs, how your feet feel on the floor."

Jim glowered at his sarcastic little slave driver, who glared back, not giving an inch. He swallowed his annoyance and focused, tensing then relaxing his leg muscles. Damn, it hurt! But it was a good hurt, the hurt of muscles on the mend. Jim knew and welcomed that ache. After eight months, it felt great to finally get out of the wheelchair. He looked at his therapist for guidance.

"Now, push your feet into the floor and stand up straight." Marti's voice rose. "Come on, I know you can do it!"

Jim hitched his pants and pushed, stubbornly willing his legs to hold his weight. Clutching the parallel bars, he hauled up his body, using the strength in his shoulders and arms. The Super Bowl ring on his right hand clattered against the metal bars. The clank cut through his harsh, raspy breaths.

He placed his feet onto the floor beneath his body. For two

exhilarating seconds his legs held firm. Joy shot through him. He pictured himself running down the field, escaping a horde of linebackers and passing for a touchdown. Then his ankles buckled. His sweaty hands slipped off the bars, and he collapsed toward the floor.

Marti and Katrin grabbed Jim on his way down, breaking his fall. "Be careful," Katrin said, as the two therapists guided him down to the mat. "Let's not get hurt."

Jim sat limply, shoulders bowed, letting his head drop into his palms. *Thirty years old, and my life's in the toilet.* He rubbed his damp face as he bit back a string of pungent curses.

"Let's try just the one leg," Marti said. "Mr. Wellman, there's nothing wrong with your left leg that a little exercise won't cure. Your file says that ankle healed months ago. It's the right that's giving us problems. Katrin, let's get him up again. Tommy, help us out."

A male attendant came forward to assist. Jim gritted his teeth against the ache as the trio helped him get onto his feet. Sweating, he leaned against one end of the therapy bars.

"Katrin, let him go. Hold on now, Mr. Wellman." Marti backed away to the other end of the bars. Her hazel-green eyes narrowed, and her little chin reminded him of a feral cat. She was as focused as any feline on the hunt.

"Come on, come to me, Mr. Wellman." Marti raised a clenched fist. "Come on, I know you can do it!"

Held by her compelling gaze, Jim found himself responding to her intensity. A sudden superstition came over him: this was the moment where it all had to happen. He'd walk now . . . or never.

Tension thickened the air. Sucking in a deep breath, he went for it.

Miraculously, his left leg held when he pushed down hard, grabbing onto the parallel therapy bars with both hands. He clenched his jaw and took a couple of quivery, hesitant hops toward Marti.

Katrin and Tommy burst into applause. Sighing with relief, Jim leaned against the parallel bars as Marti slipped a supporting arm around him.

"Yes! Excellent! Excellent job!" she cried. "Okay, that's all for right now. Good work." She smiled up at him. Again he noticed the sharp little chin, but ignored her catlike aura as Tommy pushed out Jim's wheelchair. "Not that," his therapist said. "Get a walker. No more chair."

Katrin turned, raising her eyebrows.

"He's too dependent," Marti said. "The wheelchair is the reason he can't bear his own weight anymore. He should have been out of that chair as soon as the left ankle healed. Someone with Mr. Wellman's excellent physique should have made far more progress by now." She loosened her right arm from around his waist to give him an impersonal pat on the shoulder.

Jim slid his left arm around her so he wouldn't fall, keeping a steadying grip on the parallel bars with his right. He managed to keep a grip on his resentment as well, though he didn't like her condescending little pat. He wouldn't let this woman treat him like a child.

"That's not his doctor's orders," Katrin pointed out.

Marti folded her arms across her chest. The frown that creased her mouth didn't look good with the chin. "I'll talk to the doctor, but in my professional opinion, the wheelchair is contraindicated."

Jim turned and lifted her chin so she'd have to look him full in the face. He jutted his head down toward her. "I'm sorry, but I won't use a walker."

"Excuse me?" Marti's face was less than four inches from his.

Keeping his arm around her shoulders, he fingered her chin with a practiced hand. A slight tremor ran through his therapist's slim body.

"I won't use a walker." Jim spoke gently into her right ear. "It'll make me feel like a little ol' lady." He wasn't going to use a walker until he was eighty—if then. He and his teammates had plenty of experience with injuries, and he'd never seen an athlete with a walker. He'd be damned if he'd be the first. "And please don't talk about me as though I'm not here."

Marti jerked away. "Mr. Wellman, the next step after the wheelchair is a walker. It has nothing to do with your age or your, er, manhood. It's standard therapeutic practice." She took his arm off her shoulder and placed it on the parallel bars. "Didn't the wheelchair make you feel old?"

"I don't mean to be a problem, Miss, um, Marti, but I won't use a walker." Jim stood his ground. He frowned at the pesky little female, then remembered something his mother had told him when he was a small boy. *You'll catch more flies with honey than with vinegar, James.* Fine, he'd try suave and smooth. He'd been pushed, pulled, prodded, and poked for months at the hospital, and resolved that life would be different at the rehab center.

He let his mouth relax into a smile, hoping for the usual feminine response to the good ol' Wellman charm. This time, smarty Miss Marti's skin flushed, and she ran her hand through her hair again. When she narrowed the kitty-cat eyes, he turned up the wattage of his grin. Capping his teeth had been a great investment. Not only did he make millions from endorsements, but his starch-stiff therapist was melting like the crushed ice in a margarita.

"Marti?" Katrin prodded.

Marti paused, fixing him with an impartial, analytical

stare. Jim clenched his jaw, squelching his impatience and temper.

She tapped her nails against the therapy bars. "Okay, Mr. Wellman. Try crutches, then. But in my experience, the walker is indicated." She swept out, her white Reeboks squeaking against the linoleum floor.

Jim looked after her. "In her experience? What can that little girl know?"

Katrin went to a cupboard to retrieve a pair of crutches. "There's very little Marti Solis doesn't know about the human body. She's gotten people more hurt than you up and walking. Let's see if these are the right size." She handed him the crutches.

Jim slipped the crutches under his armpits, then struggled to haul himself along. Whipping out a towel, Tommy wiped Jim down while he leaned on his left foot, which again bore his weight. The sore muscles throbbed, but not with the jabbing pain Jim knew meant injury. The good hurt, again. "Hmm," he murmured. "Maybe that girl does know what she's doing."

Uh-oh. A problem patient. And what a problem!

The news that superstar quarterback Jim Wellman was coming to Shady Glen Rehabilitation Center had shot through the staff and patients like a tightly spiraled pass. Every sports fan, including Marti, knew about Wellman's record with the Capitol City Cougars as well as his bad-boy reputation off the field. But watching him win two Super Bowls hadn't prepared Marti for hands-on contact with this superb male animal. Even disabled, Jim Wellman commanded attention.

Radiating pheromones and testosterone, her famous patient stood over six feet tall, towering over her five-foot-four.

Despite his current problems, he moved with an athlete's power and grace, a dark panther prowling the sunny therapy room. His vivid blue eyes, fringed by sooty lashes, twinkled in a very disconcerting manner when he smiled.

Marti didn't want to notice his eyes, and she didn't want to like Jim Wellman. She didn't want to remember his muscles as they flexed and released, rock-hard under her guiding hand. She refused to let her head be turned by his celebrity status or amazing good looks. It wouldn't be fair to her other patients. She'd successfully detached herself until Jim made his outrageous demand for crutches. Then, she'd been forced to see Jim as a man, with needs and feelings . . . exactly what she didn't want to see.

The sports world considered Wellman second only to the great Joe Montana in terms of raw quarterbacking talent. Unfortunately, Wellman was also the patient from hell, an arrogant, argumentative jerk. *He thinks he's one tough dude. Well, I can be just as tough!*

She strode along a light-filled, paneled hall before tapping on the open office door of Dr. Frances Murdoch, director of the center. "Dr. Fran?"

Dr. Murdoch, a white-coated, white-haired woman in her sixties, turned from the window to wave Marti in. The big picture window held a view of the lavishly landscaped entrance of Shady Glen, and Marti could see the gardeners outside as they replaced a row of faded pansies. Their flower faces danced in the mild breeze blowing off the Napa Hills, golden with the dried grasses of autumn.

Dr. Fran sat in her armchair, gesturing for Marti to sit on the patterned couch. Nervous, she perched on its edge.

"Ma'am, is it your orders that James Wellman still use his wheelchair?" The situation made Marti uneasy. The convalescence of the star football player could bring the light of media attention to flash on Shady Glen. Worse, any hitches in his recovery would be attributed by Dr. Murdoch, an intense perfectionist, to Marti's care.

Dr. Fran shook her head. "I have not examined Mr. Wellman yet, since he was admitted late yesterday. Dr. Conkling of the Cougars recommended the wheelchair until such time as the left ankle is completely healed."

"That time is long past," Marti said. "We can hardly get him upright because the muscles in both legs have atrophied. He's requesting crutches and has refused a walker."

Dr. Fran pursed her lips. "Why?"

"He said it made him feel like an old lady." The statement tickled Marti's sense of irony, considering the man's reputation. And she certainly hadn't responded to his electric touch as though he were someone's grandma.

"That's not unusual for these macho fellows. What is your opinion?"

"I'm not sure. Therapeutically, the next appropriate step is a walker. To be fair, this particular individual is in excellent physical condition, except for the involved areas." Marti hesitated.

"What is it, Martina?"

"There's something else you should know about Mr. Wellman. Er, do you follow pro football?"

"No, of course not." Dr. Fran seemed amused by the suggestion.

"Then you're not familiar with this patient's history."

"I've worked with several football players. I'm aware that they sustain numerous injuries throughout their careers."

"It's worse than that. Mr. Wellman broke his arm two seasons ago. His ulna, I believe. He apparently felt the treatment plan proposed by his physician was too slow, so he went to his garage one morning before a game and took his cast off with a hacksaw."

"What was the result?"

Marti swallowed. "He threw three touchdown passes that day."

"I see. So his faith in medical opinion may be, shall we say, challenged?"

"Yes. Frankly, Doctor, I expect Mr. Wellman to be difficult to work with, very impatient. On the other hand, I know he was cleared for a full regimen of physical therapy by his primary care physician, but you should examine him, at least for liability purposes."

Fran rose. "I'll see Mr. Wellman right away. Where is he?"

The trip from the therapy room to his private suite was exquisite agony for Jim. Tommy helped him every step and hop of the way, but Jim concluded the muscles of both legs had been underutilized for too long. With resentment, he remembered that he'd told the staff of the hospital that he'd wanted to exercise, but his protests had been ignored.

Tense with pain, he tried to relax on his bed as Tommy prepared his whirlpool bath. At least the facilities here are nice, he thought grudgingly. The suite featured a king-sized, fully adjustable bed, not a skimpy hospital bed. Its leaf-patterned comforter matched the chair pads and curtains.

He heard a tap on the door just before a white-coated lady entered the room followed by Marti Solis, the brunette cutie, who pushed a walker into the room. Sitting up, he frowned.

"I'm Doctor Frances Murdoch, the director of Shady Glen. How are you feeling today, Mr. Wellman?"

He steeled himself for yet another medical exam. "I'm all right. Will I still feel all right after you've finished?"

The grandmotherly doctor smiled. "Hopefully you'll be

better than just all right after we're done. I know you've been examined recently, but I'd like to take a look at your legs again. Could you slip off your pants and lie down?"

He hid his smirk. Many women had asked him to get horizontal but never in such a clinical manner. Somehow, the uptight doctor and her equally repressed cohort tickled his funny bone. He cooperated, wondering what Dr. Murdoch and Marti Solis would make of his underclothing.

"What's this?" the doctor asked.

Jim looked in the direction of her pointing finger and grinned. "Those are my lucky boxers, ma'am. They're probably why I could walk today."

"Minnie Mouse underwear?" Disbelief dripped off Marti's sarcastic tone of voice.

"Wore them during two Super Bowls. Won both times."

Marti raised her brows. "What happened at the Pro Bowl?"

Jim hitched himself up onto his elbows. "Proves my point. I accidentally left them at home. That was when I broke my legs."

"Are all football players superstitious?" Dr. Murdoch asked.

He shrugged. "Some are. My best friend won't play without tying a string to his baby finger. Claims it reminds him to tuck the ball while running."

The women exchanged glances weighted with skepticism. Smarty Marti even rolled her eyes.

"If you say so," the doctor said. "I won't take issue with your underwear. Let's check out your range of motion in these gams, Mr. Wellman." She bent his legs this way and that, testing his limbs and joints. "Pretty good. Have you been stretching?"

"As much as anyone will let me."

"Good. Keep doing it. This may hurt a little—" Dr. Murdoch pressed the surgical scars on his right thigh at the site of the break in the femur. He stiffened, expecting pain, but the doctor's experienced touch didn't hurt.

"Ms. Solis is right," she told him. "You should not have been in the wheelchair so long. Now let's check some basics." Lifting his T-shirt, the doctor slapped her stethoscope onto his chest.

Jim grimaced. He'd never met a doctor who didn't seem to keep the stethoscope in the deep freeze. Probably some sort of unwritten rule.

"Sounds like you're alive." The doctor's kindness contrasted with her torture implement. "I understand you resist using a walker."

"That's right, ma'am." He smiled to cover his irritation.

"I recommend a walker, Mr. Wellman." She gestured, and Marti brought one forward.

Jim sat up on his bed and examined the apparatus. The tubular structure, shaped like an open-sided cube, had wheels on two prongs and rubber-tipped ends on the other two legs. Using only one hand, he picked up the flimsy object by one of its legs and shook it. It rattled. He leaned forward, resting his full weight on the walker's wheeled legs.

The walker slipped out from under him, skidding several feet. He went sprawling.

The women gasped as he rolled out from the fall. He bet his doctor didn't know that his training as an athlete included learning how to fall without injury.

He raised an innocent gaze to Dr. Murdoch, wondering if she'd buy the act. "I just don't think the walker will work out, ma'am," he said as Tommy helped him back onto the bed.

The doctor's face did not alter, except for a slightly lifted eyebrow. "You are setting yourself up for more difficulties and discomfort."

"I play football, ma'am. I'm no stranger to pain. Pain and I are old buddies."

"Very well. Please be advised we cannot take responsibility for any setback you may experience due to your lack of compliance with our therapeutic recommendations. I will note your refusal in your chart."

Dr. Murdoch pulled his chart from its slot and flipped through it. "Where are all his x-rays?" she murmured. Jim watched as she found two films and held them up to the light, inspecting them. Marti peeked over her shoulder. After a few moments, the doctor put them back, then looked through the file some more. "Sunset Community," she said to Marti, raising her eyebrows. She pulled out a pen to scrawl notes.

"What does that mean?" Jim wanted to know.

"It's nothing for you to worry about, Mr. Wellman. We'll take care of you here. Marti, please arrange for Mr. Wellman to be transported to Napa Valley Hospital tomorrow for a full set of x-rays as well as blood work. Good day, Mr. Wellman." Lips pursed, Dr. Murdoch left the room.

"Tommy, put him into the whirlpool, give him a nap, then lunch and a short walk. He'll get more therapy tomorrow when he comes back from the hospital." Marti whirled out, a tiny, white-garbed hurricane.

"Now, how come that girl still talks about me like I'm not here?" Addressing Tommy, Jim slipped off his lucky boxers.

"Aw, don't be hard on Marti. She really cares about her patients, and she'll getcha outta here in no time. Let's get that T-shirt off—"

"If she cared, she'd talk *to* me, not about me." Jim knew he sounded like a whiny little kid, but he couldn't help himself. He still ached from the difficult morning therapy session.

Tommy eased Jim's naked body into the whirlpool bath in one corner of the private suite. The orderly began massaging Jim's neck and shoulders.

He looked down at himself. He wasn't conceited, but his body, despite numerous scars from old football injuries, had garnered its share of female attention over the years. Heck, he'd been only thirteen when his first girlfriend took him behind the bleachers to coach him on catching a forward pass. How did Smarty Marti Solis put it? *My excellent physique.* He winced. Marti's backhanded compliment, delivered with utter clinical detachment, made him feel like a microbe, not a man.

She doesn't look so bad herself, he thought. Besides, he liked her determination. She'd hauled him out of that wheelchair and shoved him along Recovery Road at her first opportunity. He wondered if she was as aggressive in the sack, and if he'd ever find out. Grinning to himself, he recalled her spontaneous response to his touch.

Last night, he'd read about her impressive qualifications in the Shady Glen promotional literature left on his bedside table. *Martina (Marti) Solis, M.P.T., magna cum laude, University of California at San Francisco; Head of Occupational and Physical Therapy.* She looked young for such a responsible position, but if she had an advanced degree, she'd be in her middle or late twenties. Just right.

The photograph in the pamphlet didn't do her justice. He remembered her from the therapy session, viewed through a haze of sweat and pain: dark hair, hazel-green eyes, high cheekbones, and—*oh yeah!*—a full, sexy mouth. Lips the devil had designed for sweet, sweet sins. Small, with a trim body and very strong hands. And that chin, of course.

As Tommy rubbed him down, Jim relaxed in the bath and started thinking about women. He hadn't had a woman since the night before two huge linebackers made a quarterback sandwich out of him at the Pro Bowl. Glenda had occasionally visited when he was at Sunset Community Hospital, but she hadn't phoned since he'd arrived at Shady Glen. He wondered when he'd see her again, if the heat between them survived their eight-month celibacy.

His eight-month celibacy, he warned himself. He'd avoided the subject of sexual monogamy in his conversations with Glenda since his injury. But in his heart, he knew the answer. Hotshot Glenda Colter, sports reporter for the *Capitol City Star*, wouldn't let moss grow on her rolling stone—or any other body part.

A jabbing pain in his right trapezius jolted him out of his thoughts. "Easy now, buddy," Jim said to Tommy. "That's flesh there, and it hurts."

"Feels solid as a rock. You bothered?"

"Yeah, well, I'm a little tense. I haven't gotten any satisfaction lately, if you know what I mean."

Tommy grinned. "You ain't likely to get much around Shady Glen, either. The ladies here are mostly married or involved with someone. Most of the patients are over seventy years old."

"What about that pretty little Marti, the one who acts like I'm not really here?"

"Marti? I thought you didn't like her."

"She's babe-licious. Besides, Katrin said, 'Ms. Solis knows all about the human body.' " Jim squeaked a little, in a mocking imitation of the blonde therapist.

"Marti's not the one-night-stand type. Believe me, I've tried, and so have a lot of the patients. There was this stunt man," Tommy continued as he massaged Jim, "good-lookin' guy, and he was really hot for her. After he got out of his body cast, he took her to all the nice restaurants, Auberge du

Soleil, Mustard's, everywhere. When he left, she wouldn't even kiss him goodbye."

She could be a challenge. Jim liked challenges. "She frigid?" He fought a yawn as his muscles relaxed.

"I dunno. Maybe she just never found the right guy, or got hurt, or somethin'. Who knows?"

Tommy guided Jim out of the whirlpool, over to an easy chair, and toweled him down before slipping him into a green robe and helping him into bed.

"Hey, whatcha doin'?" Jim demanded, woozy. "It's only eleven o'clock."

"You heard what your girlfriend said. Naptime before lunch."

Jim settled back into the pillows. "She's not my girlfriend." Damn.

Tom laughed. "Sweet dreams, lover boy."

Marti rubbed her lower back as she pushed her tray along the line in the staff cafeteria. Hauling around that quarterback hadn't improved the nagging pain near her second lumbar vertebra. Jim Wellman was big, a giant compared to her other patients, and he made her feel like a dwarf. A mischievous part of her libido wondered if all of his body parts were proportional.

She paid the cashier for her lunch, then took her avocado sandwich and mug of herb tea over to a Formica table. Through a nearby window, she could see part of Shady Glen's hundred acres of parkland. As she ate, she watched Jim Wellman and an attendant struggling along a slate footpath. Although the two were a distance away, she still recognized Jim by his physique. *Beautiful shoulders and terrific pecs. I wonder how his legs look when he's healthy*. She firmly turned her mind back to an appropriate direction.

Katrin, a mug of coffee in her hand, joined Marti at the window. "Pretty good-lookin' dude."

"He may be gorgeous, but he's as arrogant as they come."

"You don't know the half of it, boss. He called you a 'little girl.' "

"Excuse me?"

"I know you hate being teased about your height—or lack of it," Katrin said. "But our star patient seems to want to make an issue of petite little Marti ordering him around."

Marti groaned. "Maybe I should wear platform sneakers."

"Why not? Dr. Fran might decide they look good with our whites." Katrin fingered the sleeve of her white scrubs, compulsory garb for employees at Shady Glen.

"He's manipulative, too. Did you see the way he smiled at me while he argued about the walker?" Marti sipped her tea.

"Yeah. Mr. Macho Jockstrap Superstar is probably used to getting everything he wants with that killer smile and those bedroom eyes." She grinned at Marti. "Even you gave in to him."

"I gave in to his stubbornness, not his smile. You can lead a horse to water, but you can't make him think."

Katrin laughed. "I heard about his act with the walker."

"Yeah, he made it pretty clear that he thinks he's in charge. I hope his attitude doesn't become a problem around here." She glanced at Katrin, trying to gauge the other therapist's response. Marti didn't want patients, however attractive, challenging her therapy plan or labeling her a "little girl" to her assistants.

"Not for me. I'm married to a trucker, remember? I'm used to sexist jerks."

"What about Tommy?"

"What about him? Look, you're the best, Marti, and

Tommy knows that. No one else could have gotten Wellman out of that chair so fast. We told him, too."

"Thanks for the vote of confidence. But we ought to keep in mind that often these macho types wear their attitude like a shield. Underneath, I bet he's very scared."

"Yeah, he's losing his career. For these guys, it's a little like dying."

Marti sighed, knowing that she had a long journey to walk with Wellman. She looked at her watch. "Already three? No wonder I'm so tired." She stretched her arms above her head and stood. "I guess I'll do rounds and head home."

Done for the week, Marti zipped down a hall, heading for her car. Rounding a corner, she went flying as she tripped on a patient's crutch. A strong hand shot out of nowhere and jerked her upright.

Damn. It had to be Wellman, of course, returning from his walk with Tommy. "Gracious!" she gasped. "Thank you, Mr. Wellman. That would have been a nasty fall." Tugging free from his grasp, she bent over to rub her instep. Her foot had collided painfully with Jim's crutch.

A loud wolf whistle startled her. Jolted, she realized her position displayed her derriere to the watching males. Her temper shot into the stratosphere.

"Excuse me?" Marti stood up and whirled. She fixed Tommy, then Jim, with the nastiest glare she could. "Did either of you have something to say?"

"Not me, boss." Tommy dropped back a step, waving his hands. He looked as though he wanted to disappear into the linoleum.

Wellman, leaning on his crutches, looked her up and down. *Hasn't he seen enough of me yet?* Any shred of sympathy she might have had for his plight vanished like mist in the sunshine of his appreciative grin.

He seemed unaffected by her glower, so she changed tactics, giving him a big smile. "I'll take care of you on Monday, Mr. Wellman."

"Is that a promise?"

"Oh, yes," she said sweetly. "I'm sure we'll have lots of fun in therapy. Have a nice weekend, and make sure you get lots of rest. You'll need it!"

His hearty laugh pursued her all the way to the exit doors of Shady Glen.

Chapter Two

Marti loved her little cottage. She'd put several interior lights on a timer, so when she came home her house looked warm and welcoming in the cool autumn evening. Her golden retriever, Jolly, greeted her at the gate with joyful barks.

"Hey, big fella, how you doin'?" Marti stooped for a tennis ball, then threw it for the big yellow dog, who romped after it. His feathery golden tail waved as he jumped to catch it. "We're going to Dad's place tomorrow, big boy. You get to play with Lucy and Ethel."

The next morning, Marti loaded her gear and her dog into her Honda hatchback and set off for Watsonville. She had an easy drive that Saturday morning, arriving in time for lunch with her family.

She viewed her father's cottage with mixed feelings of pride and sorrow. Marti and her brother had bought the little white house for their parents several years before. But she couldn't forget that her mother, Gracia, had died in that house just two years past. Her loss left a jagged rip in Marti's heart.

When she opened her car door, Jolly climbed over her and burst out of the Honda, then leaped over the neat white picket fence. Lucy and Ethel, her father's corgis, converged on Jolly from opposite ends of the tidy front yard. The dogs briefly interrupted their rough play to greet Marti as she went to the door of the house by more conventional means.

"Martina, *mi corazón.*" Rico hugged his daughter. He pulled her into his home, fragrant with the aromas of spice cake and Chile Colorado.

She peeked into the door of Rico's small den as he urged her down the hall into the living room. The den was full of broken televisions, radios, and toaster-ovens. "Glad to see business is good, Dad."

"Never better. Don't worry about me." Rico had been able to leave work in the strawberry fields—and the pesticides that had killed Gracia—due to his small appliance repair business. "But come, see the *niñitas.*"

Oozing pride, Grandpa Rico went to the playpen set up temporarily in the middle of the living room. He lifted one of his twin granddaughters out. "Here is Annalisa . . . or is she Emilia?"

Helene, their mother, frowned. "Truth to tell, I'm not sure. Steve!" she yelled for Marti's brother. "Which one is this?"

Marti and her father exchanged glances as Steve came in from the kitchen to identify his daughters. Helene was noisier than the restrained Solis clan.

"Jeez, Helene, can't you tell yet? It's been four months," Steve complained. Steve, tall and dark, wore khakis, a polo shirt, and a smile for his sister.

"They said at the hospital that parents frequently can't tell identicals apart for up to six months," Helene said, sounding defensive. "Check her fingernails." Annalisa sported dabs of red polish while Emilia hated having her nails tended.

"She's chipped a lot of it off." Steve took the wriggling baby from Rico. "Here, Marti, this one's Emmy."

Marti took Emilia from her brother and nuzzled her niece's neck, delighting in the scent of clean baby. She looked up to catch Rico's smirk. "Stop it, Dad."

"What? Are you saying I shouldn't wish you the happiness your brother and Helene have with these little beauties?" Rico leaned into the playpen to lift out Annalisa. The baby, interrupted in her play with a rattle, squalled. Her grandfather expertly checked her diaper. He handed her to Helene. "Here, she's wet."

Rolling her eyes, Helene grabbed the pink printed diaper bag with her free hand, then headed out to change the squirming, screeching baby. Steve sat on the couch beside Marti.

She cuddled Emilia in her lap. "Helene seems to be doing a great job. For a new mother, she's really calm."

"She's the second of four, and her youngest sister was born seven years after her," Steve said. "She did a lot of babysitting, so she's used to the routine. How 'bout you? How are all of your babies?"

Marti laughed. "Same as always. I get 'em up and moving without pain, and then they fly away from the nest."

"I read that Jim Wellman was transferred to Shady Glen."

She tried not to frown, but she disliked discussing her work during her free time. On top of that, she didn't want to think about the patient from hell.

"He's a member of Stone Cliff," Steve continued. "He's single, and he's a really nice guy, Marti." Marti's brother was head groundskeeper at Stone Cliff, an exclusive golf resort.

"He's an arrogant, argumentative jerk." She stopped herself before she behaved even more unprofessionally. "Look, I can't talk about patients, and I can't get involved with any of them on a personal level. I'd lose my job."

"You get yourself a rich football player, you won't need a job." Rico settled himself into his armchair.

"But it's a different world," Helene chimed in, returning

with Annalisa. She handed the freshly diapered baby to Rico. "Big-time athletes aren't like you and Steve. Sports stars have hundreds of groupies. You think that's best for Marti?"

"Now look at what you've started," Marti admonished her brother. She handed Emilia to him and headed out of the room.

"Start what? All I said was that he's a nice guy. And he's not arrogant and argumentative!" Steve called after her.

Marti went into the kitchen and got herself a glass of water from the sink. "Is so," she muttered, staring out the window. Jolly and Ethel were at opposite ends of a rope toy, playing tug-of-war. Lucy barked at them.

Jolly and Ethel. Steve and Helene. Rico's marriage to Gracia had lasted over thirty years. Even Annalisa had Emilia. Marti felt like Lucy—the third wheel, outside looking in at everyone else's happiness.

Unbidden, an image of Jim Wellman's chiseled, handsome face and muscular torso came to mind. He'd worn a masculine, musky scent at the therapy session. Other males let themselves slip during rehab. One of them, a stunt man, had wooed her frantically. He'd never understood that his chewed fingernails and greasy hair had been a complete turn-off.

Her mind wandered. *What would it be like with Jim?* She remembered his intense blue eyes, wide shoulders, and slim hips. She imagined his hard body pressed against her as he pulled her into his arms to kiss her. His firm lips nipped sensually at her mouth, and she opened to his unspoken demand.

Rico came into the kitchen. His presence squelched the heat sweeping through her body at the mere thought of kissing Jim Wellman.

"We don't want to pressure you, *mi corazón*." Her father

slipped an arm around her. "But you are twenty-eight, time to have your first baby safely."

"Oh, Dad," Marti said, exasperated. "These days, women can have their first baby after age forty, and they're okay. There's no rush. You wouldn't want me to marry the wrong man, would you?"

"No. Oh, no. All my friends, they tell me that their kids have been divorced two, sometimes three times. And the babies get all messed up. That would be terrible."

"Besides, I really like my job. I feel as though I'm finally where I want to be in my life. The right work, the right home, in the right place. Everything's perfect. Why can't I just enjoy living?"

"But how about the right man, Marti?" her father asked. "Don't you think it's time to get over the past?"

Flinching, she pulled away as Rico jabbed a sore spot in her psyche. "I am over it, Dad, if you're referring to that doctor I dated in Berkeley. I will admit that I'm kinda cautious."

"You're not just cautious, you're gun-shy. When did you last go out on a date?"

"It's been a while. To be honest, no one's asked." She tried not to show how much that hurt.

"Pshaw. You don't encourage. Marti, you're a lovely young woman. Before that doctor, you had men lining up for you. I remember when you were a teenager. The phone never stopped ringing.

"Get over it, *chica,*" he continued. "Don't let that creep stunt you for life." He shook her gently by the shoulders, then, unexpectedly, hugged her.

She hugged back, touched by his concern.

"Now, I'm going to drop the subject for the rest of the weekend. But I want you to think about this, okay?"

* * * * *

After a fun, relaxing weekend, Marti entered Jim Wellman's room Monday morning anticipating a productive week. She liked to be aware of every aspect of her patients' lives while they were in her care, so she decided to check his early morning routine. Recalling her steamy daydream about him, she bucked herself up inside for an encounter with her maddening patient. She reminded herself that his big smile came attached to a big ego, one that seemed to demand female attention, but she wasn't going to play silly games with Jim Wellman or any other patient.

She interrupted his breakfast in bed, a forkful of steak poised halfway to its destination. "Hmm! What's this?" she asked. "Steak and eggs is an awfully heavy breakfast for someone who spends most of his time in the sack."

"Listen, sweetheart, I've been working while you've been partying. That sadist who worked me out over the weekend was even meaner than you." He placed the bite in his mouth.

"Oh, Eileen's all right. She's not hard on the patients." She pulled out his chart. "She thinks you're doing well, but I still don't know about steak and eggs."

He chewed and swallowed, then wiped his lips with the linen napkin. Glaring at her, he put down his cutlery with a clatter. "Hey, I won't be pushed around by a bitty little thing like you. I have few pleasures here. People order me around all the time. They pull, poke, and prod at me. I don't get to do anything fun. I can't walk, jog, or run. I can't throw a football. There's no sex."

At the mere mention of sex, her daydream image of kissing him leaped into her mind. Heat flooded her cheeks. She damned her thin skin, well aware that her face could be read as easily as a first grader's primer.

She tried to avoid staring at his mobile lips as he spoke. "In short, the only thing I do here that I like is to eat what I want. Steak and eggs is what I want, and that's what I'll eat. Now, if you wanted to make yourself truly useful, you would get me some coffee, with cream and sugar. Lots of cream and sugar."

She jerked herself out of her erotic fantasy of nibbling his lower lip. "Dream on, Mr. Wellman. I'm putting you on a low fat diet, starting this second." She softened her tone. "But I can get you some coffee."

I'm not a waitress! Why am I being so nice to the ungrateful wretch? Then she recalled that a successful rehabilitation of Jim Wellman could have far-reaching consequences for her career and for Shady Glen. Failure could have equal, but negative, results.

Swallowing her pride and her desire, she fetched coffee for the quarterback from hell.

Naked, Jim relaxed in the whirlpool bath, and became aware Marti had reentered the room when she put a ceramic mug into his hand. He couldn't tell if she had tried to check out his bod, but bubbles obscured anything interesting below his waist.

He listened to Marti and Tommy chatter over the gentle swish of the jets. So, pretty little Marti had gone "home" for the weekend, which meant that Tommy's gossip about her single state was probably true.

He regretted his earlier accusation of partying, but how could he make amends for his churlish behavior? He asked, "How's your foot today? That was a pretty hard bump your ankle took."

"It's fine, thank you." She sounded stiff and starchy. Damn. He must have been a real jerk.

He tried again. "Thanks for the coffee." He sniffed the steam rising from the mug. "Great aroma. Is it French roast?"

"I'm glad you like it. It's decaf, with fake sugar and cream."

Jim sipped judiciously. "Best fake I've ever tasted."

"Except for maybe your last girlfriend?" Tommy joked.

Jim smiled. "It's true that Glenda's hair color comes from a bottle. But be nice if she comes to see me."

"Your girlfriend didn't visit this weekend?" Marti asked. "No wonder you're grouchy."

"I'm not grouchy," Jim snapped. "Just . . . unfulfilled." He wondered if he dared hint that his lovely therapist could dramatically change his lack of fulfillment. He still searched for something clever and suave to say when the telephone rang, scattering the poetic, witty lines in his head.

She answered it. "It's Glenda Colter." She handed Jim the portable phone, then turned to Tommy, visibly retreating behind her professional manner. Delighted to see the signs of jealousy, Jim grinned at his therapist as she continued speaking to the orderly. "Have him in therapy in fifteen minutes. I don't want him getting too relaxed in that bath."

"Hey, Glenda, baby," Jim said into the phone, eyeing Marti, who walked over to the window. She pulled a couple of x-rays from his chart and held them up to the sunlight.

"Jim, you fox. What's up?" Glenda asked.

"Me, baby. Miss you." Was Marti reading the films or just pretending?

"Hey, me too. I'm passing by Napa on the way to the east bay. I thought I'd stop to see ya."

"Great!" Jim said. "I'll see if they'll let me out of this place. Maybe we can get some dinner."

"No can do, big boy. I have to cover tonight's game in Oakland. I can be in Napa for lunch."

"That sounds great. I don't know if I can leave, but you can share the low fat surprise lunch my therapist has arranged." He raised his eyebrows at Marti, who glared back, eyes glittering like shards of greenish glass.

"You eating healthy? This therapist must have more influence than the team doc."

"Yeah, she's pretty heavy. I've already made more progress in four days here than in eight months in that hospital." He winked at Marti and smugly watched her blush. She shoved the x-rays back into the chart, then stalked out of the room.

"Say, can I print that?"

"No." Sometimes Glenda's single-mindedness irritated Jim. "I don't want to get sued by the hospital. Give it a rest."

"Okay, don't get all huffy. See ya soon!"

Glenda hung up and Jim leaned back into the whirlpool bath, feeling rotten. Had he offended both Glenda and Marti before nine-thirty in the morning? Maybe I am whiny, he thought. But who wouldn't be? I hurt all over and neither of those girls treats me like a man.

Glenda was probably looking for a story, and Smarty Marti was a repressed little witch with the coldest bedside manner he'd ever seen. He was only a meal ticket for both women.

Marti had learned through bitter experience that the role of "other woman" didn't suit her. Though powerfully attracted to Jim Wellman, she refused to compete with Glenda Colter or anyone else for his attention.

Determined to keep a rein on her feelings as she gave Jim a massage, she felt she deserved an award for her cool performance while she kneaded and caressed Jim's muscular build. *Even his feet are beautiful . . . and oh my God, those hands!* She'd always been a pushover for beautiful hands. Jim's hands, big and broad, were strong quarterback's hands that could catch and pass a football with ease, power, and consistency. He had lover's hands, with long fingers that engendered the steamiest erotic fantasies.

She wrenched her mind back into an acceptable, clinical track, noticing that although the rest of his body was battered from injuries, her patient had somehow protected his hands. She saw no scars and couldn't sense any healed breaks when she rubbed each joint and pad of flesh with exacting care.

When she turned him over to massage his chest and legs, she remembered the old wives' tale that compared the size of a man's hands to his package. She wondered if she'd find out if there was any truth to the rumor.

"Hey, how'd you do that?" he demanded, breaking into her thoughts.

"Do what?"

"Flip me over like that. I must outweigh you by at least a hundred pounds."

She couldn't stop the self-satisfied smirk she felt crossing her face. "Tricks of the trade, Mr. Wellman."

After pouring a small puddle of herbal massage oil into one palm, she rubbed her hands together, creating friction to warm the oil. She spread it on Jim's naked chest, enjoying the slide of her fingers over his satiny skin.

She glided her palms over his pectoral muscles. The masculine mat of hair on a man's torso often impeded the easy dispersal of oil, but today she threaded her hands through Jim's rough curls with voluptuous appreciation.

Then she made a searching exploration of his lats, feathering her strokes along his sides. Eyes closed, his nostrils flared as he groaned with pleasure. She bit her lower lip to control her own response to the scent and smoothness of his skin, a delightful contrast to his rugged chest.

Someone ought to tattoo a warning on this body: therapist, beware!

She continued past the towel draped over his hips, which exhibited a slight tent in the center, clear and pleasing evidence of his reaction to her knowing touch. She went for the involved areas, his legs, massaging each limb twice, careful to keep her gaze averted from that fascinating white towel. She tenderly flexed and extended the legs, focusing her energy and attention on enhancing the healing process. Despite the inherent sensuality of the massage, she dragged her mind away from sex. Thinking about doing her patient was not only wrong, but would destroy her focus. She kept silent, afraid she'd reveal too much of herself if she talked to Jim.

She turned him over again. She shifted into deep tissue massage, working out knots of tension in his muscles. She ran her hands up and down his back, listening when each vertebra popped back into place as the muscles loosened. She came to his buttocks and swallowed hard.

They were gracefully rounded globes, covered gently with a downy fuzz. Consumed by an insane desire to nibble and kiss Jim's perfect buns, Marti broke out in a light sweat as her pulse increased and her temperature rose.

Closing her eyes, she sought to recapture a professional state of mind. She swept a towel over the tempting sight and inhaled, using breathing exercises to calm her racing heartbeat. As she headed back into the massage, she covered one cheek with the towel as she dug her fingers into the other.

Yelping, Jim jerked up off the table.

"Hot spots," she said. "Places where tension's settled into the muscles for a long stay."

"I know what they are." His voice had gone reedy from stress. He pulled away from Marti's steely fingers.

"No. Don't evade the pain, go into it." Marti kept her hands steady to probe the knots.

His body twitched.

"You're not a coward, Mr. Wellman. Breathe into the tension. Breathe in red, breathe out blue."

He took a couple of halting, painful gulps of air.

"Good, good." She gentled her tone, made it mesmerizing. "In—red, out—blue. Goood, good job." She smiled with satisfaction as the muscle loosened, became buttery and soft beneath her fingers. She treated his next cheek to the same process.

After the tension dissolved, she switched gears again, changing her touch to a mellower, more traditional massage. She felt she'd taken him as far as he could go today with the deep tissue releases. Now she'd finish with calming strokes. She rubbed his buttocks with more of the sweetly scented oil, caressing until a moan of pleasure escaped Jim's lips. She smiled again, ran her hands up his back, then turned him over to stretch his neck.

"Okay, that's enough." Marti glanced at her watch. The digital read eleven o'clock. "How'd you stay so fit, Mr. Wellman?"

"Isometrics." He grinned up at her from the padded table. The tent under his towel lowered as he brought both hands together, pressing his palms into each other. The muscles of his chest and shoulders leaped into startling relief.

She bit her lower lip. Her mouth went dry. "Impressive."

"Speaking of impressive, that was the best massage I've ever had, and I've had quite a few. What style do you use?"

"It's a mixture of shiatsu and Swedish, with a few little techniques of my own." She walked to an intercom and called for an attendant. While she waited, she found his chart, then pulled her pen from a pocket. "By the way, did you know that one of your legs is shorter than the other?"

Jim sat up. "No, no one's ever mentioned that to me."

After flipping through his chart, Marti scribbled some notes. "Without measuring, I would estimate that the right is about an inch shorter than the left. There's nothing about it in your records. Do you know if this condition preexisted your injury?"

Jim shook his head.

"Don't worry about it." She maintained a professional tone of voice. "It's often the result of a broken leg. I'll arrange for a specialist to make you custom footwear. You'll be fine."

"Will I be able to play football?"

Her lips tightened. She knew the answer, but her role didn't allow her to make diagnoses or predictions. "I really couldn't tell you, Mr. Wellman. That's a question for your coach or your team doctor." She turned as the door opened. "Hi, Tom. Same routine as Friday for Mr. Wellman. Bath, nap, and lunch."

"Are you gonna start him in the pool today?" Tommy asked.

"No, we'll leave that for tomorrow, along with the free weights. I don't want to over-stimulate him. I'll take him for a walk today at two o'clock to assess his progress."

"Yes, ma'am," both men said in chorus, and Jim saluted.

"Oh, you two!" Marti burst out laughing. She was still chuckling as she left the room to order Jim's lunch before attending to other patients. She wasn't a spiteful person, but she did order a healthy lunch for Jim and his celebrity guest. Fat-free Caesar salads with broiled salmon wouldn't hurt them.

★ ★ ★ ★ ★

She was a brunette mystery, an enigma wrapped in a challenge, a pint-sized commando with the power to bring healing or pain just from her touch.

Who the hell was she? What kind of woman was she?

Through the window of his suite, Jim saw Glenda's little Mazda sports car zip through the open gates of Shady Glen. The top was down, and Glenda's long blond hair swept behind her in the wind. Though he watched Glenda, his thoughts were on another woman entirely. Martina Solis, Nazi therapist.

She pushed him around, tossed him all over the massage table as though he was a piece of meat, and she the cook who prepared him for the oven. Jim stewed.

He didn't know if she'd been aroused as she manipulated him; he'd felt only his own struggle to control his erection as she gave him the most stimulating, sensuous massage of his life. Hell, her massage was better than most women's lovin'!

Although the therapy hurt, he'd never enjoyed pain so much. He wasn't turning into a masochist, was he? He'd have done anything to release his aching need, and, in fact, had taken care of his tension once he'd returned to the privacy of his room. But when he touched himself, he didn't think about tall, blond Glenda. His fantasies starred a wicked dark lass with an elfin chin who leaped on top of him and did mad, bad, and nasty things to his body.

Was Marti Solis mad, bad, and nasty? He wanted to find the wild woman lurking under her virgin queen facade.

Would his reaction be different if she were a battle-axe?

Well, yeah. If she weren't beautiful, he wouldn't care.

Did he care?

Yeah, he did. He sure did. But why? He knew plenty of

beautiful women. One of them was coming to eat lunch with him at this very moment.

Why did he want the therapist from hell?

Sensuous and strong.

Mysterious and challenging.

And smart. Very smart. Don't forget smart.

His reverie was interrupted by the sound of Glenda's high, spiked heels clattering on the floor outside his room as Katrin escorted her in.

Jim grinned. "Well, this is a sight for my sore eyes, two lovely ladies come to call."

Both Katrin and Glenda laughed. Glenda, wearing a red wool suit, gave him her picture-perfect smile. He'd seen the same glamorous image in today's newspaper next to her daily column.

Just seeing Glenda warmed his soul, easing his mind. After months in the hospital and out of the loop, he'd started to believe that he'd lost everything he'd struggled to achieve. Her presence made him feel as though he had a life waiting for him after he recovered.

Glenda seated herself while Tommy came in with a tray bearing their meals. He and Katrin settled Jim at the glass-topped table in the corner of the suite near the windows. He noted that the small dinette was set with silverware, patterned placemats, and fresh flowers. Yeah, Shady Glen was definitely a class operation.

Tommy cracked a fresh bottle of Perrier and filled two champagne flutes. "Have fun, you two," he said on his way out. "Remember Marti will be here in a while for your walk."

"Who's Marti?" Glenda asked.

Grateful for the remainder of his tan, Jim hoped it would hide his flush. He felt suddenly resentful of his reaction, and of Glenda. They didn't have a commitment, and he hadn't done anything to feel guilty about. He cleared his throat. "She's the chief torturer, excuse me, therapist. Physical therapist. She seems to have the responsibility for my recovery."

"What's she like?" Glenda started on her salad.

Jim kept the tone of his voice light and neutral, since his interest in Marti Solis was none of Glenda's business. "She's all right, if you like being under the control of a virginal sadist with ice water in her veins and steel in her hands. She's the strongest woman I ever met."

"Stronger than me?" Glenda batted her lashes at him.

"She has the strongest hands I've ever felt. Considering she's so small." He chewed a bite of the tasty salmon, then washed it down with Perrier. "She gave me one hell of a massage. Flipped me around that table as easy as I run a play."

"Hey, can I print any of this?"

"Aw, come on, Glenda. I thought this was a social visit."

"Well, it is. But if I get a story out of it, why not?"

"I don't know if there is a story. This place is great. I'm making a lot of progress here at Shady Glen, and hope to be back with the Cougars soon." Jim slipped into his role as professional athlete, handling the press. "Print that."

"You don't have to get snarky about it. Come to think of it, you've been pretty short with me lately. What's up?"

"Nothing's up. That's the problem." He met her blue gaze. "About two years ago, you invaded the locker room after the game with the Jets, and commented on my, uh, equipment. Since then, we've been at it hot and heavy. Then my leg gets broken, and you're gone. I've barely seen you since.

"You make me feel like a washed-up, worn-out meal ticket." He pointed his fork at her. "Why don't you tell me what's going on?"

Glenda squirmed in her chair and set her cutlery onto the table. "Jim, you know we never had a commitment."

"I know that. I'm an adult."

"And your injury was pretty bad. What kind of companion have you been lately?"

He stared at her. The selfishness behind her question washed his mind blank. "I . . . I thought we were friends, at least."

"Oh, we are! Nothing will ever change that. But, you know, people's lives go on though you're not a part of what's happening anymore." Her brilliant smile didn't match her words.

"So, I'm not what's happening."

"You're a great guy and I hope that we'll always be pals. But yeah, I have to live my life whether or not you're a part of it. And lately you haven't been a part of it."

"Hmm." Appetite gone, Jim pushed away his plate. "You're giving me mixed messages. I'm not quite sure what you mean."

"I'm not sure I do either, babe. Why don't we just give it a rest for now?" Glenda stood, looking at her watch. "Geez, it's getting late. I'd better be going. I wouldn't want to upset Monster Marti, the Sadist Therapist!"

They both chuckled as Marti entered. She eyed Glenda as the blonde's laughter increased.

Glenda bent down to kiss Jim lightly on the cheek in parting. "Don't try to get up, I know it's difficult for you. Till next time, baby. Ciao!"

Marti stared at Glenda's departing back. She turned to Jim. "Get up." Her eyes were baleful chips of jade ice.

"You're jealous," he said.

"Excuse me?"

"I know what I see. You're jealous."

Marti raised her left eyebrow. "Trust me, Mr. Wellman, there is nothing about Ms. Colter I desire to imitate. I am a health care professional and happy with my life."

Jim reached for his crutches and hauled himself to his feet. "I have to admit, you're very competent. I've made more progress here in a few days than I did at the hospital in eight months."

"I'm so flattered," she said, sarcasm edging her voice. She led him to the nearest exterior door and opened it. A gust of October wind blew her hair into his face as she held the door for him. As he stumbled by her on the crutches, he caught her scent, a potpourri of citrusy cologne and crisp autumn leaves. In an obvious fit of pique she let the metal door, pushed by the wind, slam behind them. He jerked slightly, startled by the bang.

Chapter Three

The chill wind lifted Marti's hair and flicked at her nape. She followed Jim as he limped down the path, which wound through wide lawns dotted with clumps of trees and patches of flowers. The breeze blew red and yellow leaves into whirls and eddies over the green fields. The cloudy sky hinted at the coming winter.

Marti brooded with the weather. With some bitterness, she realized that Jim was right; she *was* jealous. She felt like a cauldron, boiling over with a venomous brew composed of every bad emotion: shame, envy, even hate. She loathed these feelings and was surprised she had them. Through her mother's illness and death, she'd worked hard to maintain a happy demeanor for her patients and family. No one in her life needed to see another sad face to add to their troubles.

But Glenda Colter had what Marti wanted: Jim.

Though she struggled, she couldn't stop her irrational feelings. The suddenness and intensity of her need overwhelmed her defenses. She didn't like him—how could she? She didn't know him. But his overwhelming maleness struck her as fiercely as any primal force of nature, a tsunami that swept away her emotional walls.

Though distracted by her conflicting thoughts, she still monitored her patient, noting that his use of the crutches had improved. He'd even begun to lean some weight on his right leg.

She led him to a bench placed in the lee of a copse of birches. The graceful trees, golden with autumn, swayed in the brisk wind. Jim looked tired by the time he lowered himself down on the bench after the short, five-minute walk.

"What do you feel?"

He sighed. "A lot of different things. Mostly, I'm depressed."

"Why? You're doing great."

"Glenda reminded me that I don't have a life left."

Marti huffed. "How sweet of her."

Jim raised both brows, visibly astonished at her cattiness.

She groaned inwardly, realizing she needed to keep a rein on her smart mouth. "I'm sorry. That remark wasn't called for, Mr. Wellman. It's not my place to comment on your friends."

"I'm not sure she's my friend," he said. "She says she is, but her life has moved along while I'm going nowhere. I get the feeling she's leaving me behind."

"I'm sure you're wrong about her. She—she seems very nice," Marti lied, sitting on the bench beside Jim. She hesitated before taking his hand in both of hers. She believed in the healing power of touch, and told herself that she was doing this for him. It had nothing to do with the fact that she couldn't forget how great he'd felt when she'd massaged him . . . all over.

"She is. She's a nice person and I bet you're right." He sounded more confident. "But it's as though, umm . . . she's a symbol."

"Excuse me?" His large palm warmed her smaller, chilled hand.

"She's a symbol. See, I studied psychology and philosophy in college. I've figured out that she symbolizes my success. Lose her, lose success."

"What does all that have to do with friendship? You don't dump your friend because his life has changed. That's crazy." Holding Jim's hand was even crazier. If being around him was a tsunami, this was Noah's flood. But she couldn't stop. He felt too good.

"You're right. That's nuts. I think I'm thinking too much." He squeezed her hand, then released it.

Desire, a hot, sweet torrent, cascaded through Marti. She closed her eyes, trying to stem the tide. She wanted that warm, strong hand back, darn it, and this neediness was all her fault. Why had she touched him in the first place?

"Thank you for hearing me out." Using the crutches, Jim hauled himself up and headed back toward the rehab center in a rapid hop.

Marti frowned as she watched his halting progress. She didn't like emotional upsets in the lives of her patients. Stress could limit recovery in unexpected ways. Jim needed to feel that he had a life waiting for him. If not, he'd lack motivation to heal.

She wanted to believe that her interest in Jim's emotional health was limited to his rehabilitation and had nothing to do with her attraction to him. But he'd hit the mark when he told her she was jealous of Glenda Colter.

The bottom line was that Marti wanted him. Badly.

Her hand still tingled where he'd squeezed it. Well, at least he's treating me with more respect, she rationalized. She had learned to manage bullheaded patients. Usually it took only a day or two of her competent care to win over the most stubborn. Fortunately, Jim Wellman was no different. He was different only in her mind and heart. She had never reacted with such primitive need to any patient before.

But maybe her attraction had more to do with her boring

social life than anything special between her and Wellman. They had nothing in common. *Dad's right. I need to get out more often.*

Still, she hated to hear Jim's worries about his relationship with Glenda, especially since her visit had an adverse effect on him. He should dump that bimbo, she thought. He'd be a lot happier with . . . well, with me!

He interrupted her insane train of thought by stopping. Leaning on one crutch, he waved the other at the glass-walled facility. "Why's it designed that way?"

"Excuse me?"

"Shady Glen. Looks like a glass caterpillar with, well, a big phallus at the end."

She raised her brows. "That phallus is your favorite place."

His eyes widened, and one brow jerked up. "What?"

"That's the therapy tower. It's placed at the south end of the building to receive maximum natural light. That's why the whole building is glass. Dr. Fran believes that patients need exercise, good food, and sunlight. Shady Glen is the embodiment of her therapeutic approach."

"Sounds like you're really into this therapeutic approach thing."

"Of course. I wanted to work for Dr. Fran ever since I heard her lecture at my school ten years ago."

"So you're exactly where you want to be in life." The expression on his face confused her.

Hoping to shake off her patient's strange mood, she changed the subject. "I hear that you know my brother, Steve Solis. He works at Stone Cliff." She helped Jim through the main gate of Shady Glen.

"Steve? Ol' Steve's your brother?" Visibly startled, he scanned her face.

Marti grinned, aware that she and Steve looked like an interracial Mutt and Jeff. "I look more like my mother, who was Romanian. Steve takes after the Latino side of the family."

"Interesting combination," Jim said. "How did that come about?"

"My parents met at the Immigration Office in San Francisco." She ushered him through the glass doors into Shady Glen's lobby. "My father's from Pueblo, Mexico."

"I think I mighta met your dad at the club with Steve. Older fellow, shoots about ninety-five?"

"I wouldn't know what his golf score is." She pushed a button to call the elevator. "I know he plays at Stone Cliff as Steve's guest, and that you're a member."

"Yeah, it's a great place. I missed going there this summer. They didn't let me out to go golfing."

A light flashed on inside Marti's head. "Why don't you go soon? After all, you're not a prisoner here."

"I'll go if you take me," he wheedled.

"Oh, no, I couldn't do that. I can't socialize with the patients." She waved him into the elevator. "But I can arrange for a limo to take you when you're stronger. You're not quite ready to drive so far or to play golf. But if you keep up your good effort, you will be soon. Perhaps in a month or so."

"A month, you think?"

"Yes. If you keep working." She wasn't above manipulating her patient to get the desired result.

"I'll make you a deal. I'll work hard and if I earn that golf game in one month, *you* have to take me." That bedroom smile came at her again. "I'll fix it with Dr. Murdoch." He left the elevator, then went down the hall toward his suite.

She hesitated, balancing her desire to be with Jim and assist his recovery against her need to keep a job she loved. Dr. Fran would never allow her to socialize with Jim Wellman over a golf game. "Why don't you ask your friend Glenda Colter?"

His eyes narrowed. "I just might."

Great move, Marti. Her heart jumped into her throat. Why had she said such a stupid thing?

After making his way through the door of his room, he staggered over to his bed. He let his crutches fall.

"Why didn't you say something? I had no idea you were so tired!" she cried, genuinely shocked. She paged Tommy, and said, "I'll have Tommy put you into bed properly."

"Don't forget our deal," Jim called as she flew out the door.

Jim gimped down the sterile linoleum hall toward Shady Glen's common room. He hoped there'd be a few people watching Monday Night Football, because company always made sports a lot more fun. A burst of cheering met his ears as he reached the open door.

Patients and staff crowded the room. Good. Attired in motley garb ranging from bathrobes to sweats to jeans, patients sat in their wheelchairs or on the big, comfortable couches arranged in an L-shape in front of the giant-screen television. Jim recognized staff, dressed in their white scrubs, perched on couches and chairs. He looked around, but didn't see Marti Solis.

Entering, he greeted several staff members, who plied him with questions about the game.

"Hey, Jim, how's Hansley gonna stack up against Oakland?" Tommy asked.

Jim shrugged his shoulders as best he could with crutches. "I hope for the sake of the team Randy will rise to the occasion," he said, keeping his voice calm as jealousy roiled in his gut. "But you have to keep in mind that the Raiders have a lot of experienced players. Hansley has never started in a NFL game before tonight. That's a lot of pressure." Especially on someone as talentless as Randy Hansley, who moved like a slug and threw like a ten-year-old girl. The Cougars' second-string quarterback, scion of a wealthy banking family, had gotten his job the old-fashioned way: by greasing the right fists.

Someone poked his rump, and Jim looked around for the owner of the bony finger.

Seated in her wheelchair, she had to be at least ninety and didn't appear to recognize him. "Sonny, sit down. You're blocking my view of that cute Carl Worthing."

"Jim, this is Mrs. Stockman, one of our long-term guests," Katrin said. "Donna, this is Jim Wellman, from the Cougars football team."

"I know that!" the elderly lady snapped. "What do you think I am, senile?" She peered at Jim through thick spectacles. "You better shape up soon, young man. That second-stringer can't even pass gas."

"Yes, ma'am." Jim found himself a spot on a sofa near Mrs. Stockman's wheelchair, but out of reach of her claws. He stared at the screen, his innards churning with anger and jealousy. His mood lifted as Hansley was tackled before the quarterback could pass the ball. "He should have avoided that," he murmured.

"Huh?" Mrs. Stockman asked. She reached up to adjust her hearing aid.

"He should have avoided that sack." Jim used a normal tone of voice. "He coulda rolled out sideways for a pass and gained some yardage, or even thrown the ball out of bounds. You ever see me get sacked like that?"

"Heck, no." Katrin grinned. "Looks like your job's secure."

"They'll have to punt," Jim said.

A few moments later, a player with the number zero on his jersey took the field to kick the ball away.

"I bet you could do this professionally." Katrin reached for a handful of popcorn.

"What?"

"Provide play-by-play commentary. You're great."

Jim smiled, trying to remain modest. "Let's watch the Raiders take this snap. They're great."

Dr. Murdoch poked her nose into the room, distracting him. Before Jim could seize the initiative and approach her, she entered, making her way through the group around the TV.

"Hello, Katrin. Mark on the road again?" the doctor asked.

"Yep. I like to watch Monday Night Football with company, so I come here."

"Very good. Hello, Mr. Wellman. Enjoying yourself?"

"Surprisingly, yes. I thought I'd be jealous, but I'm all right. It doesn't seem as though I have to worry about my job." Jim grinned, remembering the sack.

"The only thing you have to worry about is getting back on your feet," Dr. Murdoch said. "Ms. Solis thinks you're doing very well."

"Yes, ma'am. Your Miss Marti's a miracle worker."

"Ms. Solis does have a special talent."

"I was wondering if I could ask a little favor. In regard to Ms. Solis." Jim paused, unsure of the best approach for the enigmatic doctor. "She says that I might go golfing in about a month if I continue to improve."

"That's a wonderful idea. Why not?"

"You see, I want her to take me."

Dr. Murdoch pursed her lips. "This is an unusual request,

Mr. Wellman. I don't encourage the staff to socialize with patients. It's not professional."

"But this is a special situation. With my injury and all, I would feel more comfortable with my therapist present." Jim hoped he didn't sound too devious. "And Marti's brother works for my golf resort."

"Was this your suggestion or hers?" His doctor's voice was cool, her expression impassive.

Hey, this lady's tough. He pasted an innocent, wide-eyed look on his face. "The golf was Marti's recommendation. I think she should come along, just in case something should happen, with the leg and all." He flashed his thousand-watt smile at her.

Nevertheless, she hesitated. "I'll consider your request, and let you know within the month."

The rosy dawn light peeked through the lace curtains in Marti's bedroom as Jolly nuzzled her awake. She swatted her dog aside, then turned her head to check her bedside clock. Jolly was right, as usual; it was time for their morning run. Marti sleepily pushed the coverlet away and fumbled for her sweats, socks, and shoes.

Dressed for running in gray sweatpants, a faded blue jersey, and new Nikes, she pulled her hair back and fastened it with a red gingham scrunchy. Jolly, eager as always for their run, beat her to the door.

They left the cottage, located on a side street outside Napa, and Marti headed toward the small town of Yountville. Jolly paced her, his flowing tail waving in the chill breeze, while she jogged in the soft morning light for about twenty minutes before turning back.

Few cars broke the country morning's serenity. The golden, dried grasses, damp with dew and morning mist, gave forth the particular spicy scent that she associated with autumn. They ran past the occasional cow or horse cropping weeds in the fields bordering the lane.

Though close to home, they stopped at their favorite café for breakfast. Jolly liked Edward's Place because the proprietors, Edward and Zelda Deaver, tolerated the big retriever even during the seven a.m. coffee rush. Marti liked the café because the couple served great coffee and baked the flaky croissants on the premises every morning.

They also kept an assortment of free newspapers lying about for her reading pleasure. Marti didn't bother with a subscription because Edward and Zelda got the *Napa Valley Tribune*, the *San Francisco Chronicle*, the *Sacramento Bee*, and the *Capitol City Star*.

The café's interior featured a multitude of small round tables and cane-backed wooden chairs scattered over squares of black-and-white linoleum. A coffee bar with a polished chrome espresso machine dominated one wall of the large room.

Amazon tall, with four earrings in each lobe and eyeshadow matching her teal shirt, Zelda Deaver greeted Marti with a sunburst smile. "The usual? And how are you, sweet thing?" She stooped to pat Jolly around the ears.

"The usual," Marti said. As Marti took Jolly out to the patio in front of the café, she heard Zelda washing her hands before setting out Marti's plain croissant and black coffee at the counter.

"Eddie taking the kids to school?" Marti took her seat.

"Yes, he should be back in a minute."

Edward breezed in as Marti sipped her coffee. A transplanted Londoner like his wife, he had a clipped black moustache, retro love beads, and a Cockney accent.

"Morning, m'dear. Read the news today?" he asked Marti.

"No, haven't got to it yet. Anything?"

"Oh, spicy, spicy. Your shop got a mention in the sports section."

"No way."

"Way. See here." Edward reached for the sports section of the *Capitol City Star*. He flipped it open to Glenda Colter's column, "Hotshot's Hot Tips," pointing to a paragraph midway down the page.

Marti read:

> *In an exclusive interview, former Cougar quarterback Jim Wellman revealed that his progress toward health has improved greatly since he was moved to the posh Shady Glen Rehabilitation Center in Napa Valley. While he characterized his therapist as a "virginal sadist with ice water in her veins," he appeared, to this reporter, to be in good spirits.*

"That jerk!" Marti whacked down her mug so hard that coffee slopped onto the counter.

Edward and Zelda looked at her, round-eyed. "Marti, Marti, why the violent response?" Zelda asked.

"Look at this!" Marti thrust the paper at her friend.

As Zelda read, her dark brows drew together into a frown.

Marti continued, "Wellman's my patient. Mine and Katrin's. So he's talking about one or the other of us. I can't believe he'd say something like this. We're working our tails off for this guy." Without finishing her breakfast, she flung a five onto the counter and slammed out, intent on confronting Jim about his loose lips.

A "virginal sadist with ice water in her veins"? Her anger combined with excruciating self-doubt. Jim's smile made her sparkle like diamonds in sunlight, but if he saw her as repressed, mean, and cold—boy, her instincts were totally out to lunch!

Yeah, she had the hots for him. Beyond that, she thought she'd established a rapport with this patient, a connection which would help push him faster down the long, hard road to recovery. Despite his initial burst of progress, her experience told her that he would have difficulties, both physical and emotional. He had to face the pain and monotony of the long rehab process. Plus, his life would never be the same. She didn't know for sure, but it was her best guess that he'd never play pro ball again. Heck, he might not even walk normally.

Marti had been pivotal to the recovery of scores of patients. She'd thought she could do the same for Jim Wellman, but that was before he flapped his lips to his equally big-mouthed, bleached-blond pal.

What a creep! How could be say such a thing? Marti burned with righteous anger. She wasn't a virginal sadist with ice water in her veins, but she'd be damned to twenty hells before she went out of her way to prove it to Jim Wellman.

Chapter Four

While still in bed with his decaf coffee, Jim skimmed the *Capitol City Star*. Flipping to the sports section, he read about his team's exploits. He paid special attention to Glenda Colter's column. Amidst the usual discussion of the team's stars and best plays, he found his unauthorized, off-the-record comment.

Former Cougar quarterback? What the hell was she saying? He was on injured reserve, not dumped! He'd be back!

Wouldn't he? Did Glenda know something he didn't? She kept tabs on all the latest Cougar gossip. Was his job up for grabs?

He knew the trading deadline was within a few weeks. If his team needed another quarterback—and from what he'd seen last night, they sure did—he could get cut from the Cougars' roster to make room for another high-priced player to fit under the salary cap.

Alone in his room, he swore loud and long, then grabbed the telephone from the bedside table. He couldn't call his agent or his attorney at this early hour, but he punched in the number for Glenda Colter's desk at the *Star* and left a message for Colter to call, immediately. Then he tried her home phone.

A male voice answered. A familiar male voice. Randy Hansley's voice. Now the former second-string quarterback of the Cougars was the starter, and obviously enjoying all the perks of the position. I guess I should have seen this coming, Jim thought ruefully.

"Randy, my man." He made an effort to sound affable. "It's Jim, Jim Wellman. May I talk to every quarterback's favorite reporter?"

"Uh, er, she's in the shower," Randy stuttered.

"Just tell the young lady to give me a call. I want to discuss her latest column. I'm sure she'll know exactly what I mean." He banged down the phone before Randy had a chance to respond.

Jim turned and punched his pillow in frustration, then winced as the twisting motion irritated his injured leg. His anger would hurt no one but himself, so he tried to calm down. Before he was able to completely collect himself, Marti exploded into the room, waving the morning paper at him.

"Just what were you thinking? A virginal sadist with ice water in my veins? Thank you very much!"

"I didn't mean it that way!"

"How dare you say such a thing about my work!" Red-faced and furious, she whacked the rolled-up newspaper on his bedside table. "I'm a great therapist!" *Whack!* "Who hauled you out of that wheelchair where you'd been sitting like a potted plant for eight months, huh?" *Whack!* "Who?" *Whack! Whack!*

"Now, Marti, calm down. I know—"

"I haven't worked my butt off for ten years to let you destroy me! It's my job to push you so you can grow." *Whack!* "If you think I'm sadistic, so be it!" She threw the paper at his head.

He grabbed the paper out of the air. "Hey, I can explain this."

"There is no adequate explanation. Except—did you actually say this?"

"Yeah, but she wasn't supposed to print it. That statement was in a private conversation. I had no intention of embarrassing you publicly."

"Is this what you really think about me?" A harsh note of pain edged her voice. "Find yourself another golf buddy!" She stormed out of the room.

"I didn't mean it that way!" he yelled as the door slammed shut. "I was only joking around!"

Damn. Absorbed in his own selfish concerns, he hadn't even thought of how the column would hurt Marti. He'd been out of circulation way, way too long. He'd never blown it with a woman so badly.

Scant minutes later, Dr. Murdoch came to call.

"Mr. Wellman, I don't mean to intrude on your conversations with members of the press, but I am deeply concerned about this statement. To which therapist were you referring?"

Jim momentarily buried his face in his hands. "Dr. Murdoch, please believe me when I tell you that I was joking at the time the statement was made. I wasn't referring to any therapist in particular."

"I hope not, because both Ms. Solis and Ms. Young, who are primarily responsible for your care, are very distressed by this column. We feel that you have made remarkable progress," his doctor said. "We are also aware of the relationship between your happiness and your healing. If you are unhappy with any of the personnel, your caretakers can be changed. No one person is essential in this facility."

Dr. Fran left. Jim pulled the comforter over his head, hoping to shut out the world. But Tommy came in, accompanied by Eileen Stuart, the therapist who had treated him over the weekend.

"Up and at 'em, big boy." Tommy tugged the comforter off Jim. "No resting on laurels for you. Into the therapy tower you go!"

"Nice to see you again, Mr. Wellman." Eileen handed him his crutches. "I'll be taking over your care at this time, since you weren't happy with Marti and Katrin."

Jim groaned with exasperation. He wondered if explaining himself was worthwhile. "I *am* happy with Marti and Katrin. The statement was taken totally out of context." That broad better print a retraction, he thought. "However, it's nice to see you again, Ms. Stuart."

Jim dragged himself into the therapy tower, feeling lower than pond scum.

The rest of the week crawled for Marti. She fought hard against wanting Jim, missing Jim, even thinking about Jim, but her treacherous body betrayed her at every turn. She surreptitiously read his chart, watched him in the therapy tower, and even spied on him while he walked with Eileen or Tommy.

She burned for the man, but she hardly knew him and what she did know wasn't good. He'd said vicious things about her behind her back, statements attacking her professionalism. Thank God he hadn't used her name, otherwise she'd really be in the soup.

Implying a woman was frigid was the nastiest kind of male contempt. Just because she wasn't like Glenda Colter didn't mean she was inadequate, but a big lunkhead like Wellman couldn't be expected to know that.

This is what happens when you let your fantasies get ahead of reality, she admonished herself. Someone like Jim Wellman couldn't possibly want me!

What had she been thinking? How could she have been so

naive to dream about being with someone like Jim? Marti hadn't been so reckless with her heart for years. She hadn't opened herself at all, preferring to remain untouched and alone in her cozy little cottage.

Staying close to home was smart. Letting someone like Wellman into her cocoon was the ultimate stupidity.

On Saturday morning, Marti slept late. Jolly snuffled at her face at six o'clock, but she pushed him away, checked the time, and rolled over for another snooze. She awakened at nine o'clock, stretched, then pulled on her running clothes.

She snapped her fingers at Jolly. "You must be hungry, fella." He nuzzled her hand. "Late breakfast today after running, okay?"

They ended up at Edward's Place after jogging on side streets to avoid the inevitable Saturday morning tourist traffic. Zelda and Jolly greeted each other enthusiastically. Café patrons smiled as Zelda led Jolly to his favorite spot by the fence in the front patio, before bringing him a dish of water and a day-old scone.

"You spoil that beast," Marti told Zelda with mock annoyance. "He's gonna turn into a fat ol' dog." She settled herself at the coffee bar with breakfast and opened the nearest newspaper.

A volley of yaps and barks soon disturbed her serenity. Zelda, Edward, and Marti looked up and all dashed out to the patio, together trying to jam through a door meant for only one.

As Jim squirmed out of Glenda's small sports car, he was distracted by the sound of raucous canines. Frowning, he adjusted the crutches beneath his arms.

He'd scented trouble the moment he'd seen Glenda had brought her little mop-head of a pooch with her. He didn't know how Glenda tolerated the drive all the way from Sacramento to Napa with the fleabag. The damn thing never sat still. During the short drive from Shady Glen, it had climbed all over him, poking its irritating little snout into his face, his armpit, and his crotch. By the time Glenda stopped the car in front of the trendy-looking coffee house, long white hair and dog spit soiled his burgundy and gold Cougar sweats.

He hobbled closer to the source of the racket. Glenda's tiny mutt yelped and yipped at a big golden retriever seated by a green metal fence bordering the patio. Head cocked on one side, the golden seemed to examine the mini-beastie with amusement in his large brown eyes. The retriever's feathery tail began to swish back and forth over the tiled patio. The dog extended his nose toward the fluff-ball cautiously, then jerked back as the fleabag snapped.

"Now, that's a cool dog! A real dog, not a sissy excuse for a dog!" He turned away from Glenda's scowl to admire the gorgeous retriever. The beautiful golden was both well-mannered and well-groomed, and Jim envied its unknown owner.

Commotion from the doorway of the coffee house distracted him from the pooches. A tangle of bodies, all talking and shouting at once, blocked the door. To his surprise, his therapist—no, his former therapist—popped out of the crush and advanced.

Jim met Marti's eyes. He had come to recognize that look. She was pissed. Her eyes glittered, cold and green. Her amber skin wore red flags on her cheekbones.

"What is that thing, and why is it terrorizing my dog?" she asked. "Is this your animal, Mr. Wellman?"

Glenda scooped up the little mutt. "Did the big nasty dog scare you, sweetums?" she cooed to the squirming white mop. "It's okay, Mommy's here."

Marti raised her eyebrows and jabbed her vixen chin into the air. A short, tense silence fell. "Jolly, come," she commanded. The retriever rushed to her side, nuzzling her hand. She stroked his head. "I'll see you later," she said to her companions.

She stalked out. She didn't give him another glance, making him feel as though he'd been sideswiped by an iceberg. Her dog pranced by her side.

Despite her chilliness, he gazed at the pair with longing. She looked pretty good in a sweatshirt and leggings, like she worked out. He preferred a woman who wasn't constantly worried about her clothing, as Glenda was.

"Nice sweats, baby!" Glenda snickered as Marti left. Many of the café's patrons, including Jim, were attired in comfortable, aged sweats. Several glowered at her, visibly offended by the remark from Glenda, attired in fuchsia lace.

Glenda settled her pet into her oversized zebra-print satchel, then swept into Edward's Place. She spotted an empty table near the back, and took it. Jim struggled with his crutches through the café, crowded with occupied tables. He reached Glenda as a server arrived.

She shouldn't have brought the dog inside the restaurant, but he kept his lip buttoned. After all, he had asked for the meeting and wanted a favor from her. The nearby, crowded coffee bar also bothered him, and he prayed there wouldn't be another scene that would reach the tabloids. After Glenda's latest prank, he'd had enough lousy press.

After they ordered coffee and pastries, he confronted her. "That column you wrote got me into a lot of hot water at Shady Glen. Now I told you what you could and could not write. Why'd you say that stuff about my therapist?"

She raised her tweezed eyebrows. "You've never objected to anything I've written before. What's the problem now?"

"The two best therapists there got taken off my case because the director of the place thought I was unhappy with them. Because of what you wrote."

"Didn't you explain?"

"Of course. But they all think that what I told you was what I really feel. I was joking at the time." He noticed the server clearing an empty table a few feet away, so he tried to keep his voice low. "I told you to write only that I was making progress at Shady Glen. You need to publish a retraction."

"No way." Their orders arrived.

"What?"

"I said, no way. This isn't important enough."

"It's very important to me. Why not?"

She sipped her latte. "Look, Jim, it's time you saw reality. The paper doesn't care if you're offended. You're history, you know what I mean?"

Her contempt hit him like a blow to the belly. He didn't expect to be told he was yesterday's news so rudely. "What are you talking about? I'll be back."

"Dream on. Rumor is that your team is angling for a new quarterback, and when that happens, you're out. No way can they keep you active without blasting through the salary cap."

His gut twisted while he fought to keep a calm demeanor. He wouldn't let her know she'd slipped the knife through his ribs to his vulnerable core. "That might be, sweetheart, but I'm only thirty. Surgeons can do amazing things these days. Rest assured; I'll be back. And when I'm active again, you're gonna want those tasty little bits of insider gossip I can give you, so you just better do something about the mess you made."

"What mess?"

He picked at his croissant. "I'm not making the kind of progress I did with Marti. She was very upset by the column."

"That's really it, isn't it?"

"What?" Aware of the server wiping tables nearby, he hoped the conversation wasn't being overheard.

"You're not pissed off because I stepped on your precious privacy." She tore her pastry in two. "I've put plenty of personal stuff in the column before, tidbits that you didn't want me to print. It's never been a big deal to you." She paused. "It's this Marti, isn't it? Are you boinking her yet?"

The server tripped over a chair. Jim's mouth dropped open. Glenda could be blunt, but this deliberate crudeness came as a surprise.

"Are you jealous?"

She laughed harshly. "You wish." She thrust her left hand into his face, showing off the big diamond on her fourth finger. "I can't believe you didn't spot this on the drive over. Isn't it gorgeous?"

"Very nice. Randy give it to you?"

"Nope. I'm engaged to Carl."

"No way. No way!" Jim tried to jump up on his bad leg. Wide receiver Carl Worthing had been his buddy since elementary school in East Oakland. When the kids lined up in first grade in alphabetical order, Wellman and Worthing always ended up together. They had earned scholarships to different universities, but, to their delight, they were both drafted to the Cougars after graduation. "Girl, you know I gotta tell him!"

"Tell him what?"

"Didn't Randy give you my message? I called your home on Tuesday morning, and he answered the phone. Does Carl know who you were with on Monday night?"

"It's none of your business. If you tell Carl anything, I'll tear you to shreds in my column! You'll never work in sports again!"

"You try that and my lawyers will be on you and your paper like ants at a picnic. You'll have more legal problems than O.J. Simpson!"

Glenda stood, picking up her satchel. Her dog whined and scrabbled for air. "I'm leaving. Have Shady Glen send a car for you. Or maybe your new girlfriend will come to pick you up."

"You just make sure that retraction gets printed!" he called after her.

A public argument. Great. *Touchdown, Wellman!* He rubbed his face as he watched Glenda flounce out of the café.

Both relieved and sad, he realized she truly was a symbol to him. She represented a part of his life that was over, when he'd stood at the top of his world.

Football hero, Heisman winner, M.V.P. at two Super Bowls, Jim had everything he'd ever wanted before he broke his legs. He'd been named one of the world's most eligible bachelors by *People* magazine. He squired the model-perfect women he bedded to Hollywood parties in a three-thousand-dollar tux and drove a ninety-thousand-dollar Aston Martin. He kept the restored antique vehicle with the rest of his car collection at his house in Beverly Hills.

He also owned a nine-thousand-square-foot mansion located deep in a forest in the Sierra foothills. His home, a showplace that had won several architectural design awards, boasted three hot tubs and five fireplaces. One of each was in the spacious, elegant master suite. The enormous estate was completely paid off.

None of it meant squat if he couldn't play football.

He didn't mourn the passing of his relationship with Glenda, but he stared into his empty coffee cup, silently grieving for the life he had lost. He had single-mindedly pursued just one goal since childhood: to be the best quarterback in the NFL. He'd set record after record, winning a place in football history. But now, he looked his future in the face and found no smile in fortune's eyes.

Marti came home on Wednesday evening to find Rico's corgis digging up her roses. Her father's elderly Cadillac blocked her driveway. She sighed, realizing that she'd been blessed by a visit from Daddy.

Since Gracia's death, Rico, a sociable soul, made frequent visits to either Marti or her brother. Steve, because of the grandchildren and access to great golf, was the usual beneficiary of Rico's company. But for whatever reason, this week she was the favored child.

She found her father in the kitchen, cooking enchiladas with Jolly underfoot sniffing for scraps. "Dad, can't you ever phone?"

"What for? You aren't gonna turn away your dear old dad, are you?"

She squirmed. "Well, no."

"So, why should I waste money on a long-distance call?" He tossed Jolly a shred of tortilla, and he caught it out of the air with a snap of his jaws.

She sighed again. She didn't know if she wanted her dad around, on top of the emotional turmoil at work. But what choice did she have?

The next morning, Marti and Rico drove together to Shady Glen. She wore her usual white scrubs. Rico, dapper in gray Dockers and a matching sweater, had brushed his silver hair until it shone. She hoped that her father could stay out of trouble by taking walks and chatting with the patients in the common room. Dr. Fran was a stickler for professional conduct, and Marti had never discovered how her boss reacted to her father accompanying her to work.

She settled Rico in the common room with a cup of coffee, then went to attend to her newest patient. Andrea was adorable, a four-year-old whose small body had been traumatized in a traffic accident. Marti had the pleasure of helping Andrea learn to walk again. Few of Marti's patients had been so gratifying.

Working with Andrea made Marti long for children of her own. With a pang, she realized she might never become close enough to a man to marry and have babies. Who would want a virginal sadist with ice water in her veins?

She told herself to snap out of it. The blow dealt to her ego by Jim Wellman via his "friend's" column need not smash her dreams of marriage and motherhood into dust.

Wrenching her mind away from her own issues, she watched as Andrea gripped the handles of her tiny walker with determination and maneuvered herself down the long main hallway. Voices emanated from the common room, and she turned into that doorway with Marti close by. To her surprise, she saw her father and Dr. Murdoch chatting in front of the big TV. Andrea made a beeline to Fran, then tugged on the doctor's white coat. Dr. Fran looked down at Andrea, smiling.

"Hello there, Andrea." Fran stroked her hair. "How's our favorite little girl today?"

"Fine. Can I watch cartoons?"

Dr. Fran looked at Marti. "That depends. Have you been good for Marti?"

"She's been very good, except she becomes bored quickly," Marti said. "I'd recommend more frequent, but shorter, therapy sessions for Andrea. She's doing well, but she tires easily."

"Well, then, it sounds as though you may watch cartoons right now," Dr. Fran said.

"And you may have a snack. What would you like?" Marti asked.

Andrea scrunched her little face in thought. "I want Ho-Hos and milk."

"We don't have Ho-Hos," Marti said, "but how about some nice fresh oatmeal cookies?"

Andrea nodded enthusiastically, so Marti settled the child on a couch in front of the TV. After locating the clicker for Andrea, Marti eyed the odd couple—Fran and Rico—as she left to fetch her patient's snack.

Better to let well enough alone, Marti decided. Both Dr. Fran and her father seemed to be getting along okay. But what could those two have to talk about?

Marti's father settled himself into the cushions of her Honda for the drive back to her cottage after work. He clicked on his seatbelt and announced, "I did you a favor today."

Marti's heart sank. Her father's surprises could be more like bombshells, such as the time he'd decided to stop by her Berkeley apartment. She'd been entertaining one of her friends, and Rico subjected the poor fellow to an interrogation that smacked of the Spanish Inquisition. She'd never heard from the man again.

She stopped at a traffic light and silently counted to ten. "What did you do for me, Dad?" She tried to keep her voice calm and even. As the light changed to green, she drove away, making a point to gently depress the accelerator.

"I got you back on that nice football player's case."

"You did *what?*" She clutched at her hair, then grabbed the steering wheel. "You got me back on Wellman's case! Why did you do that? Didn't you hear what he said about me?"

"Oh, relax, Marti. I talked to him about it. You're being unfair. He said he had a misunderstanding with that reporter."

"You talked to Wellman about me? Oh, Dad, how could you do that?" She halted the car at a stop sign and took several deep, relaxing breaths before continuing to drive. Why did she let the Wellman problem get to her?

"What's the big deal? Fran thought it was okay."

"You talked to Dr. Fran about this? Oh, no!" She pulled into her driveway, stopped the car, and faced her father. "Dad."

"Yes, darling?"

"You need to understand that I am a health care professional." She smoothed her hair behind her ears, pleased by her control.

"I know that. I'm very proud of you, *mi corazón.*"

"You cannot go around adjusting my professional life for me. Now, what Mr. Wellman said showed that he isn't happy with my care. He won't heal unless he's happy. We changed therapists for Mr. Wellman's health."

"That's not what he thinks."

"No?" She stared.

"No. He thinks you're mad at him."

She counted to ten. Again. "I'm not mad at Mr. Wellman. I just want Mr. Wellman to heal, go home, and have a nice life."

"But he doesn't like Eileen Stuart. Says she doesn't care."

"What did Dr. Murdoch say?"

"Dr. Murdoch examined Jim and said that he's not making the same kind of progress he made while you were his therapist."

"After one week?" Despite her exasperation, a burst of pride warmed her. Nice to see Mr. Macho Quarterback reduced to begging for her services after the humiliation he'd dealt her.

"She said that you're the most talented therapist she's ever met, and that you're back on the case. So there!" Rico sounded triumphant. "He's a nice guy. I think he's interested in you."

"Excuse me?"

"You heard what I said."

"But why? He's got this gorgeous girlfriend."

"Not anymore. He said he broke up with her on Saturday."

"Dad, that doesn't mean he's right for me. Please don't try to fix me up anymore, okay?" She got out of the car and shut the door.

"Now, don't get angry with me, Marti." Rico followed her up the walkway to her house.

She turned and eyed her father, whose gaze didn't quite meet hers. She knew that look. Dad had something up his sleeve, and he wouldn't tell until he was good and ready. She prayed his little secret wouldn't have any additional impact upon her career. "I'm not angry, Daddy." She sighed. "I just need some time to think about all this, okay?"

"Sure do love the autumn."

Marti watched her problem patient tip his head back to admire the yellow leaves of a birch tree set against a brilliant blue sky. The afternoon sunlight blazed on the Napa hills, burnt golden. A line of vivid green, running along the base of the slope, marked a creek at the boundary of Shady Glen's grounds. Warm, but with an edge of chill, the bright fall days seemed to laugh at the possibility of winter's cold. The brevity of the season made these days intense and precious.

She looked at her biggest challenge, walking with her along one of Shady Glen's slate paths.

Jim wore a muscle-T that showed off his well-developed pecs and biceps. The breeze raised his nipples, which pointed, sharp and definite, through the thin cloth of his shirt. A pleasant, sensual heat flowed through her as she checked his gait.

He continued, "It's always been my favorite time of year."

"Wouldn't you normally be playing football?" she asked.

"Yeah, that's why I like it so much. I love to train. Football's been my life since I was thirteen. I miss playing." His voice caught in his throat.

She injected a lighthearted note into her voice. "Look on the bright side. Ever have a chance to watch the leaves turn?"

"Nope. Too busy working. So what's with you?"

"Excuse me?" The abrupt change of subject startled her.

"I'm concerned," he said.

"What's on your mind, Mr. Wellman?"

"Jim. My name is Jim."

She hesitated. "Okay, Jim. What's up?"

"You are."

"Excuse me?"

"You've been acting strange today. Kinda funny but quiet."

She winced. She'd tried all day to keep her heart and her hands in line. She hoped she'd behaved normally, but apparently her mood hadn't gone unnoticed.

"Are you unhappy about being put back on my case? She printed a retraction, you know." He stopped to pull at a crumpled bit of newsprint protruding from the back pocket of his tight jeans. One crutch slipped, and he grabbed it before it fell.

"Marti, could you please help me?"

She reached down to his hip to tug at the paper, trying to remove it from his pocket without touching his firm buttock. Tough job, since Jim's faded jeans clung like a second skin. The flimsy newsprint ripped.

"You have to stick your hand inside the pocket to get anything out," he said. "Sorry."

Marti eyed him suspiciously. He didn't sound apologetic, but he returned her glance with a look of utter innocence. She slipped her hand inside the pocket, running her fingers over his taut rear end. She got the clipping out, but not before her mild pleasure escalated into total turn-on.

She forced the feeling away, then read the clipping.

Hotshot's Hot Tips and this paper extend an apology to quarterback Jim Wellman and the staff of the Shady Glen Rehabilitation Center. Mr. Wellman's remarks, printed in this column on October third, were quoted out of context.

"Oh. Well." Marti reconsidered. Holding onto the grudge would make the situation very unpleasant. She couldn't work with Jim while staying mad. She took a deep breath. "I'm not upset. I realize what happened wasn't your fault."

"Really? I did say that, you know."

She sucked in another breath. Why had she grown so hot? "I'm sure you didn't mean it the way it was printed."

He looked relieved. "That's exactly right! That's the problem with Glenda. Everything's a story. You joke around and—wham! You're in her column, getting heat from everyone."

"What did it take for you to get a retraction?"

He shrugged. "Not much. That's what lawyers are for. One phone call, and it was done."

"She must not have liked it."

"Who cares? She had already burned her bridges with me."

"What about this symbol business you mentioned last week?"

His jaw tightened as he continued down the path. "There's no use pursuing something that won't work out. Glenda's moved on without me. I wish she had told me she's dating one of my best friends as well as the second-string quarterback."

"A busy lady."

"I'd say so, but she doesn't matter anymore." He stopped, balanced a crutch under his arm, and extended his hand toward Marti. "Truce?"

"Truce." She shook his hand, but he kept it when she tried to pull away.

"Friends?"

She nodded, shaking his hand a second time. "Friends." She tugged. "Mr. Wellman—Jim—you really have to let go of my hand. I'm sure I'll need to use it again sometime."

He chuckled. He squeezed the pad of flesh under her thumb, then rubbed slowly along the ridge of her index finger as he stared into her eyes.

She couldn't look away from his bright blue gaze. An erotic thrill leaped from her hand all the way up to her heart, which took flight along with the autumn leaves swirling freely with the wind. Her knees went weak. *I wonder if he knows what he's doing, how that feels.* Jim's knowing smile told her that he understood exactly what he was doing to her.

He let go of her hand, then tucked the crutch back under his shoulder before continuing down the slate path. They passed his favorite bench under the birches.

"Did you look at the rest of the column?" he asked.

"No. Is there something else?"

"Oh, yeah. Check it out."

Marti opened the bit of paper, which she'd scrunched in her hand when he'd caressed her. She shoved her embarrassment to the back of her mind, then read:

> *In less happy news for the Cougar quarterback—or should we say, the former Cougar quarterback?—a hot rumor says that the Cougar coaching staff is frantically searching for a new starting quarterback before the trading deadline passes. Talks have opened with Colts star Drew Langley . . .*

She gulped. Another therapeutic challenge, courtesy of the bleached-blond bimbo. *Thank you, Glenda Colter.* However, Marti wasn't surprised. As soon as she'd noticed that one leg had healed shorter than the other, she figured Jim's career as a professional athlete was over.

How could she help her patient handle this disastrous news? She kept her voice calm and even. "Do you know if there's any truth to this?"

"Yep, there sure is." Jim continued down the path. "My attorney and my agent made some calls and confirmed that the Cougars have to replace me soon, or the season is shot to hell. My back-up just isn't performing. Unless they cut me, the team can't get another quarterback without violating the salary cap."

"What about other franchises, after you've recovered?"

"There's no way anyone will take a chance on a player who's over thirty and had a serious injury to boot. I'm finished, Marti, washed up." Jim's expression was bleak, his eyes as blank as the cobalt blue glass for sale in the Napa antique shops.

"You're right," she said.

He looked at her. His mouth hung open slightly.

"You're one hundred percent right, Jim. You should just pack it in. I'll get a gun and you can end it all right here."

"What?"

She shrugged. "After all, it's not as though you're handsome, rich, and famous. You have no brains and can't do anything except throw an old piece of pigskin and run around in circles."

He managed a little laugh. "All right, I get the message. But can't I mourn?"

"Yeah, you can mourn." She allowed her voice to soften and slipped her hand into his, giving a gentle, comforting squeeze. "Just not for very long."

"Okay, I'll stop feeling sorry for myself right now. You really take the cake, you know."

"Take the cake? What does that mean?" She tried to disengage her hand.

He held onto her, keeping control. "It's just something my mother used to say. Hey, come out with me tonight." He ran a finger along her palm.

Her flesh rippled, an unfamiliar sensation that warmed her but brought shivers at the same time. "Excuse me?"

"Let's go out for dinner." He continued stroking.

"You d-don't like the food here?"

"Aw, come on, Marti. I'm asking you for a date."

Her body heated and her mind spun madly. What would happen on a date with Jim? "Why not? But not tonight. I'm always tired after a day at work. How about Saturday?"

"Whatever you want." Jim kissed her palm, then let go. "My schedule is completely clear."

Marti's heart stuttered. Kissing her hand had quite an effect. "Then let's say . . . eight o'clock Saturday night. Shall I, uh, pick you up?" Was her voice wobbling?

"Heck, no. A lady hasn't picked me up since my mom stopped in kindergarten. I'll pick *you* up."

"How are you going to do that?"

"You'll see," said Jim.

Chapter Five

Rico blew back into town Saturday afternoon, claiming he had an engagement for dinner at seven and a date for a round of golf at the Silverado the next morning. That was fine with Marti. She didn't want her father around when Jim came to call for her.

Though she didn't know if she wanted to pursue a physical relationship with him, she took unusual care when dressing that evening. She desired this man with a longing that was so powerful that it frightened her, but rather than rush the relationship, she decided to use the event to brush up on her dating skills. It had been a very long time since she'd cared enough about any man to primp for him.

She took a long, sensuous bubble bath, scented with her favorite *Eternity* perfume, then sprayed more of the fragrance into her hair as she arranged it into a French twist. She stared at her face in the mirror and rubbed her pointed chin with one hand. Short of plastic surgery, she couldn't do much with her knife-sharp chin. Sighing, she lightly dusted blusher onto her cheekbones, then augmented her already dark lashes with mascara.

Still naked, she rubbed lotion into her legs as she sat on her bed, then checked out the contents of her closet for the millionth time since he'd asked her out. She didn't have many choices. Would Jim prefer her in black lace or green silk? She caressed her breasts with more cream. Reveling in the sensual, animal heat in her body, she decided to skip wearing a bra.

He's gonna get a few surprises tonight! she thought smugly. She took a patterned silk dress out of her closet. The green jacquard silk was a long-sleeved wrap style featuring a low-cut, surplice front. Ending above the knee, it showed plenty of leg. Because Jim had never seen her in any clothes other than scrubs and sweats, Marti wanted to knock his socks off.

She pulled on sheer nylons before sliding her feet into high heels, which had been dyed to match her dress. She examined her reflection in the cheval mirror. The green silk clung to her body, outlining every curve. The jacquard pattern almost disguised her erect nipples, which pushed at the soft fabric. Her flesh tingled. The leaf green of the silk lit her hazel eyes with a gentle emerald glow. Hearing a knock, she stroked her lips with a subtle mauve lipstick, then hurried to answer the door.

Marti opened her door to see a long, white limousine parked outside her cottage. Jim, attired in a tuxedo, stood on her porch. She lifted her brows in surprise as he bowed slightly and presented her with a bouquet of red roses with a flourish. The dogs, penned in the side yard, barked at the stranger.

"Oh, they're beautiful," she bubbled, burying her face in the flowers to inhale their scent. "Please come in."

He hobbled through the doorway with fair grace. A professional chunk of her consciousness noticed that he'd jettisoned one crutch and handled the remaining one with skill. She invited him to sit on her couch, upholstered in blue chambray. He arranged two of the gingham pillows to support his right leg while she bustled to her kitchen to fetch champagne and to place the roses in water.

Returning with a bottle, she eyed him, and decided that,

for this one time, she'd manipulate *him*. "Jim, could you open this for me, please?"

"Cristal." Taking the bottle, he raised his brows. "A lady of unexpectedly sophisticated tastes."

She grinned. "Usually I stick to the local vintages. This was a gift from a grateful patient."

Jim uncorked the champagne with practiced ease as Marti brought out two cut crystal flutes. He poured for them both as she went to the refrigerator and took out the shrimp canapés she'd hidden from Rico on a back shelf. She put them on the low table in front of the sofa.

Then she had nothing to do except sip champagne and enjoy the moment. She was aware of his admiring scrutiny as she perched on the edge of her rocking chair, and she took the opportunity to look her fill.

She'd already noticed that Jim was a handsome man, but she'd never permitted herself to be completely open to his rugged masculine presence. In fact, until this second, she'd done everything she could to fight her attraction .

Even seated, he dominated the room, groomed to perfection from the top of his newly trimmed hair to the soles of his shined shoes. His hands, always remarkable, tonight looked unusually elegant. She realized he'd even had a manicure. She blinked to erase the fantasy of those hands caressing her body.

The tux, which looked as though it had been tailored to emphasize his broad shoulders and slim hips, was icing on a delicious cake. His cobalt eyes twinkled as she checked him out.

Everything about him made her feel special, treasured. Her bright mood dimmed when she guessed that he probably did this for every woman he dated, including Glenda Colter. She shoved the thought firmly from her mind. She decided to resist his seductive presence while she savored his company. Safe, yet fun.

"A toast," she said. "To your good health and recovery."

He smiled back. "To you. You're the one who's responsible for my recovery, you and no one else."

"No way. Jim, you're a hard worker. I just encourage."

"So that's what you call pushing me around."

She chuckled into her champagne flute as she sipped. They nibbled the tasty canapés while they made small talk. He mentioned the difficulties arranging for the limo and the tux. "I finally had to get my sister to drive down from my house with my own tux—they just didn't have my size anywhere in the Napa Valley."

"You really went out of your way. Thank you."

He shrugged it off. "If I'm going to take you out, I might as well do it right. It's been awhile since I dated. I feel as though I need to get back my social life."

"I was thinking the same thing when I got dressed. It's been a long time for me, too. And so far, you're doing great. This is already the best date I've ever been on."

"Better than . . . the senior prom?"

Marti blushed, remembering what she'd done after her senior prom. "Not exactly. But very similar. Flowers, tux, limo . . . this is really special."

The limo driver tapped at the door to remind Jim of the dinner reservation at Domaine Patrice. Jim escorted Marti out the door of her cottage and helped her into the limo. Slightly tipsy from the champagne, she giggled as she slid across the leather seat. The leather beneath her thighs felt sexy. Smelled good, too, reminding her of Jim's musky, male scent.

They pulled up to the entrance of Domaine Patrice just as two familiar figures stepped out of the wide, carved doors of the winery. "Oh, my God!" She gasped and fell back into the limo. She wrenched the door from the chauffeur's hand and slammed it closed. She lowered the window slightly, gesturing for the astounded driver to stand aside. Jim leaned across her to see what had attracted her attention.

Rico Solis and Fran Murdoch, dressed to the hilt, emerged from the restaurant. Natty in a navy, double-breasted blazer, Rico held Fran's elbow as if he cradled precious porcelain. Fran wore a dark red evening suit with soutache trim. An orchid corsage adorned one satin lapel. Two heads of silver hair glistened like searchlights beneath the beams of the outdoor lighting.

Marti's mouth dropped open, and she flopped back into the leather seat. Eyes wide, she turned to Jim.

He grinned. "Shall we ask them to join us?"

"Are you out of your mind? Dr. Fran can't see me dating a patient. I'll lose my job!"

"But they're a handsome couple." His broad shoulders shook with laughter. "Who wouldn't want to double date with her father and her boss?" He guffawed.

"I know you think this is a scream—" she started. "Oh look, they're leaving." Relieved, she watched Rico unlock the passenger door of his Cadillac.

"Oh, no." Jim chuckled. "Maybe I can catch them!"

"Oh no you don't," she said. "No running. Not yet."

"Excuse me, sir," the driver said. "Are we stopping here?"

"Yes, we will." Jim's laughter subsided.

The chauffeur again opened Marti's door, looking wary. He held it for her, then went to Jim's side of the limo to let him out. She peeked over the top of the limo and nervously watched Rico drive off with Dr. Fran in his car. Only then did Marti allow Jim to take her arm and escort her into the restaurant.

The Domaine Patrice dining room looked like a traditional French country restaurant, with whitewashed walls, dark wood trim, and fine table linens. Lit by numerous beeswax candles, the room was full of well-dressed diners nibbling gourmet delicacies.

From past visits Marti knew that their table, which was placed near a window, normally held a panoramic view of the Domaine Patrice vineyard. The winery's spectacular grounds, located on rolling hills near Yountville, were dark, and few lights disturbed the quiet autumn night.

"This is weird for me," Marti said as she picked at her salad. "To think of my dad dating—" She shook her head.

"Why not?" Jim demanded. "My mother's single and I hope she has a gentleman friend."

"You're right. It's been two years since my mother died."

"I got news for you, girl. Rico's around Shady Glen a lot."

Marti was stunned. "He is?"

"You don't see him 'cause you're busy working, and you don't come in on weekends. He's taken her to lunch a few times, I think. I bet he drives up for only the day, so you don't see him."

The waiter removed the salad plates and brought their entrées: seared ahi for Marti, filet mignon for Jim. She didn't comment on his dinner, though beef wasn't part of the fat-free diet she ordered for him at Shady Glen. She continued on her previous line of conversation as their waiter poured her Chardonnay and replenished Jim's Pinot Noir.

"Hmmm. I'm not sure I like my father dating my boss."

"You got a choice?"

"Hmm. I guess I don't." She cut the tender fish with her fork, noting it was perfectly prepared: seared on the outside, rare in the interior of the steak. She ate a bite and licked her lips.

"I don't know how you eat that stuff. That fish is practically raw," Jim said.

"Oh, it's great. It's just like sushi. Want a taste?" Marti extended her fork, bearing a bit of ahi, to Jim.

He jerked back as though she'd offered hemlock. "No, thank you. I prefer my food cooked, not flopping around on the plate getting scales everywhere."

"Well, I don't know how or why you still eat beef. It's very, very unhealthy, all that fat. With ahi, I can have steak without worrying about my health."

"Maybe it's because we never got decent food when I was a kid."

She wondered if she should pry into his past, whether he'd be offended by her nosiness or flattered by her interest. She took a deep breath. "Tell me about your childhood, Jim."

"It was pretty classic. Single mother, three kids, Oakland projects. I was too young to really remember, but I guess my dad left when Mom got pregnant with my sister, Shawna. Couldn't handle the idea of another baby." He gave her a bleak smile. "My mom would make meals a game. She'd give us a casserole and tell us to search for the mystery meat. Later I realized that there wasn't much to go around."

She stilled for a moment before saying, "I guess it was great for your mother, seeing you become a success."

"Yeah. I enjoyed buying her a house like the ones she had to clean when I was a kid. She cried the day the maid came." He smiled at the memory.

"What do your brothers and sisters do?"

"I only have one of each. My sister goes to Sierra College, and she's taking care of my place while I'm here. My younger brother is also in football. He's a kicker for Dallas."

"Oh, that's right. Jack Wellman. He was at the Pro Bowl when you got injured, wasn't he?"

"Yeah." Jim quieted. "I still remember way too much of that day. I heard my leg snap like dry kindling. Incredible pain, and my brother's face looming down over me while I lay on the field. Even now, I can't believe I got hurt at the damned Pro Bowl, for God's sake. That's supposed to be a junket to Hawaii for football players and the press, not a serious game."

"How did it happen?"

"That's no secret. The offensive line was porous—probably staring at the pretty Hawaiian cheerleaders! So two gung-ho linebackers nailed me. I remember going back for the pass, spotting my man, and bringing my right arm back. Then I got hit. Somehow, my cleats got stuck in the turf and my legs went when they sacked me. Hank Chester fell on the right thigh, and Jefferson Buttrell got the left ankle."

She swallowed more fish. "The injuries were unusual. I'm not surprised about the ankle, but one of the joints would generally go before the femur. That's the strongest bone in your body."

"Guess I just got unlucky."

"I noticed from your chart that you were in a cast and traction for an unusually long time. What's the story on that?"

"I don't really know," he said. "But all sorts of specialists came by and there was sure a lot of publicity. I figure with all the attention that the care was all right."

"Hmmm." She knew Sunset Community Hospital had a bad reputation for long-term care, but she wouldn't suggest his lawyer take a look at the case for possible medical malpractice. It wasn't her area of expertise; besides, she didn't want to spoil the mood of the evening. She shifted the conversation toward the future. "So what are you going to do now?"

Jim surveyed the remains of their dinners. "Order dessert, I think."

"Oh, no. I couldn't eat another bite."

"Sure you can," the waiter said, wheeling the dessert cart closer. Marti and Jim scanned the selections. Fresh fruit tart, New York cheesecake, crème brûlee, chocolate decadence, tiramisu; the waiter also mentioned that fresh melon sorbets were available.

Marti selected the sorbets, and Jim indulged himself with the tart. She thought that was a good pick. "If they hadn't had sorbet, I'd order the tart. I love desserts with fruit."

"Not a chocoholic?"

"No, not really. Though there are times when nothing will do but a Hershey's kiss."

"I don't have any Hershey's kisses, but I have plenty of the other kind."

The waiter brought coffee and desserts as Marti felt herself flush. She lifted her gaze from her coffee cup to meet Jim's glance. He stared deeply into her eyes, as if willing her to respond to his desire. She read his erotic intent as easily as she had understood her dinner menu. She shifted in her chair and sipped her coffee.

She wasn't sure yet if she wanted any of the other kind of kisses from a man who had the potential to hurt her. Despite the sensual promise in his glance, she couldn't help remembering his earlier betrayal. And he might still be on the rebound from Glenda Colter.

Even a kiss from Jim would be dangerous. Rumor was he'd had many women. She'd never stoop to the level of just another football groupie. She had more to offer than a one-night stand. But did he have anything more than hot sex to give? She drank her coffee thoughtfully, tantalized by his mouth, his eyes, his smile. *What would it be like with him?* The question haunted her.

She wrenched her mind away from useless speculations.

For goodness' sake, Marti, it's only a date! She dipped her spoon into her sorbet and focused on enjoying the moment, as well as every bite and nibble of the tasty dessert.

"Hey, let me try that." Jim put down his coffee cup.

"Sure," she said. Three different sorbets adorned her plate: cantaloupe, honeydew, and watermelon. The pastel spheres were arranged with a triangle of crispy pastry.

He used his coffee spoon to sample each. "Do you want to try a bite of tart?" he asked, handing her his fork.

"Thanks." She flaked a slice of kiwi off the top of the small pie. She scooped some of the underlying custard with it, avoiding the strawberries.

"Don't like strawberries?"

"No. My parents worked the strawberry fields for years."

"So how long was Rico in the fields? He seems like a pretty sophisticated guy for a retired farm worker."

"Don't forget, my parents emigrated to this country nearly forty years ago. Dad's an American, through and through. He also has a knack for fixing appliances, and that got him out of the fields after a few years." Marti looked down at her plate. "We needed the two incomes, so Mom wasn't as lucky."

"You sound bitter."

"I am bitter. My mother died from the pesticides they used. No, I don't like strawberries, and I don't eat them."

"I'm sorry." His voice was gentle. "Two years hasn't been long enough for you, has it?"

"Long enough for what?" Something in her chest clenched.

"Long enough for you to accept your mother's death."

Her mind and heart froze, icy as her dessert.

"Oh, I'm sorry, I'm sorry. I was being an armchair psychologist. I had no right." Jim extended his hand across the table to her.

Somehow, she recovered. "No, *I'm* sorry. You're—you're probably right. I just can't talk about it very easily, that's all." She reached over and put her hand into his, seeking comfort. She missed her mother every day.

His voice softened. "I hope one day you'll be able to talk with me about anything and everything that bothers you." He bent his head to kiss the tip of each of her fingers. Heat flashed through her body, startling and sweet.

He smiled at her. "Your blush is very flattering."

Her heart danced some more. "Should I be embarrassed more frequently?"

"Do I embarrass you?"

"No, not at all. I'm just not used to this, uh, kind of date."

"Neither am I. It's been a very long time." Jim handed the waiter a credit card. "I understand there are lovely gardens here. Would you like to take a walk?"

"Yeah, that would probably do us both good. Maybe walk off some of this dinner."

Softly glowing in the night, Domaine Patrice's garden featured a fountain and a pond. The water splashed as Marti walked with Jim along a flagstone walkway. A few late roses shimmered in the moonlight. Alone with him, she again became aware of his exhilarating and seductive presence, a presence that made her breathless with anticipation.

When he switched his grip from Marti's arm to her hand, lacing his fingers with hers, she turned to him willingly. He raised her hand to his lips, kissing the back of each finger and then the palm. "Such wonderful hands," he murmured.

A shiver rushed through her body.

"Are you cold?" he asked.

"It wasn't that kind of shiver."

"Oh. What kind of shiver was it?"

"A very good kind of shiver. A hot shiver, not a cold shiver."

"Hmm. These hot shivers, do you get them often?"

"Only when I'm with you," she flirted. Something about this man and this night made her feel wild and free. Was it his cologne, or the wine? She didn't care. Maybe it was the way his eyes twinkled. She'd always liked his little-boy grin.

As if on cue, he smiled into her eyes, then led her over to a stone bench set under a grape arbor. The leafless vines allowed moonlight to dapple his face as he turned to her.

The bench cooled Marti's thighs and bottom, but Jim's breath warmed her face as he took her chin in his hand. He leaned down and touched his lips to hers, tentatively at first, she thought, sampling her flavor as though she were a new dish.

He stroked the sensitive inner lining of her lips with his tongue, an enticing promise of bliss. He made her want more before he eased in, probing her depths. A husky purr emerged from her throat as he leisurely explored her mouth with his.

She felt she was a part of the moonlight and the stars spinning above. It had never been so good or so right in a man's arms. And he made her realize she had never been properly kissed. Her tongue met his and twirled together with it in utter rapture as he wrapped his arms around her, pulling her into his embrace. Nothing she'd ever experienced had prepared her for this magnificent male animal's assault on her senses, and he seemed determined to make her lose her head.

When they finally drew apart, he murmured, "Oh, yeah."

She giggled, trying to cover a burst of nerves. She sensed from the one kiss that they'd be very, very good together. Damn. She couldn't avoid intimacy with Jim on the grounds that he was a crummy kisser or that they'd be lousy in bed. No, they'd be great. Wonderful. The earth would move, and angels would sing the *Hallelujah Chorus*, if that kiss had been any example.

She again shoved her concerns aside to enjoy the moment for what it was: just a first date. She kissed him again, a happy smacking kiss more for fun and friendship than for passion. She was ecstatic with him and with the evening. This one kiss had shown her that her past hadn't ruined her, that she still could attract and want a man.

One unique, spectacular man.

Jim bent his head, sniffing the scent in her hair. "You're delicious."

"Delicious! What am I, dessert?"

"Well, yeah. Aren't I dessert for you? There's nothing wrong with it."

"You're right." She cuddled into his shoulder and rubbed her face against him.

Hugging her close, he bent his head to her lips again. As they kissed, he drew her onto his lap and slid one hand up her thigh. She felt his large hand on the flimsy silk dress as he stroked her hip. It burned through the thin fabric, igniting her desire. His other hand toyed with loose tendrils of hair at her nape.

She sensed the strength of his muscular legs beneath her, and then the pulsing hardness of his masculinity against her thigh. As a sensual heat leaped through her limbs, she wriggled slightly, before pulling away. Though excited by him, she was also embarrassed and unready for the intimacy of the contact. He released her, moving both hands to trace the contours of her cheekbones.

Voices floated over the splash of the fountain, interrupting their solitude. Other diners had discovered the moonlit garden. Marti slid off Jim's lap to sit beside him. She shivered, already missing the warmth of his arms.

"Ready to go? I'd like to continue this elsewhere."

"I guess so," she said, deliberately vague. *What exactly does he mean? This is only the first date.*

Fingers entwined with Jim's, Marti ambled out of the winery toward the waiting limo. A thrumming sensuality flowed through her body like champagne going to her head.

As she settled herself into the luxurious leather seats of the limousine, he pushed the button to raise the partition, cutting off the driver's view of the back. She tensed before she remembered that the drive from the restaurant to her cottage was not so long that she would lose control over the situation.

"You okay?" he asked.

Jolted, she realized that he'd seen through her calm act to her nervousness. His perceptiveness made her even more edgy. Swallowing, she said, "Yeah, I'm fine. Better than fine, actually." But Marti wasn't used to the level of attention Jim lavished on her.

He took her chin in his hand to smile into her eyes. She could drown in his twin blue pools. "Don't be nervous. I promise I'll give you nothing but pleasure."

He embraced her again as they were driven through the night. With a happy moan, she let her mind float away as he plundered her lips with his. His fingers drifted down past her neckline, exploring the sensitive valley between her breasts. The gentleness of his hands, so at odds with their size and strength, entranced and excited her. He caressed one nipple over the thin silk and nibbled at her mouth.

Sweet languor pervaded her, escalating the fire that threatened to burn away her caution. She slid both hands into Jim's hair, bringing him closer. His teeth and tongue savaged her lips, which now felt deliciously tender. She sighed as he left her mouth to feather his lips over her throat. She shivered with delight at his gentleness; his delicate touch reminded her of a night bird's wing.

The car stopped at Marti's cottage, behind Rico's Cadillac. She rubbed her face against Jim's, reveling in the slight stubble of his beard and his musky, masculine scent. "This has been such a wonderful night. Thank you."

"It doesn't have to end, you know."

"I know. But for now, this is enough." She had enjoyed herself thoroughly, but didn't want to lead Jim on.

"Well, I'll see you soon. Monday, in fact."

"Monday." She kissed him again—a brief kiss goodnight—and stepped out of the limo when the chauffeur opened her door. "Don't get out. I know it's hard for you."

"I generally walk a lady to her door."

"Thank you, but no. I'm actually doing you a favor. Believe me, you don't want to deal with my father. I think he's home now."

"Oh, I see. Are you ashamed of me?"

"No!" Anxious to explain herself, she hopped back inside the car. "But you can't imagine the pressure. He'd want to know everything about everything. He'd interrogate both of us as though we were felons. This night has been so terrific—I just don't feel like ending it as a threesome."

"I understand. I had to swear my sister to secrecy when she brought my tux. I do *not* want to have to talk about my personal life with my mother." They both laughed.

They kissed again—another sweet peck—and Marti left, trailing her hand back to hold his until the last moment as she walked away.

Jim watched her go to her door and unlock it. She waved goodbye before she closed it against the night, against him. A mixture of regret and pleasure sank through his limbs. He leaned back against the leather cushions of the limo, telling the driver to take him back to Shady Glen.

Her scent lingered in the car and on his fingers where they had become so pleasantly entangled in her hair. He lifted his hand to his face and sniffed. He recognized the fragrance. *Eternity*. How appropriate for Marti, he thought. She's a woman I could be with forever.

Chapter Six

The next morning, Marti skipped her usual run in favor of spending some quality time with her dad, figuring that breakfast at Edward and Zelda's café ought to do it. She settled into a chair near the coffee bar, with her father opposite her at a small round table. She eyed Rico. How could she tactfully broach the subject of the relationship between her father and her boss?

Her chatterbox father solved the problem for her. "Hey, I heard that you and that football player guy are playing golf at Steve's in a couple of weeks." Rico stirred his cappuccino.

"Is that so? No one told me."

"That's what I heard. He really seems interested in you, *querida*."

"Who told you about the golf?" she probed.

"Fran Murdoch."

"You're awfully chummy with Dr. Murdoch. What's going on?"

He fidgeted. "It's been two years since your mama passed on."

"Are you dating Dr. Fran?"

"I guess so." He hid behind his upraised cup.

Her voice rose. "I'm not quite sure if I want my father to date my boss. It, um, might bother the rest of the staff."

"Martina, you're always telling me that your personal life

is no one else's business." Her father put his cappuccino cup into the saucer with a clatter. "Now, who's being nosy?"

Abashed, she sat back in her chair and regarded her father. What she saw gave her pause. Here was a well-groomed gentleman in his sixties, with impeccably cut silver hair and a trim physique. For the first time she recognized that, for some women, her father was a catch.

"I don't mean to be nosy, Dad," she said, feeling as though she was walking through a minefield. "I just never thought—"

"You didn't think, Martina, but that's all right," he said. "I don't expect you to think about my personal life, but I do have one, you know."

"I guess so." She drank coffee while trying to wrap her mind around this new set of thoughts.

He broke her reverie. "I did arrange something else."

"What?" She nibbled her croissant.

"We're all going to play golf."

She put down her mug. A sinking feeling dropped through her body. She swallowed, then chose her words carefully. " 'We're all going to play golf.' Who, exactly, do you mean?"

"You, Jim . . . me and Fran."

"You and Dr. Fran! I don't want to golf with you and Dr. Fran!"

"Why not? She's a nice person, and it's good for you to have a social relationship with the boss."

She clutched her hair in frustration, then let go, recognizing that she was allowing the Wellman situation to drive her crazy—again. She folded her hands and smoothed her voice. "I don't want to double date with my boss and my father. And, Dad, you know I don't play golf. I was only going to tag along to make sure that Jim doesn't get hurt."

"But Jim says he won't go unless you do. Fran didn't think

it was professional for the two of you to go alone, so I told her we could all go."

"How do you think the rest of the staff will feel if the four of us go to Stone Cliff to play golf?"

"I never thought about it. But everybody likes you, *muchacha*. It's not like anyone's jealous of you, or anything."

"Let's sure hope you're right." She crossed her arms, letting sarcasm sharpen her voice.

"I'm sorry to disappoint you, Martina, but the world does not turn on what you think is appropriate." Her father's tone was firm. "Now, you'll go golfing and have a good time, you hear?"

"Dad, you have to quit talking at me as though I'm still a little girl."

"Sweetheart, you'll always be my little girl, and it's up to me to set you straight." Rico checked his wristwatch. "*Dios mio!* I'm supposed to meet Fran at the Silverado at nine, and it's already eight-thirty. Gotta go, hon!" His chair scraped the floor loudly as he stood.

"You're just leaving me here?"

"*Querida,* there's no reason to cut your breakfast short. I'll just dash back to your place to get the car by myself. Bye, now!" He buzzed out.

Flabbergasted by Rico's attitude, Marti finally remembered to close her mouth, which she'd let sag open for several seconds after he left. She'd had always taken it for granted that she was the center of Rico's world, along with Gracia, Steve, and later, the twins. But she'd been unrealistic to assume her vital, healthy father would remain single forever with no other interests in life.

"But what about Mom?" she cried to herself. Jim was right. She hadn't gotten over her mother's death. How could Rico move forward so fast?

A hand flapped in front of her face and a cheerful, Cockney voice called, " 'Allo? Anyone home?"

"Oh, Zelda! I'm sorry. I'm really distracted, I guess."

"Problems with the old man?" Zelda pulled out a chair and sprawled her long body onto it. Today she wore rose pink, and her nails, eyeshadow, and hair all complemented the outfit. She must have seen an old Pink video, Marti thought.

"He's dating my boss. Boy, what a mess."

"It is? Why, what's the big deal?"

"What if they break up? She could decide I remind her of him and I could lose my job. What if the rest of the staff thinks I'm getting too many perks because my father's going steady with the boss? I don't want to be the teacher's pet."

Zelda grinned at Marti. "If this is the worst of your problems, chickie, your life is smooth sailing."

Marti rolled her eyes. "It's not remotely the worst of my problems."

"Come on then, out with it."

Marti hesitated. She liked Zelda and needed to unburden herself. "Don't you have to work?"

"I have a few minutes. The Sunday morning coffee rush is closer to nine o'clock."

"Promise not to tell anyone? It could get me in trouble." Marti knew that Edward loved to dish. If Zelda told him anything, it would be all over the Napa Valley by sundown.

Zelda made an X across her chest. "Cross my heart. Not even Eddie. You know how he likes to talk."

"Well, okay. There's this man."

"Yes, Jim Wellman."

Marti stared at her, shocked. "How did you know?"

Zelda chuckled softly. "Marti, you know my husband considers that the major fringe benefit of running this shop is the gossip. Believe me, not much happens in our little town that Eddie doesn't hear. What he knows, I know."

She leaned across the table toward Marti. "A certain chauffeur spent a couple of hours here last night while his clients were eating at Domaine Patrice. He boasted that he was driving the star football player, Jim Wellman, and described his date to a T. It wasn't hard for us to put two and two together."

"So you know. Oh, God. What a mess." Marti rested her chin in her hand.

"What mess? Jim's been in here, and he's brill."

Marti sat up straighter. "He's a total horndog. He'll chew me up and spit me out like yesterday's bad meat."

Zelda smirked. It was the smirk of someone who had a nice bit of info to share. Marti didn't normally like gossip, but she'd listen if it had anything to do with Jim.

"Let me tell you something, babe. Jim Wellman is a nice ripe plum ready to be picked."

"Excuse me?" Marti couldn't see Jim as any kind of fruit.

"He was in here a few days ago. He had a big fight with some woman who left—walked right out on him. He had to call a cab to get home."

"Yeah, I know. Glenda Colter. Edward told me Glenda dumped him." Marti stirred her coffee. "That means his next girl is a rebound relationship. Everyone knows they never last long."

"Not necessarily." Zelda arched her brows, newly bleached and tinted pink. "He seemed depressed, so Eddie stopped by his table to try to cheer him up. You know how he is."

Marti again rolled her eyes. "Yeah." Edward would talk with a fencepost if he thought the conversation would sell more coffee.

Zelda grinned and continued. "They chatted for quite a long time. Jim mentioned settling down with the right woman. Even said he liked kids."

"Kids? Jim Wellman said he likes kids?" Marti frowned. She couldn't picture the tuxedo-clad devil who'd kissed her so seductively wiping a child's dirty face or burping a baby.

"Don't most people?"

"I guess so."

"Don't you? You seem to get along with Lizzie and Phil just fine." Twenty-something Zelda referred to her two younger siblings, both teens. Their "short visit" had extended to months.

"Well, yeah. They're great. But that's not the point."

"So what's the point? You want to settle down, don't you?"

"Eventually, sure. Sometime. Whenever." Marti picked at her croissant. "But Zelda, Jim's doing really well, and he'll be leaving Shady Glen in only a week or two. He won't hang around the Napa Valley forever just to be with me."

"You don't know that. You don't even know where he lives."

"I kinda do. He said his sister is taking care of his home while she's attending Sierra College."

"Hmm," Zelda mused. "Sierra College is in Rocklin. It's one of the community colleges we're checking out for Lizzie. So he probably lives within an easy drive of Rocklin, which is just east of Sacramento."

"Several hours away from here. Long-distance relationships never work."

"That could be an issue, yes, but I've seen them last."

Marti ignored her. "Plus, he probably just thinks he likes me. A lot of patients think they're in love with their care providers. It's called transference, and it's not real. He'll forget about me as soon as he gets well and leaves."

Zelda's voice was gentle. "But it's not transference for you, is it?"

Marti looked down, unable to meet her friend's searching gaze. "No. No, it's not. I'm really starting to care."

"So it was a hot date?"

Lifting her head, Marti smiled. "Yeah, it was great. And, darn it, so is he."

Zelda grinned back. "You're blushing."

"Am not." But a liquid, glowing happiness spread through her body as she remembered last night's encounter in the winery garden.

"Are too. If you like him, why don't you go after him?"

"Oh, a lot of reasons." Marti clutched her hair. "For one thing, he's a patient. Dr. Fran will hit the roof if I have a relationship with a patient on the grounds of the facility, and she'll have a good reason to be mad."

"Other people at Shady Glen have dated patients, or each other." Zelda stood up. "Fran Murdoch knows she can't stop people from being people. Marti, he's one hell of a catch. You'd have to be made out of stone to walk away."

Again, Marti couldn't meet her friend's scrutiny.

"You're falling for him, aren't you?" Zelda asked.

Marti buried her face in her hands. "Halfway there and going down fast."

Zelda laughed. "If I were you, I'd go for it."

Marti watched her well-meaning friend and her husband start to serve the Sunday morning coffee rush. She paid the bill for herself and her father, then walked home, still in chaos.

Her brain said no.

Her body said yes, please. Pretty please, with sugar on it.

Her heart was the same barbed-wire bundle of confusion it had been since she met Jim Wellman.

She wanted to believe she had a chance for something real with Jim, but she knew she could only be a passing fling for the superstar athlete. Why on earth would a celebrity like Jim be interested in someone as ordinary as she?

So far, he'd offered her nothing but a brief affair. While she guessed sex with Jim was likely to be great—no, make that mind-blowing incredible—she really was not the kind of woman who could wholeheartedly enjoy a fling, then walk away as though nothing had happened. The thought of a tawdry one-night stand made her feel grubby. She wanted the real thing, the whole enchilada, the big tomato: she wanted to fall in love with someone who loved her madly.

And the odds of Mr. Macho Celebrity Quarterback also being Mr. Right were between slim and none. So why bother?

No doubt about it. She was gonna dispose of the Wellman problem on Monday morning.

Upon her arrival at Shady Glen, Marti went to the staff lounge, which functioned as the employees' mail room and conference center, to check for mail and new assignments. It was a few days before Halloween, so the room was decorated with orange and black streamers, paper cutouts of black cats, and a fluorescent plastic skeleton. She smiled. The weekend staff had done a good job. She made a mental note to thank Eileen and the rest of the crew.

Then she spotted a vase of flowers set prominently on the large table in the middle of the room. The enormous bouquet consisted of two dozen red roses, with a big card adorned with a huge red heart and her name, written in calligraphy. *How impressive. How embarrassing. Why doesn't he just rent a billboard?*

"Hmm." She tried to control her cartwheeling emotions.

Katrin sat at the table, coffee mug nearby. " 'Hmm?' That's all you can say? Open it. I'm dying to know who it's from."

Marti pressed her lips together. Short of offending her colleague by telling Katrin that it was none of her business, Marti had no alternative but to open the card.

She found a poem, beautifully inscribed with a calligrapher's beveled pen on what appeared to be hand-made paper. The heavy, textured card read:

Enfolded in dust
your soul is sweet rock
and the flow of rain.
My blood is seawater and rust
I am cobalt-eyed
open and infinite.
The vital world is before you
offered to you for your delight
and delectation.

"Oh boy, he is really going for it!"

"Who?" Katrin asked. She hovered near Marti's shoulder, no doubt trying to catch a glimpse of the sender's name, but the card wasn't signed.

Marti breathed a sigh of relief. "Nobody. Well, this man I went out with on Saturday night."

"Some nobody," Katrin said. "I wish Mark would write me poetry."

"Mark's better than poetry, honey. He's a good man who loves you. This one . . ." Marti let the card fall to the table. "Fancy flowers and poetry are no substitute for the real thing."

"Are you telling me you're immune to dates, poetry, and two dozen red roses? Don't you like to be wooed?"

"Well, yeah. I'm a woman. But will I know what he's like underneath, once the wooing's done?"

"You never do. I didn't know about Mark. We eloped within three days of meeting each other. But we've been together for ten years now."

Marti stared at her. Sure, Katrin was a competent physical therapist, but Marti had always regarded her as something of a flake. Katrin's conversations generally centered on cosmetics and celebrities. Her favorite reading seemed to be *People* magazine. While Marti knew Katrin was married, she hadn't realized Katrin could keep a relationship together for longer than ten days, let alone ten years. Appearances can certainly be deceiving, Marti thought.

Marti reread the poem and sniffed. *Cobalt-eyed, open and infinite*—indeed! She read on: *The vital world is before you, offered to you for your delight and delectation.* Easy to understand what he was talking about. Did he think she could be seduced by such mushy sentiments?

"I guess it's time to see to Mr. Wellman." She set her jaw. Despite flowers, poetry, and a great date, she'd decided to give him the brush-off. Theirs was going to be a strictly professional relationship.

Jim wasn't in his suite. Surprised, Marti checked the therapy tower, finding him on its third level with Dr. Fran and Tommy, the orderly. Her heart made its usual, Jim-inspired flutter. Darn.

Holding a chart, a pen, and an intense expression, Dr. Murdoch observed Jim's performance on the various training stairs and ramps that were set up to help convalescents regain mobility. Despite her mixed feelings about him, Marti proudly watched her patient negotiate the various obstacles with ease and competence.

"You've made excellent progress, Mr. Wellman," Dr.

Fran said. "No, I don't see any problem with the golf date you have scheduled for November the first."

Marti's heart bounced.

His gaze swung to her. "Great! I take it there's no problem with Ms. Solis coming along?"

"No, not at all," Fran said. "Feel free to make any arrangements you wish. I will also be accompanying you, to make sure that your condition does not degenerate."

His brows knit as he heard this new crimp in his plans. Marti could practically see the gears and wheels spinning in his remarkably devious mind as he sought a way around this new roadblock to his goal: her body in his bed.

She wished she could decide whether to respond or run.

Dr. Fran continued, oblivious. "Tom, please fetch a quad cane for Mr. Wellman from storage. One crutch, Mr. Wellman, is not therapeutically appropriate."

Fran and Tommy left the room. Marti noticed uneasily that Dr. Fran hadn't said anything to her at all. Then she noticed, with even more unease, that she was alone with Jim. Since an encounter couldn't be avoided, she stepped farther into the room as he sat on a bench beneath a window.

"Hey! Isn't this good news?" he asked. "I don't particularly want Fran Murdoch along, but I bet we can ditch her as soon as we get to Stone Cliff."

"Dream on. My dad told me that he's going, too."

"That's even better. They'll be all wrapped up in each other, and we can go and have a good time." He lounged back into the window seat and propped his leg up.

She shook her head. "I don't know what you think is gonna happen on that trip. You're going to play golf. I'm going to watch you. My father, my brother, and my boss will be watching us. Believe me, nothing other than golf will take place." Which is just fine. Safety in numbers, she thought, with mingled relief and disappointment.

He grinned at her, his vivid blue eyes crinkling at the edges. Lines from his poem tripped through her thoughts. *Cobalt-eyed, open and infinite.*

"You don't know me, sweetheart. I'm apt to get what I want."

"Really? And what might that be?" She sat next to him, careful not to get too near the source of her unease. The closer she got to Wellman, the more overheated her body and brain became. She told herself she was making sure she didn't bump his leg.

"I don't want to tell you. You might lose your charming modesty and become all conceited."

"Well, you have a nice opinion of me."

"As a matter of fact, I do. Say, did you like the flowers?"

Reminded of her manners, she flushed. "Yes, I did. I meant to thank you. They're beautiful."

"No more beautiful than you."

She shot Jim a sidelong glance. "Flatterer. Everyone wants to know who they're from."

He shrugged. "Let 'em wonder. No one will ever guess it's me. Everyone thinks football players are big lummoxes who can't write poetry." His tone changed as he ran a fingertip underneath her chin. "Hey, come by tonight."

"Excuse me?" She flinched away.

His little-boy smile appeared. "Stop by tonight."

"What for?"

"Aw, come on, Marti. Do I have to spell everything out for you? I really missed you yesterday. I just want to spend some time together. We can eat popcorn and watch Monday Night Football."

"In your room, by ourselves?"

"I usually watch in the common room with the other patients and staff."

"That really doesn't suit me." *That's too public!*

"So come by my room afterwards."

That's too private! "I'll think about it." She changed the subject. "But now it's time for a whirlpool bath. It looked to me as though Dr. Fran worked you out pretty hard."

"And a massage?" he wheedled.

"Okay, a massage. Then I have to see to my other patients."

Tommy came back holding a quad cane.

"So what's this?" Jim asked.

"This is your quad cane," she said. "It's a specially designed walking stick with a four-footed base, for extra stability. Give it a try on the training stairs."

"Not bad." He thumped up and down the stairs. "Okay, let's go. I think I can deal with this myself, Tom," Jim said to the attendant, who winked as he left the room.

Alone again . . . with Jim. She stiffened against the onslaught of sensual energy between them, palpable and real as his touch on her chin. She walked him to his suite, wishing for a machete to cut through the sexual tension in the air.

When they arrived, she realized with some embarrassment that he'd strip off his clothes and get into his whirlpool bath. Her feelings confused her, since she'd never been shy around a patient before. She went over to the bath to fiddle with the temperature dial. He closed and locked the door.

"Er, how hot do you want it?" she asked, as nervous as a kid buying condoms.

"As hot as you can take it, baby."

"Now, Jim—" She meant to say, *Let's keep this under control, okay?* But when she turned to face him, his shirt was already off. Although she saw Jim semi-nude every day, she was again floored by his sheer masculine perfection.

His light tan complemented his chiseled pectorals and toned abdomen. A crinkly mat of dark hair ran over his chest and down, making a soft line toward his navel. She wanted to stroke it forever. Today he wore a leather thong around his neck from which a silver pendant was suspended. The oval pendant fitted into the hollow of his tanned throat. The lapis in the pendant matched his eyes.

He walked toward her, smiling. She knew by the predatory glint in his gaze that he sensed the breakdown in her resistance. She wanted him desperately.

Jim thrust his hands into her hair and pulled her mouth to his. Needy, rougher than he had been on Saturday night, this kiss was sheer sexual torment: demanding, fierce, and long, lighting a fire that scorched along every vein. When he finally released her, she jerked away from him. Despite her own desire, she was unnerved by the intensity of his passion.

"Jim, this is not like me."

"Hey, I thought everything was okay."

"I cannot do this at work. I absolutely can not." Marti enunciated every word clearly, trying to convince both of them.

"Come on, Murdoch will never know."

"I will know. And I am important."

He shook his head, looking gorgeous and confused. "I never meant to imply that you weren't. I'm sorry. I guess I misunderstood your mood."

"Please, just get into the bath." Though upset, she managed to control her hysteria. She knew she teetered on some kind of intangible edge, dancing on the boundary between her stable, secure life and the infinite unknown he represented. Holding her breath, she watched him like a mouse watches a cobra.

He stripped off his sweatpants and slid into the tub. She wanted to touch him, to run her fingers along the hard length of him, but didn't dare. She closed her eyes. She wanted to cry.

She was terrified of what she knew he would demand from her. This man had the power to overset her life completely, to take from her everything she had to give, and then to walk away, leaving nothing but a drained husk. God help her, she wanted to give him everything he demanded, and more. But instead of taking off her scrubs and joining him in the tub, she sat on the edge of his bed and drew her knees into her chest. She wrapped her arms around her legs, watching the back of his head as he lay, relaxed, in the bath.

The jets shut off automatically after ten minutes. He stood, the water shining off his muscled torso, supple back, and rounded buttocks. Her gaze was drawn to the flex of his muscles as he reached for a towel, which he ran over his sleek, powerful body before wrapping it around his hips.

He turned to Marti, still seated on his bed, feeling small and waiflike, arms cocooning herself. He sat down next to her.

"Marti, it's me, Jim. Please, trust me."

She couldn't speak for the emotions clogging her throat.

"I don't know what happened before, I don't know who did this to you, but it wasn't me."

Her sigh came from the depths of her soul. He put his arm around her, hugging her to him. Gradually she loosened and dropped her feet to the floor. Pulling out of his grasp, she stood to stretch, realizing how cramped she'd become in the upright fetal position into which she'd twisted. She wondered if her tight, bound heart could release as easily as her muscles.

She looked down at him. "I'm sorry. You're a wonderful man, and you deserve better, you really do."

"Sweetheart, we deserve each other." He took her hand. "Let me show you. Come by tonight."

She hesitated. "I don't know."

"Aw, come on, Marti. It's just a football game. How much trouble can we get into?" He again gave her what she recognized as his best little-boy grin. Damn it, that look always made her melt.

"All right, but only for awhile. And I think it's better if Katrin or Tommy gives you your massage today, okay?"

Jim's smile stretched wider. "It's definitely not better for me, but I know what you mean. See you later, then."

Marti escaped his room with a sense of disbelief. As she paged Katrin, she realized that he'd bamboozled her again. She had intended to break things off before anyone got hurt, but somehow he'd conned her into another private little tête-à-tête in his room.

What a manipulator! She knew that quarterbacks were often the smartest football players on a team. They frequently called their own plays and, because they were natural leaders, were generally team captains. So far, Jim was a classic: an intelligent, calculating predator. He was a risk-taker, too. Hell, Mr. Macho was so sure of success that he didn't hesitate to put his massive ego on the line.

She shivered. She'd learned on Saturday night that his natural talent, aggression, and drive had lifted him out of the Oakland slums to the top of the heap as a high-scoring celebrity athlete. The word "failure" wasn't in his vocabulary.

He doesn't have much to occupy himself, she reasoned. Working on his recovery is time-consuming, but not intellectually challenging. He's got way too much time on his hands—and it seems as though he's found himself a new project—me!

Unease slithered up her spine. She saw herself as a rabbit in the sights of a high-powered rifle wielded by an especially clever hunter. She was a challenge to her bored, restless patient, nothing more. There was no way someone like Jim Wellman could have a real interest in her.

She couldn't, however, say that he had bad intentions. Oh, no. He wanted to give her nothing but pleasure. Or so he said.

Marti grimaced. Of all the feelings in the world, she hated insecurity the most. She liked to know what was going to happen in her day, every day. She didn't want an uncertain new love to confuse and upset her. Her feet belonged on firm soil, not shifting quicksand.

Yep, she was definitely going to give Jim the ol' heave-ho that very evening.

Chapter Seven

Marti avoided Jim for the rest of the day, tending instead to her other patients. She feared they'd been neglected as a result of her growing interest in him. She instructed Tommy to take Jim for his afternoon walk, certain that if she went, the stroll would turn into tonsil hockey behind the birch trees.

That afternoon, she worked with little Andrea up in the therapy tower. Through a window, she spied Jim and Tommy walking briskly over the slate paths that wound through the grounds. She noticed the difference between Jim's gait this day and the first time she had observed him. Jim now moved easily, with confidence. *Soon he'll be gone, and then what?* Again depressed by the thought, she became more determined to tell him the truth. Their relationship could go no further.

Dressed in dark sweats, feeling like a ninja spy, Marti parked her Honda in the middle of a row of cars at the far end of the Shady Glen employees' lot. While the facility was only lightly staffed in the evening, she saw that there were an unusual number of cars parked. All the better, she thought. Nobody will notice mine.

She planned to slip in, find Jim in his room, and tell him that they had to maintain a strictly professional relationship in the future. She walked around to the back entrance near the common room. As she eased the door open and sneaked inside, she met a burst of laughter and chatter. Startled, she let the metal door slam shut behind her. She'd forgotten Monday Night Football, the sports institution, was also a big night for the patients and evening staff at Shady Glen. Everyone would be in the common room, even those who weren't sports fans. Companionship was scarce anywhere else at Shady Glen on Monday nights in the autumn.

"What was that?" a voice called over the racket in the noisy room. Someone else answered, "Oh, it's just the wind. Pass the popcorn!"

She could hear crowd noises coming from the TV, and the patient from hell lecturing about the game.

"See, the secondary's gonna go wide, while the primary defenders come in to pressure the quarterback. That's what they call a 'blitz.' "

She heard a female voice—Katrin?—say, "Oh. That's a blitz?"

How lame, Marti thought. Everyone knows that! Discretion abandoned, she pushed open the door to the common room and entered. Everyone was focused on the last two minutes of the game, which tonight featured the Bengals against the Cowboys.

She watched as Jim took the opportunity to school the ignorant, particularly the females, in the finer points of football. A group of admiring women surrounded him. She would have felt jealous except their average age was eighty years, typical of most convalescent facilities.

"But it's risky to blitz when the offense is in the shotgun formation. Let me show you, Mrs. Stockman." Jim touched the shoulder of an elderly woman in a wheelchair, pointing at the screen with his free hand. The old biddy was transfixed, not by the football, but by Jim. Marti grinned as she saw Mrs.

Stockman, who had to be ninety if she was a day, scrutinize Jim's buns as he gestured.

"A shotgun formation is when the passer goes way back." He drew his right hand back over his shoulder. "The quarterback earns more time to find a guy open and to throw the ball." He faked passing an imaginary football. "But there's fewer men on defense out there to cover the wide receivers. See?" A burst of crowd noise accompanied a completed pass.

Marti perched at the end of one of the couches, feeling like a Martian in a chocolate factory. What was she doing here? Planning to leave, she stood.

"Hey, Marti." Katrin grabbed her arm. "Listen to this guy. He knows everything about football!"

"Sure he does," Marti said. "He was M.V.P. at the last two Super Bowls and won the Heisman Trophy when he was in college. Of course he knows everything about football."

Jim looked over at her. "I didn't know you followed my career."

"I didn't really. Just the basics every sports fan knows."

He staggered toward her. Despite his clumsiness, he managed to avoid hitting anyone with his cane. He draped an arm around her and hauled her down onto the couch. "You came, I can't believe you came," he purred into her ear.

She sat upright and rigid. "Are you aware everyone is watching us?" she muttered.

"Are not. They're watching the game. Bengals are about to score. Maybe a historic moment, at least for this season. Besides, so what? I'm not mysterious Marti's mysterious lover, the one who sends her flowers and poetry. Nope, I'm just ol' Jim, dumbo quarterback."

"Why do you say these things about yourself?"

He grinned at her. "Aw, I'm just playin' around. Hey, game's almost over. Wanna take a walk?"

"Sure," she said. "To the women's room."

"See you in my room in five?"

She paused to reflect. "Well, okay. But no funny business, you understand?"

Five minutes or so later, she went to the door of Jim's suite and raised her hand to tap on it before entering. She heard his voice, sounding as though he was talking on the phone. She heard him say, "Yeah, Glenda," and laugh.

That rat, she thought. He's back with her!

Marti turned and vanished, a wraith in the night.

The next morning, Marti worked with Andrea in the therapy tower, fobbing Jim off onto Katrin and Tommy. Due to Andrea's particular needs, therapy with her was more play than work, only lasting a few minutes until the little girl became bored or tired.

Marti sensed Jim's eyes on her back, but she ignored him as she led Andrea, still using the walker, over a training ramp used to teach patients mobility. He climbed a small flight of training stairs in the same area, but without cane or crutches. This workout was another step toward complete independence from the cane. She saw he was having difficulties, so after Andrea began to show signs of fatigue, she sat the child down and approached Katrin, who monitored Jim's progress from the bottom of the stairs.

Katrin turned to Marti, brow wrinkled. "I don't get it. He seems to be relapsing."

"Maybe he's just hit a plateau. Try letting him relax a bit," Marti said.

"You're doing it again," Jim interrupted.

"Excuse me?" Marti asked.

"You're talking about me as though I'm not here." Jim wiped his brow. "I thought you'd stopped that."

She managed to hold her tongue. She wanted to snap at Jim that her conversation wasn't his business, but she could hardly tell a patient that his therapeutic progress was none of his concern. Instead, she adopted her most distant professional manner and asked, "Mr. Wellman, how are you feeling today?"

"Disappointed."

"Excuse me?"

"I was supposed to get a visit from a friend last night, and she stood me up."

"Oh." Marti, the responsible party, was disconcerted by that statement.

"Listen, Jim." Katrin jumped in. "I realize that your relationships are important to you, but you can't let the acts of another person affect your health. Do you feel that this one event is slowing your progress?"

"Oh, definitely." He glanced at Marti.

"Then you should probably contact this person and get the matter straightened out," Katrin said. "Keep in mind that no relationship is more important than your well-being."

"Yes, I'd like to do that." Jim continued to skewer Marti with his icy blue gaze. She tried not to squirm.

"In the meantime, let's take Ms. Solis' suggestion and let you relax for a while. How about a whirlpool, followed by nap and lunch?" Katrin nodded to Tommy, who came forward to accompany Jim to his suite. "Marti, I think you should work with this patient today. He seems to make the most progress with you."

"That's fine with me," Jim said promptly.

To her irritation, Marti saw Tommy smirk. "Okay," she said reluctantly, seeing no way out. But she'd get a chaperone. "Tom, please meet us in Jim's suite at two."

"I'm sorry, Marti," the aide said. "I have a dental appointment after lunch in Santa Rosa. It'll take the whole afternoon."

"And I have other patients to consider," Katrin said. "I'm sure you can deal with Mr. Wellman alone."

Marti scrutinized Jim. Cornered, she had to admit to herself that he'd handled the situation—and her—like a master.

He gave her his little-boy smile, guileless and sweet. "Guess it's just you and me."

"Guess so." But Marti wasn't going to go down easily. "Andrea, do you know Jim?" she asked the girl.

"Sure. Everyone knows Jim."

"Do you want to walk with us this afternoon?" Marti asked.

Andrea frowned. "Is it during 'Rugrats'?"

"Umm, it might be," he cut in. "Tell you what, let's take a walk right now to the cafeteria and get a snack. That way, you won't miss 'Rugrats.' "

"Gee, thanks, Jim," Andrea chirped.

"Gee, thanks, Jim," Marti said.

At two o'clock, Jim stretched on the floor of his suite as he waited for Marti to arrive for their walk. He bent toward each foot, slowly relaxing the hamstrings.

Baffled by her attitude, he mentally reviewed the progress—if it could be called progress—of their relationship.

They had met.

She was sympathetic toward his problems, more so, he felt, than the average therapist would be.

Then he discovered, from Tommy and later from her father, that she was single and available. So far, so good.

They went out. Had a great date.

He'd pushed her a little too hard yesterday, but everything she'd done had led him to believe that she'd welcome his advances. Remembering the passionate way she'd kissed him in the winery garden and then yesterday in his suite, he broke into a light, lustful sweat. She'd sent a message his body was all too ready to receive, but then she'd recoiled as though he was gonna rape her. He shook his head. Something sure had this girl scared, really scared, of normal human contact.

He stood and bent one leg back toward his butt, grabbing the toes to stretch the quad. He breathed deeply for ten counts, then repeated the process with the other leg.

At least he'd managed to get her calmed down and to agree to stop by after football. Everything had seemed fine, but then she didn't show up. Worse, she was trying hard to avoid seeing him alone, which meant she didn't want to discuss the situation.

He twisted his torso from side to side, releasing back tension.

Fine. If Marti didn't want him, he knew plenty of women who did. Just because none of them were at Shady Glen meant that he'd better get well fast, go home, and return to a normal routine. But what would that be? he wondered for what must have been the millionth time. *What am I going to do with myself?*

He was the same kid who'd dragged himself out of the slums and into success. He'd be a winner, no matter what this sorry world dished out to him. He'd create a new life, with or without Marti Solis. *I like a challenge, but I'll be damned if I'll chase her!* he thought as he did shoulder shrugs.

He wished he had free weights in his room. The trek to the basement workout room annoyed him every time he wanted to do just a few bicep curls.

What the hell was going on in her head? He had to know before he walked away. He'd given her every reassurance possible except a declaration of undying love and an engagement ring. That might happen, but he wasn't ready for it yet and neither was she.

But he wanted her more than he'd ever wanted any other woman. He'd promised Marti nothing but pleasure, and meant it. He'd make her body sing.

He could sense that she'd never been fulfilled by any man. He figured she knew her own body—hell, she was a modern woman, and a health professional to boot. But he'd bet his last dollar that he'd be the first lover to make her lose control. And he could hardly wait. He loved watching his partner peak.

He stopped stretching as the mere thought of making Marti climax in his arms made him hard. He imagined her gentle moans and pants of joy as her tight little body gripped him while they kissed.

No, he wouldn't give up. The victory would be all the sweeter for her resistance.

Still, he was mystified and just plain frustrated, dammit. He hadn't made love for months. His body was a raging inferno of pent-up need that no amount of stretching and weightlifting could relieve.

Marti was taken aback by the glare on Jim's face as she entered his room.

"Let's go." He stood. "I want to see if I can make it to the creek today."

She raised her eyebrows. "All the way to the creek? That's a half-mile round trip. Think you're up to it?"

Jim narrowed his eyes. "That sounds like a challenge. I like that." He pulled a sweatshirt over his head. "Better take a sweater. It's gray and windy out there."

"I didn't bring one."

"Borrow one of mine. It's cold outside."

She pursed her lips. She didn't want to encourage intimacy on any level, but didn't want to get chilled either. "I guess so."

He went to the chest of drawers and took out a faded burgundy Cougars sweatshirt. Great, she thought. If anyone sees us, they'll know it's his! However, she felt it would be a little foolish to make an issue over the sweatshirt. She'd just take it off as soon as they got back from their walk. She pulled it over her head. The shirt fell in folds over her, enveloping her in his spicy, musky scent. The sweatshirt hung, tunic length, to the middle of her thighs.

Both warmly attired, they proceeded down the elevator and out the back door of the facility. This exit faced the foothills and the creek. Winding through a wide lawn, the path to the creek was paved with the usual slate for part of the way, then turned to rammed earth, gradually coming to resemble a well-maintained hiking trail.

Jim looked grimly determined, tramping along the track with an almost fierce demeanor. Marti paced him and watched his progress closely.

He was right—it was cold, and the sky was gray. Fog had persisted all day, and still hung low over the hills. It was not the kind of gorgeous autumn day typical of the Napa Valley. But even in poor weather, the valley had its own mysterious, brooding beauty.

Neither attempted to break the tension between them with small talk. They reached the creek, and turned right to follow a side trail which ran along the water's edge. The creek, though shallow, was full enough to feed a band of greenery—willows, ferns, and wild grasses—which grew along its banks. The water clattered over myriad rocks, and eddied in constantly moving swirls.

Marti came to a portion of the bank that jutted out into the stream and squatted, watching. She heard Jim step behind her. She turned to him, finger to her lips, then pointed.

Across the creek, an olive-green bullfrog the size of a saucer sat on a rock and regarded the cloudy day. Suddenly, his throat expanded, and he emitted a croaking squeal that broke up both Marti and Jim completely. They laughed so hard that the frog, with an insulted air, leapt into the creek and disappeared.

He managed to choke out, "I suppose he thinks we spoiled his great mating call."

"Yeah, we wrecked his date for the evening." She groped for a tissue in her pocket and wiped her streaming eyes. "This is a great spot, isn't it? I come here a lot."

"Yeah." He smiled. "Sometimes I watch you from the window of the common room."

"Oh, so you're spying on me."

"I wouldn't call it spying. Sometimes if I'm taking a break and resting my eyes on the scenery, there's an extra added beauty spot walking along the path to the creek. Now I know what you do down here."

"Yes, I watch the wildlife. I've seen all kinds, egrets, turtles, you name it." She stood up and stretched.

"You should come to my place if you're interested in nature. Wanna see a cougar?"

"I'm seeing one right now."

"No, I mean a real cougar."

"So do I." She grinned.

"No, really. A mountain lion. Colfax is prime mountain lion habitat."

"You live near Colfax? That's a lovely area."

"Yeah. My house is in a forest. There's a creek like this one, but it widens into a pond on my property."

Marti was both intrigued and discouraged. She knew that

Colfax, a small community on the road to north Lake Tahoe, was a drive of several hours from Napa. She'd passed the Colfax off-ramp on the way to the lake and noticed the beauty of the region, located inside the timberline of the Sierra foothills.

"That sounds wonderful," she said. "I'm very attracted to running water. That's one of the many reasons I like working here. I love this walk, but I think we should start back. It's getting dark, and I don't want your leg to stiffen up from standing too long. When we get back, I want you in the whirlpool right away, you hear?"

"Yes, ma'am. I hear and obey." He turned back toward the main trail.

"Oh, you! You make me sound as though I'm some sort of meanie. Everything I do, I'm trying to help you get stronger, healthier." *Even though you'll leave when you're well,* she added silently as she followed him.

"I know that," Jim said, unabashed. "I like to tease you, you know. You're kind of an easy mark."

"Excuse me?"

"You're fun to tease, that's all."

"Hmm." She wasn't sure she liked that.

"I don't know why you're so surprised. I'm surprised that the men you've been with haven't told you you're fun."

"I haven't been with many men," Marti said, aware of the gap between her experience and Jim's.

"I know that. Quit twisting my words. I'm just saying you're fun to flirt with, that's all." He continued down the path. "Lighten up, babe."

"I'm not your babe."

His cobalt eyes narrowed. "That's a pity." He stumped down the path. "Look, Marti, I get the message, all right?

Let's just be friends and forget everything else that's happened. It was obviously a big mistake for both of us."

"I don't think anything that's happened between us was a mistake. I just can't figure out how to fit you into my life. In a few weeks, you're outta here. Why should I get involved with someone who won't be around?"

Jim was silent for a time as they walked. "Maybe you shouldn't," he said. "But who says I'm not going to be around? I have no idea what I'm going to do after I leave Shady Glen. It'll depend upon my physical condition. If I can't play—and it looks as though I can't—I might go into coaching, or sports journalism. I don't really want to deal with people like Glenda Colter anymore, though."

"I thought you were back with her."

"Hell, no. Why would you think that?"

Marti blushed. She didn't want Jim to know she had been eavesdropping. "That's just the rumor."

"The rumor's wrong. It's over."

"Hmm." But she knew what she'd overheard the night before, and wasn't sure she wanted to give him the benefit of the doubt.

"The point is," he said, "I can do anything I want and be anywhere I want to be. And I just might want to be with you. I don't know yet."

"Hmmm."

"At least you can put up with my company for a while, all right? You don't really have a choice. You're my therapist for the duration. So, let's try to make this as pleasant as possible, okay?"

"Okay," she said. "Truce?"

"Truce. Friends?" He held out his hand.

She took it. "Well, all right, friends."

"There, that wasn't so hard, was it?"

"You make me feel so silly, sometimes. I can't help my feelings. I just don't want to become attached to you unless it's real. What's wrong with that?"

"Nothing at all." Jim squeezed her hand for emphasis. "But sometimes you just have to take a chance, to find out if it's real. I'm willing to take a chance on you. Why are you so scared to do the same for me?"

She took a deep breath, counted to ten. "Well . . . there was this doctor in Berkeley . . . he was, er, married."

"I'm surprised." He raised a brow. "You're pretty smart. What made you get involved with a married man?"

She shrugged unhappily. "The oldest line in the world. He told me he was separated."

"Oh, baby." He enfolded her in the comforting warmth of his embrace. "He was just a jerk. A two-timing, double-dealing, two-faced bastard."

Marti rubbed her face against his shirt. "What made it worse was that it was my first really intense relationship, at least in my own mind. I mean, I had a boyfriend in high school, but I didn't get involved seriously with anyone else until Terrence, and haven't since."

"Isn't it about time?"

"Yes. Maybe." She pulled away from him. "But what made it worse was that everyone at the hospital knew that Terrence hit on the new interns, and no one warned me. Everyone knew he was married. I was never so humiliated in my life."

"Humiliation and betrayal. You think I'd do that to you?" His voice rose with outrage.

"I don't think you'd intend to," Marti said quickly. "But that mess with Glenda Colter made me nervous. You're a celebrity, Jim. I feel intimidated by you—by everything about you. You're so different from me. I'm just a little physical therapist in a little town."

"You have a very negative self-evaluation."

He sounds like a shrink. Remembering that Jim had majored in psych, she blew out an exasperated breath.

He continued, "I was at the top of my profession when I got hurt. So what? You're at the top of yours. Otherwise, I wouldn't be here. And, we're not much different, at least in the things that matter. We were both raised poor and made something of our lives. That's important. We both like the country—that's why I live in Colfax and you in Napa.

"You're focusing on the negative external stuff," he said. "Look at the broader perspective."

"Hmm."

They had reached Shady Glen, and both Marti and Jim reached for the doorknob at the same time. As their hands collided, Jim clasped hers. He raised her hand to his lips, then nibbled on the palm. *Instant turn-on. How does he do that?*

"Marti, you're a very beautiful, unique woman, and I want to see you and be with you. Saturday night?"

Marti looked down at the ground, embarrassed by the flattery. "You think I'm beautiful?"

Jim laughed. "Are you serious? Honey, you're a walkin', talkin' reason to live. Why do you think I recuperated so fast? So I can hang around with you! So how 'bout Saturday night?" He squeezed her hand.

"I'm sorry, but I'm going out of town," she mumbled, still floored by his compliment. "Gotta see Dad."

He narrowed his eyes at her, looking comically suspicious.

"Really, I'm telling the truth. This isn't an excuse. I'll let you know if my plans change, okay?"

He relaxed and smiled, letting her hand go. "All right. But will you have dinner with me at Stone Cliff on the evening of the first?"

"That's our golf date, right?"

"Yeah. Fran Murdoch said I could make any arrangements I wanted, so I decided that we're going to spend the night at Stone Cliff. I told her that the drive is so long, I felt that I'd be too tired to drive both ways and play golf all in one day. There's a guesthouse I've rented for the night."

"You'd better fix this with Dr. Fran. This doesn't sound like the kind of thing she'd approve."

He chuckled. "You've said yourself, darlin', that I have lots of experience with the opposite sex. Don't worry about the boss-lady. I can twist her around my little finger. Besides, your dad will be along. The old folks will be so excited about each other, they won't have time for us."

"You might be right." She opened the door, ushering Jim in.

He groaned. "I stiffened up standing out there. I'd better get into the bath." He awkwardly turned toward the elevator.

"Wait." She stripped off his sweatshirt and held it out.

"Keep it," he said.

"I don't need it for what I'm doing now."

"And what's that?"

She shuddered. "Taking Andrea to the hydrotherapy pool."

"What's wrong? I love my swim workouts. Tom and I have a great time."

Marti turned left toward a staircase, then stopped. "Andrea has some kind of aversion to the water she won't talk about. I can't seem to make it fun for her, and it's not working at all. I'm almost about to give up."

"Aw, you never give up. Determination is your middle name."

She grinned. "Funny you should say that. It's what I think about you."

"You just keep that in mind the evening of the first, sweetheart. Hold onto the shirt. You'll need it for your ride home. See ya tomorrow!" he called as the elevator doors closed behind him.

Chapter Eight

Marti's fingers stabbed into Jim's back as her beeper buzzed in a code: one long and two short tones. She whipped a towel over his naked form and said, "Gotta go."

She was out of the room before he was aware he'd been ditched. Still dazed from the massage, he rolled over and sat up on the padded massage table. He groped for his sweatpants and T-shirt as he heard footsteps running down the hall outside his room, with the distinctive squeal of rubber-soled shoes against linoleum, accompanied by the clatter of a cart.

What the hell was going on? He poked his head out the door of his suite. Fran Murdoch raced down the hall. "Code Blue! Code Blue!" The doctor's normally calm voice was raised.

He heard Marti shout, "Where's that crash cart?"

The clattering cart was hauled into a room down the hall.

Mrs. Stockman's room.

Jim grabbed the lintel of his doorway for support. He'd forgotten his cane in his haste. The hall was full of white-clothed figures moving in a frantic, but well-choreographed dance as medical personnel fought for the elderly patient's life. A siren screamed as an ambulance arrived, and Napa Valley paramedics shoved into Mrs. Stockman's room.

Sorrow swept him. He knew Donna Stockman was in her

nineties. He had met her son and daughter and overheard their anxious, whispered conversations in the hallway outside his suite. *They say she's doing as well as can be expected, but her heart's weak . . .*

Suddenly all was quiet and still.

A gurney bearing an inert figure, covered entirely by a white sheet, was pushed out of Mrs. Stockman's room.

It was followed by Dr. Murdoch, Marti, and other Shady Glen personnel. All wore the same stony expression. They walked down the hall toward the elevators.

Jim waited until the hall was empty, then went to Mrs. Stockman's room. Inside, Tommy was making the bed with fresh sheets; for the next occupant, Jim supposed. The young man's face was quiet and set.

"She's gone, isn't she?" Jim asked.

Tom leaned against the bed after tucking in the last neatly mitered corner. "Yeah, she's gone."

"She was a nice lady."

"Yeah, and she had a pretty good run. She was ninety-four, I think."

"Wow. We should all be so lucky."

"Yeah." Tommy straightened up. "Well, I better go find Marti."

"What about Marti?"

"Dr. Fran says this is a place where people learn how to live, not come to die. Everyone takes it pretty hard when something like this happens, Marti more than anyone. You know about her mother, don't you?"

"Yeah." Jim glanced around the room. His attention was drawn to the open curtains, through which he could see the ambulance leave through the open gates of Shady Glen. He went closer to the window. Several white-garbed figures watched the ambulance as it departed, bearing the body of

Mrs. Stockman. Instinct told him that Marti also stood there. "Excuse me, Tom."

He left the room, and caught up with Marti as Dr. Fran, who seemed to have recovered her composure, issued orders in a dry, crisp tone. "I'll see the section heads in my office promptly at eight a.m. tomorrow for full reports in regard to Mrs. Stockman. At this time, all of you will please make rounds and calm the rest of the patients. We don't want to have any relapses as a result of this unfortunate incident."

Marti's mouth tightened at Dr. Fran's last phrase, "unfortunate incident." Nice way to refer to someone's passing, he thought.

Marti's face was pale, and her lips bloodless. As the staff dispersed, Jim grabbed her sleeve to halt her flight.

"Oh, Mr. Wellman."

"You're back to calling me Mr. Wellman again?"

"I'm . . . I'm sorry." She sounded dazed.

"That's all right. I know this is difficult for you, honey, because of your mother."

Her head jerked up. She stared at him.

"Am I right?" he asked in his gentlest tone.

She was mute as he guided her toward their favorite stand of birches, which had been rendered nearly leafless by autumn winds. Their stark branches thrust toward the gray sky.

He worried about her. The hand he held was ice cold. Her usually graceful walk was awkward, like a badly tuned robot. Their easy chatter had been replaced by a painful silence.

She dropped onto the bench and buried her face in her hands. Sitting next to her, he put one arm around her quivering shoulders. She turned her face into his chest and cried without shame or restraint. He pawed through his pocket for a tissue, offering it to her.

"Mom had ingested a chemical called methyl bromide,"

Marti started, in a soft, choked voice. "They fumigate the fields with this gas, and the workers follow the trucks and cover the ground with tarps to prevent the stuff from escaping. It's a Category One acute toxin, kills everything it touches. My mother was no exception."

Sighing, she rubbed her nose with the tissue. "Mom started to cough one day. We thought it was just a cold or something, but she began to cough up blood. It had affected her lungs mostly, like a severe case of pneumonia. Her lungs kept filling—" She stopped to bury her face in her hands again. He massaged her shoulder lightly, reminding her that he was there for her.

"They had tubes down her nose, down her throat, in her arms, everywhere. She was on a respirator to help her breathe. It was ghastly.

"They did everything they could, but another effect of the chemical is a generalized muscular weakness. Her heart was failing. One day they told us they couldn't do anything more for her." She gulped. "We had a choice. We could leave her there, put her in hospice care, or take her home. Mom wanted to go home."

She rubbed her face on his chest. "The hospital staff was awful, didn't support us at all. It was weird . . . in this day and age, most hospitals are used to people taking family home for their last days. But they refused to help us, told us we'd be accessories to her murder if we took her away.

"And I was the worst kind of selfish bitch."

He stirred. "I don't understand."

"I was the one with the medical training. I disconnected her from her tubes and IVs." She broke into tears again. "I'm a healer, and I pulled the plug. God help me, when I took her off the respirator, I was worried about me, not her. I remember my hands were shaking so hard because I wondered if I would be spending the night, or even the rest of my life, in jail. I wasn't thinking about my mother, who was in agony. I was worried about myself." Her voice had grown hard with self-loathing.

Abruptly, he was incensed. He grabbed her by the shoulders and shook her. "Don't you ever let me hear you say that again, and don't you ever think it!" He seized her chin, forcing her to look him in the eyes. "That's the most courageous, compassionate, selfless act anyone could ever do."

"But I wasn't thinking of her."

"That's not the point. What did your mother think?"

Her voice dropped to a whisper. "She was wonderful. We took her home. We rented a hospital bed, set it up in the living room. That was where she died. I don't know how my dad still lives in that house. I couldn't stand it." She wiped her wet face with the shredded tissue.

"Were you there when she went, sweetheart?"

"Yeah. We all were. It was . . . it was a holy moment."

"How?"

"She knew she was going. She made sure we all were there, that she was clean." Marti started to laugh. It was a jerky, grating sound. "She said that when she met her Maker she wanted to be in a fresh nightgown with her teeth brushed."

"She sounds like one hell of a feisty lady. Like her daughter." He squeezed her tighter.

"She was great. She told me how proud she was of me and how much she loved me." Her eyes filled again.

Her internal wall had finally broken. Her release was as powerful as sex and just as gratifying to him. He was pleased—no, make that honored—that she finally trusted him enough to share her most private emotions.

He continued holding her close. Without impatience, he waited for her to collect herself. He treasured the moment, knowing in some deep and primal way that she was his to support as well as to love.

Love. The word blazed across all of his synapses like a comet igniting the sky.

He loved her.

No, he was in love with her. Even better.

Jim looked down at the small, dark-haired woman cuddled against his chest with a rising tide of joy in his heart. He had never thought it would happen to him, but he was in love, and it felt like forever. This new, delightful, all-encompassing adoration was as far beyond anything else he'd ever felt for a woman as a human is different from an amoeba.

He hoped she loved him too, and suddenly knew with utter certainty that she did. Jim couldn't picture Marti, a very private person, unburdening herself so completely to anyone she didn't love and trust.

How should I tell her? Not now. She was involved in intense emotions of a different sort, a cleansing that was necessary and right.

He smiled with sheer anticipation. One part of his mind started to make plans at the same time he comforted her.

After a few moments he began to kiss the tears away, to dot her sweet face with his most tender, light kisses. Her eyelids were puffy. He kissed them too. Her mouth trembled. *Gotta kiss there. That lower lip needs attention.* She snuggled deeper into his arms and returned his kiss, but with more affection than desire. That was okay. He could wait.

Standing, he held out his hand to her. She took it, and they walked back toward the facility, remaining silent. Everything necessary had already been said.

When they reached the building, Jim opened the door for her. "I'll go to my room now. You makin' rounds?"

"Yes." She turned to walk away. "Jim?"

"Yeah?"

"Thanks for being here for me."

"Oh, honey." He swung back to her. "You're here for me every day. Believe me, it's the least I could do." His eyes raked her. "And you know I'd like to do a lot more."

She smiled and ducked her head. "Perhaps in time."

Rico called late Friday to say that since he was taking Fran to dinner in Napa on Saturday night, Marti's visit to Watsonville for the weekend was canceled. She wondered if she should tell Jim about the change in her plans, and to try to get together for a date. The notice was too short, so she decided to surprise him with flowers on Saturday evening.

After Rico left her cottage at seven o'clock on Saturday for his date with Fran—dressed to the nines, of course—Marti pulled on Jim's Cougars sweatshirt over a turtleneck and leggings. She figured she could return his sweatshirt at the same time.

She piloted her little Honda through the evening-dark valley, humming to the tune coming from the radio. Some country crooner wailed about his lover's cheatin' heart. She was uncomfortably reminded of the telephone conversation she'd overheard after *Monday Night Football*, when Jim had been speaking to Glenda Colter. Marti hoped the conversation had been innocent. Even after he had comforted her on the bench beneath the birch trees, she was still unable to trust him wholeheartedly because of that one nagging loose end.

She punched another button on the radio, picking an oldies station. Leslie Gore sang that it was her party and she'd cry if she wanted to. Worse and worse. Frowning, Marti slipped her favorite CD into the player: Vivaldi's *Four Seasons*. The soothing baroque strings drifted through her mind, reminding her that she'd finally had a stress-free week after Mrs. Stockman's death on Wednesday. In the tender warmth of Jim's support, Marti felt cradled and loved rather than rushed.

She wondered what would happen Tuesday night in the guesthouse on the grounds of the golf resort. Probably nothing at all, since her father and her boss were going to be there too.

After turning in at the gates of Shady Glen, she parked her car, then made her way up to Jim's suite. At eight o'clock on Saturday night, most of the patients were in their rooms. With only a skeleton staff, Shady Glen was quiet as a school library during summer vacation.

She heard voices and laughter coming from Jim's room. One of the voices was female. Marti remembered the motifs of the songs she'd heard during her drive over. She sighed, angrily recalling that she had been sighing an awful lot lately. *Well, if it's Colter, I might as well confront them!* She tapped on the door, then turned the knob and entered.

To her surprise, she found three people in the room. All were fully clothed, she saw with relief. One, a large man with skin the color of French roast, seemed vaguely familiar. Well-built and striking, he epitomized the phrase "tall, dark, and handsome." His large brown eyes had the longest lashes she'd ever seen, and she couldn't help a twinge of envy.

The owner of the female voice was a younger, feminine version of Jim, with the same mink-brown hair and bright blue eyes. She was even dressed the same way as Jim, in faded jeans and a Cougars T-shirt.

Jim turned to her with delight. "Hey! It's you! Now all my favorite people are here. Everyone, this is Marti. Marti, this is my sister, Shawna. I told you about her. She came down to drop off my golf clubs and clothes. And this is my best friend,

Carl Worthing. We grew up together. He's a wide receiver for the Cougars."

Marti's memory sparked. "Of course I know who he is. I'm pleased to meet both of you. And these are for you," she told Jim, handing him a bouquet of flowers.

"Ooh, Jimbo, flowers from a lady," Carl teased. He winked at Marti, who grinned back.

"From your garden?" Shawna asked.

"Yes," Marti said. "How did you know?"

"Oh, lucky guess." Shawna glanced at Jim. Marti suspected she'd been the subject of at least one conversation between brother and sister.

Jim busied himself finding a vase for the flowers. "Thank you, Marti, they're great."

Carl's voice had a deeper rumble. "They are. Surprising, too, so late in the season."

"We've had unusually good weather," Marti said. "Which will be good for golf."

Carl rose to offer her his seat.

She waved a hand. "Thank you, but I don't want to interrupt what you're doing."

"Sit down, you're not interrupting anything," called Jim from the suite's bathroom. He emerged, carrying a vase full of water. "Carl, make her stay."

Carl turned to her, a twinkle in his brown eyes. "Marti, stay."

She laughed and complied, sitting at the glass-topped dinette in the suite's corner. Flat cartons with the red and blue logo of Domino's Pizza littered the table.

"Jim, are you getting pizza delivered here?" she demanded.

He sheepishly shrugged. "I had to serve them something. Those meals you order for me couldn't feed a flea."

"What had I ordered for you tonight?"

"A really good chef's salad," Shawna said. "I ate it."

"I'm glad you enjoyed it." Marti glanced at Jim's waistline.

"Never mind that," Shawna said. "We were just getting to the juicy stuff. Carl, I'm not letting you out of this one!"

Carl explained, "We were just comparing notes on the lamentable Ms. Colter."

Marti shuddered. "Glenda Colter? What's she done now? Jim, did you tell them about that article?"

Seating himself, Jim said, "That's nothin'. Believe it or not, but she had the gall to date Carl here, as well as Randy Hansley, at the same time she was still stringing me along. She had told them both that we had broken up."

Carl rubbed his shaved head, the color of coffee beans. "Yeah, and when you called me on Monday night, we were discussing a wedding date. She was hella mad when she heard it was you on the phone."

Marti broke out into a real smile for the first time in nearly a week as the rest of them laughed. That weight was off her shoulders—but what a fool she'd been! Why did she always think the worst about Jim? She should have guessed there was an innocent explanation. It had been Carl Worthing with whom Jim had been talking on Monday night, not Glenda. Marti had heard Glenda's name through the door because Carl and Jim were discussing her.

"I gave her a chance to explain," Carl said. "She denied being with Randy, said you were jealous because she had dumped you. But I called Randy up right away, and after he finished stuttering he admitted he'd been drilling her also. So I took back the ring."

"Bet she didn't like that." Shawna chuckled. "I heard it was a big one."

"Yeah, she tried to take me for four carats," Carl said. "But it's over now. To tell you the truth, I'm kinda relieved. That Glenda, I think she's a little too much woman, if you know what I mean!"

They all laughed. Marti met Jim's eyes and smiled.

Carl and Shawna apparently noticed, because the two of them began stumbling over their words and feet in their haste to leave. Marti would have thought it funny if she weren't so embarrassed.

"Well!" Carl and Shawna chimed in unison. *Had they practiced?*

"I guess it's time for us to be going!" Carl said.

"Yeah." Shawna turned to Marti. "Marti, it's been really nice to meet you. You've done so much for Jim. We wish we could stay longer, but after Carl takes me back to Sacramento I have to drive up to Colfax. It's a long way, so we really have to go."

"But I just got here," Marti protested. "I feel like I chased you away."

Carl said, "Marti, you may just have gotten here, but we've been here for a while. Shawna's right, gotta go before it gets foggy going over the I-80 causeway."

"It was really nice meeting you. Shall we see them out?" Marti asked Jim.

As they walked Carl and Shawna to the glass-fronted lobby of Shady Glen, Jim asked, "What happened? I thought you were going out of town."

"Dad came here, so I didn't go there," Marti said. "He's out with Dr. Fran tonight. My father is dating my boss," she told Shawna and Carl. "I'm having trouble getting used to the idea."

"What's the problem?" Shawna asked.

"Oh, I don't know. I feel like my boss is treating me differently. She's more distant. Lord only knows what my father's telling her. He tends to be a chatterbox."

Carl said, "It's not as though you have a choice, do you?"

Marti shook her head. "Good point. So I guess I just have to put up with it."

Carl took her hand and tucked it in his arm as they walked. "Don't worry," he said, patting her hand in a fatherly way. "Things usually turn out for the best. Just ask Jimmy, here—look at him! Eight months ago he thought life was over. He was the saddest sad sack you ever saw."

" 'Sack' being the operative word," Shawna put in with a wicked gleam in her eye. They all chuckled, even Jim.

Marti opened the glass doors of Shady Glen, and they stepped out into the night. She breathed deeply of the frosty air.

"I was gonna give you back your sweatshirt tonight," she said to Jim, "but it's so chilly that I think I'll keep it until Monday. You can do without it, can't you?"

"Sure I can."

"Besides, it looks better on you than it ever looked on him," Carl said. "Marti, Jim, it's been great to see you."

Brother hugged sister. "You look so good," Shawna said. "Marti, you don't know how bad it was at Sunset Community. That place was awful."

"I wasn't happy with Jim's condition when he arrived, but we got him squared away," Marti said.

Carl said, "Jim, you ought to see about suing those people."

Jim fidgeted.

"At least check it out." Carl turned to Marti. "Hey, do you think they treated him right at Sunset Community?"

"I'm not an expert, and I wasn't there. But I can tell you that their reputation for long-term care isn't good."

Jim said heartily, "Let's not spoil the night by talking about lawsuits. But I've already asked my lawyers to look into it. I'll call them on Monday to get an update. In the meantime, have a safe ride home. Shawna, thanks for bringing my gear, and Carl, thanks for driving her."

Carl and Shawna crammed themselves into Carl's Porsche. Marti and Jim watched as they drove off.

"Well, I guess it's time for me to be going, too."

"Not necessarily," Jim said. "How about a tub?"

"I don't think so. Dad will be coming back from his date with Dr. Fran, which means she could stop by here. The last thing I want is for my boss to think that I'm conducting a personal relationship with a patient on the grounds of the facility. I could lose my job."

"All right, I understand that. I know you love your work. Where's your car?" He walked her to the Honda.

She fished her keys out of her purse. Before she could unlock the door, Jim twirled her around for a kiss.

Like Dorothy in the whirlwind, a cyclone had taken hold of her, spinning her around and around until she didn't know where she was. Time and space seemed suspended, irrelevant as his lips plumbed hers. His arms wrapped around her, strong and sinewy, as he pressed her against the car. While he had her pinned, he took his fill of her mouth, probing slowly, grinding his hips against hers as she moaned. Passion whipped through her and she responded, pressing herself against his erection which burned hot and hard through his jeans. She was breathless and aroused when he released her.

He took the keys out of her boneless hand. Opening the car door for her, he said, "Nighty-night, *mi Martina*."

He turned and made his way back to the facility, using the cane skillfully.

Marti watched him go, dazed. He waved goodbye to her as

he entered the building, closing the door against the night. She felt cheated, like a child whose dessert had been taken away. She got into her car, fastened her safety belt, and drove home, her mind in a cloud.

Marti worked late on Monday afternoon. She decided to visit the patients' therapy pool at about six o'clock, after everyone else had gone home or was watching football. She needed some peace and quiet.

She went to the women's locker room and retrieved her one-piece blue Speedo. Her free locker plus use of the pool and the adjoining weight room were fringe benefits of employment at Shady Glen, more reasons Marti prized her job.

She occasionally used the shallow pool for after-hours swims when she was especially stressed or tired. And yeah, she was certainly feeling some tension tonight.

The kiss last Saturday night in the parking lot had really thrown her for a loop. She had the major hots for Jim, but had somehow suppressed what he could do to her with his touch and his mouth. When he'd eased her against the side of her car and taken what he wanted, she'd remembered all too well just how seductive and sexy he could be.

A pleasurable warmth, at odds with the unheated locker room, spread through her flesh at the memory.

And then he'd just walked away from her as though nothing had happened between them at all.

Surely Jim hadn't given up on her. It wasn't like him to give up on anything. But he hadn't said anything all day to her of a personal nature, hadn't flirted or even talked about their upcoming trip.

As she pulled off her white scrubs, she wondered if he was waiting for her to feel completely right and comfortable with her feelings and his. But that was ridiculous, way too touchy-feely for a macho dude like Jim Wellman. No, it was far more likely that the master manipulator adapted his plans to one of her requirements. She figured that he intended to seduce her at Stone Cliff, primarily due to her insistence that their romance couldn't take place at work.

She shivered. What were his plans for her? She recalled what he'd told her during their date: *I promise I'll give you nothing but pleasure.*

The tile floor was cool under her feet, so Marti pulled on her swimsuit quickly, eager to get into the warm water. She clipped her hair onto the top of her head to keep it dry.

After Marti went to the door and opened it, she heard the sound of girlish giggles, followed by a husky male voice.

How embarrassing. She'd apparently caught other employees using the therapy pool for an after-hours tryst. She didn't want to interrupt. It wasn't her business. Considering what she wanted to do with Jim Wellman, she had a certain amount of sympathy for whoever used the pool as a meeting place.

She stopped and frowned. The giggles were too high, almost squeals. Then she recognized the man's voice. Yeah, it was Wellman, all right. Anger flashed through her.

What was that sneaky quarterback up to this time?

Chapter Nine

Marti hated herself for spying. But why shouldn't she? As head of therapy at the facility, she had a right to know what went on.

She peeked beyond the open door. Most of the lights were switched off, since patients weren't scheduled there after four o'clock. Evening came early in late October, so the big windows let in no illumination. The room was dark but for the eerie turquoise of the pool light. Marti's gaze zeroed in on the water.

Andrea's small body, clad in a hot-pink tank suit, was supported by one of Jim Wellman's big hands under her stomach. The little girl giggled as she splashed and played in the shallow pool. Jim wore wild leopard-print swim trunks.

"Now flap your arms, sweetie, like a birdie." His tone was gentle.

Marti watched Andrea flap. One waving hand missed whacking Jim's head by only a hairsbreadth.

He jerked back. "Now put your arms forward, like Superman. Flap some more for me, honey."

Andrea obeyed.

"Do the little scoop thing I taught you. Remember to kick!"

Andrea scooped up water in front of her and began to dog paddle across the pool while Jim paced her. Marti was amazed. Andrea wouldn't put a toe into the water for anyone else. In fact, the first time Marti had tried to put her into the pool, the child had screamed to high heaven, as though Marti had tortured her.

Reason had failed. The four-year-old was unimpressed by anything Marti had to say about the benefits of hydrotherapy.

Sternness had failed. Andrea pouted.

Bribery with Ho-Hos and cookies had brought Andrea only to the second step.

But somehow Jim had charmed Andrea into the pool and appeared to be successfully teaching her how to swim. "Hot damn," Marti breathed. She kept quiet, reluctant to interrupt.

He continued talking as Andrea flailed and giggled her way across the shallow pool. "Great job, honey." He let her go and she continued flapping, scooping, and kicking.

He's so sweet with her! Tears prickled Marti's eyes as she watched him with the child. He didn't need to work with Andrea—he actually didn't have to do anything for anyone else at all. If he wanted, he could just focus on his own recovery and damn everything and everyone else to hell.

But he wouldn't do that, she realized in a moment of blinding clarity. She'd been misled by the sensational press as well as her first, negative impression of Jim as a selfish, arrogant celebrity. A sinking, sick feeling of guilt crawled around her belly. She'd unfairly misjudged him from the very first day they'd met. *Not only is he good with her, but he's—well, he's as unselfish as—as a father would be . . .*

An image of Jim holding a baby drifted into her mind as he laughed and played with Andrea. For the first time, Marti didn't push her dream away.

That could be my baby.

This man could be the father of my children.

The thought staggered her. She clutched the doorpost for support.

Oh my God.

I'm in love with Jim Wellman.

I want him to be the father of my children.

Oh my God.

Marti's guts turned to mush. She backed away, planning to change back into her street clothes and go home. She didn't think she could look him in the eye after these revelations.

Too late. She must have made some sort of sound, because both Jim and Andrea's heads turned. *Damn. They've seen me!*

"Hey, Marti!" Andrea yelled. "Lookit me! Lookit me! I'm swimming!" Her face was radiant.

"Yes, honey, and you're doing really well." Marti went over to the pool steps, hoping that neither her voice nor her legs quivered the way her heart throbbed.

"Come on in, the water's fine," Jim said. He splashed her playfully, drenching her hair.

Mood shattered, she jumped in and splashed back, nailing him right in the face.

"Payback's a bitch, huh?" she asked him as he gasped and spluttered. Andrea prudently paddled over to the far side of the pool, out of the firing line.

"All right, this is war!" he yelled. Scooping up two palmfuls of water, he tried to heave them at Marti.

She evaded the attack, laughing. She got him again, good, right in his mouth when he gasped for breath. "Gotcha, Wellman!"

"You are a bad, bad girl, Martina Solis!"

By this time she was laughing so hard she had to grab onto the side of the pool for support. She flapped one hand at him helplessly. This time the feeble splash didn't go six inches. His facial expression was a scream.

He shot across the pool. Grabbing her around the waist, he dunked her in. As she came up to the surface, the wake he'd created smacked her in the nose.

"Oof!" She sneezed, blinked the water out of her eyes, and looked for him. The coward was hiding behind Andrea, who was giggling madly at the adults' antics.

"Help me, Andrea, she's gone nuts!"

Andrea whooped.

"You chicken, hiding behind a little girl!" Marti advanced on him.

"You're beating up on a helpless cripple! What else can I do?"

"You're about as helpless as a killer shark, you punk!"

"I am *not* a punk! Do you hear what she's saying about poor little me?" he asked Andrea.

"Sissy face!" Marti splashed water up from her right, trying to hit Jim from the side. He still used Andrea as a shield.

"Them's fightin' words, Solis!" He seated Andrea on the side of the pool, then dove for Marti.

He clutched her around the waist and they both went down again. When they came up, she found his arms around her and his lips on her forehead.

"Truce?" he asked, a tender note in his voice.

She narrowed her eyes at him, then winked. "I'll think about it."

"Jim, are you gonna kiss Marti?" a small, high voice asked.

Marti gasped. Her eyes flew to Jim's face.

He grinned, then winked. "I'll think about it."

Halloween had always been Marti's favorite holiday. The entire staff of Shady Glen celebrated, had a little fun, and lifted the spirits of the patients. Most of the staff and the patients wore costumes, and the common room was decorated for the evening Halloween party.

Marti took Andrea trick-or-treating around the facility. The child wore a pink fairy costume, complete with iridescent wings, antennae, and elfin slippers with turned-up toes. Shiny wings, attached by Velcro tabs to her shoulders, flapped ridiculously while she worked her walker. A pink trick-or-treat bag dangled from one of the walker's bars as she made her way around the halls of Shady Glen, visiting her new friends.

Marti wore a vintage, high-collared white lace blouse. Her skirt, of a deep forest green, flared from a wide waistband and draped to her ankles. She'd piled her hair atop her head in a Gibson Girl style.

Late in the afternoon, they tapped at the door of Dr. Fran's office.

"Why, hello, Andrea!" Dr. Fran was costumed as Alice's White Rabbit. Her outfit aped the Tenniel illustration, complete with floppy ears, a tunic decorated with red hearts, and a large gold pocket watch over leggings. Her feet were shod in gray bunny slippers.

"Trick or treat! Trick or treat!" Andrea chanted.

"Let's see what we can find here. I wouldn't want to risk any trick you might think of, Andrea." Fran rummaged in her desk, retrieving a small wrapped gift.

Andrea squealed with delight. Marti looked at Fran, and their eyes met.

"Thanks, Dr. Fran," Marti said softly. "That was a really sweet thing to do."

"I'm a sweet person," Fran said, smiling.

Andrea tore apart the patterned gold wrapping and opened the small box to find a tiny brass hummingbird with a crystal suspended from its beak. A red ribbon loop was tied to its wing.

"For the sunny window in your room," Fran said. "You can watch the rainbows it makes when you're resting."

"This is so cool!" Andrea bubbled. "Marti, let's go and hang it up right now!" The child grabbed her walker, her face shining. She looped the red ribbon around her wrist before she made her way to the hall. Marti followed.

"Marti!" Fran called after her.

Marti turned. "Yes, Doctor?"

"I want to congratulate you again on Andrea's progress." She paused. "I know you're uncomfortable with my relationship with your father."

Marti squirmed. "I guess I'm getting used to it. I hope that you're both happy."

"We are, and I wanted to reassure you that you are an enormously talented therapist, my dear. Regardless of what happens between Rico and me, I'm sure you will always have a job. I would hate to lose you because of a personal relationship," Fran added, with a lift of one gray eyebrow.

Marti was about to respond when Andrea called, "Marti, come on!"

She waved her hands in the air helplessly. "Thank you, but I guess we'll have to continue this discussion later. Princess Andrea calls!" She hurried out.

Andrea wandered down the hall, moving less briskly than earlier. *All the trick-or-treating is getting to her . . . too much excitement.* Marti strode after Andrea in a swirl of green gabardine, ready to grab the child if she collapsed. At the same time, another part of her mind worked overtime on her personal problems.

Exactly what did Dr. Fran mean? Marti didn't know, but had noticed that Dr. Fran hadn't assured her of always having a position at Shady Glen. Fran's last statement might have been a reference to Marti's growing intimacy with Jim

Wellman. From the attitudes of Katrin and Tommy, Marti knew that she and Jim were an "item." A rumor could have reached Dr. Fran's ears.

Marti pushed the rambling worried thoughts out of her mind as she followed Andrea down the hall. As she passed Jim's suite, the door opened.

Andrea stopped. "My legs just got tired."

"You've walked around a lot today, sweetie, and you've done really well," Marti said. "Why don't you have a little nap, and I'll wake you up in time for the party."

She led Andrea into her room, then put her to bed. Marti took the headband with the antennae, placing it on Andrea's dresser before pulling the wings off the rest of the costume, which consisted of a leotard and tights. Lastly, she tugged the fairy slippers off Andrea's unresisting feet and draped a light comforter over her.

Marti turned. Jim stood in the doorway, watching. He was attired as a pirate, with torn black pants, an extravagantly collared shirt, and a rakish eye patch. He wore red sashes, one at his waist, the other tied as a kerchief around his head. His Nikes contrasted with the costume. "You're good at this, you know," he murmured.

Her heart tripped as she was reminded of the gossip Zelda had shared, something about Jim being a ripe plum ready for a relationship. She envisioned a pregnant plum in a pirate costume. The bizarre juxtaposition was both disarming and charming. She grinned at him.

In the few weeks she had known Jim Wellman, she'd gone from fear and loathing to love and need. She was astounded and delighted by her feelings, when she wasn't terrified at their intensity.

"Marti!" An imperious little voice issued from the bed. "I want my hummingbird."

"Here it is, honey. How about if I hang it from your window, and you can watch it from bed."

"Okay," Andrea said.

Marti took the small brass ornament and slipped its ribbon over the curtain rod of Andrea's window. "Rest, now." She dropped a kiss on the child's forehead, then stepped out of Andrea's door and smiled at Jim.

Jim smiled back, taking her in. The white lace blouse Marti wore concealed her slender body while it outlined her curves. A strapless bustier peeked through the lace-work. His curiosity teased. He didn't know if Marti liked sexy lingerie. He sure hoped so, and wanted to find out right away.

Offering her his arm, he walked her down the hall to his suite. He closed the door of his room behind them and took her into his arms, stroking her back. One hand freed pearl buttons from tiny loops. He opened the shirt while softly kissing her lips, and ran his fingers over the pale amber swells of her breasts where they thrust from the bustier.

She murmured against his mouth, "I'm scared."

"Scared of what?" he asked, still caressing her breasts. He lifted one out of the bustier and rubbed his thumb over the tender nipple. It puckered instantly. He bent his head to nibble at the enticing nub.

"Someone may come in," she said weakly.

"Door's locked. You'll keep your job today, sweetheart."

"But—"

He stopped her protest with a kiss, then loosened his hold. "Marti, I'm not into forcing you. Whenever you feel uncomfortable, just tell me to stop." He stroked her cheek. "I promise you won't be sorry."

She hesitated.

"Make a choice, now." He knew she didn't want to tell him *no*.

She gulped. "I'll stay. For a while, at least."

Jim tried not to let his surge of masculine triumph show on his face. "That's all I ask." He walked her over to his big bed and lowered her onto it, gazing down at her.

She had never looked so exciting. The high-collared blouse contrasted with her flagrantly exposed breast. She was mind-numbingly sexy. The pirate outfit made him feel like an outlaw seducing a prim and proper Victorian virgin.

Erect and flushed, her nipple glistened where he had licked it. Her hair partially escaped from the old-fashioned style, framing her face with soft wisps that begged for his touch.

Jim joined her on the bed so they lay side by side. He captured her in his arms and kissed her mouth thoroughly, voluptuously. He groped at her side to find a row of buttons securing the high, tight waist of her skirt, and unfastened them as she stroked his chest through the pirate's shirt. Arousal sparked through his body like electric shocks with every caress of her knowing hands.

He again took her breast with his mouth, sucking the nipple before gently nipping it with his teeth. It rose, hot and hard on his tongue, and he tugged on the sexy little point. She was tasty as hell and he wanted to eat her right up.

He slid his right hand underneath the waistband of the long, old-fashioned skirt. She ran her hands through his hair to pull his head even closer to her breast. Her moan of desire incited him, made his body swell with need.

His fingers danced over her flat abdomen, then searched further, encountering her panties. With pleasure he realized that they were lace also, and apparently matched the bustier.

He wanted to strip her, so he pushed the skirt away to see Marti's seductive body, clad only in white lace.

He crouched over her, wanting her, as determined and as dangerous as any wild pirate claiming prey. He eased her other breast from the encasing bustier and worried it with his teeth as he slipped his hand under the elastic of her panties.

He rubbed the thatch of dark hair and the sensual mound beneath until her moans increased in pitch. His fingers found her wetness, and he pushed into the furrow until he felt her vibrate and writhe. He slid another finger in, deliberately opening the narrow passage while continuing to rotate his palm against her bud, hidden beneath the sultry folds of her sex.

He felt passion pulse through Marti's body, and she reached for his head, bringing his lips to hers. He responded, his tongue in her mouth echoing the motion of his fingers in her slick depths. Her hips rolled wildly against his hand. She moaned, incoherent.

"Yes, baby, yes, yes." With a flash of primitive male satisfaction he realized he finally had her where and how he wanted her: sprawled on his bed, helpless with lust and need. "Give it to me, baby, right now," he demanded, pushing against her harder until her body rocked with her climax.

"Oh, baby, you are so beautiful." Amazed and delighted at her responsiveness, he took her into his arms and hugged her until her body stopped quivering. He kissed her eyelids as she relaxed against his rock-hard shaft. He rubbed against her thigh.

"Oh, darling, I want you so much," he whispered into her ear. "I can hardly wait until tomorrow night when I'll have you all to myself. I'll love you like no one else ever has."

Marti breathed deeply, then chuckled. "You think a lot of yourself, don't you?"

"That sounds like a challenge. I like that." Jim massaged her again through her damp panties.

She hummed deep in her throat. "Maybe you're right."

He stretched. "Let's blow off the party, stay here, and get naked for the rest of the night."

"Oh, my gosh! The party!" Her eyes popped open. She pulled away from him, tugging her skirt back into place. "I hate to go, but I have to go help set up for the party before I'm missed." She grabbed her blouse.

He watched her go, willing his arousal to subside. It sure seemed as though he did a lot of watching Marti leave. He remembered her hand as it trailed to hold his when she walked into her cottage after their dinner date. The same mixture of regret and pleasure flooded him as she closed the door of his suite behind her. He also felt like he was going to explode from sheer sexual tension.

Heading into his cold shower, Jim realized that he had never before been so controlled with a woman. No one else had ever needed him to be so self-disciplined. The difficulties of the situation, given Marti's commitment to her job as well as her particular emotional landscape, forced him to be more responsible than he'd ever been in a relationship.

He was growing up, only because the woman he loved needed him to give more, to *be* more, than anyone else had ever wanted.

In the past, women had been readily available, probably too available. He'd had numerous "no strings attached" affairs and one-night stands with football groupies and celebrity wannabes like Glenda Colter. Hell, sometimes he had taken two or three at a time!

Marti was different, in every way. Her continuing diffidence and her determination to hold on to her heart while withholding her body were frustrating—he was used to women tumbling into his bed at a snap of his fingers.

Her sharp humor and quick mind were also unusual, but fun and challenging. He liked challenges, all kinds.

Amber skin free of make-up, dark hair plainly styled . . . so different, so simple, and so sexy, in a healthy and honest way. He liked that. She appealed to his yearning for the basics, simplicity and structure in his life.

He knew he was at a turning point. Money, yeah, but no job. No relationship. He felt rootless and adrift. He envied Marti, securely grounded as she was in home, hearth, job, and family.

Well, he was going to get what he needed, and with Marti. Nothing had ever stopped him when he'd decided what he wanted, and this—she—was what he wanted. His old life was gone, and it was time to create a new one.

"Our Halloween party was a complete success." Dr. Fran settled herself into the back-facing seat of the limousine Jim had rented for their excursion to Stone Cliff. It was eight o'clock, early enough in the morning to drive to Stone Cliff Resort and arrive on time for lunch and an afternoon of golf.

Marti nodded. "Yeah, I think everyone enjoyed it."

"You really missed out, Mr. Wellman." Fran sounded regretful.

Marti repressed a grin. She had a good idea of what Jim had done after she had left his suite. She felt badly about leaving him in so needy a condition, but it was his own fault because he had created the situation.

She sat upright, facing forward. Seated beside her, Jim leaned over and explored the limo's minibar as the chauffeur drove southward out of Napa.

"Orange juice, Doctor?" he asked. Fran accepted the juice with a smile while Marti curled up in her corner to take a nap. She had selected comfortable garb, pleated khaki trousers and a green polo shirt, because she wanted to catch up on her sleep. Jim, in faded jeans and a chambray work shirt, seemed to have similar ideas as he relaxed against the cushions of the limo.

Fran broke the silence as they drove down the highway. "What about our accommodations, Mr. Wellman?"

"I've rented a guesthouse on the Stone Cliff property for myself, plus two rooms in the main resort for you and Marti. That should be enough space, since Rico's staying in Monterey."

"More than enough, I should think," Fran said.

Marti kept her eyes half-closed as if she was sleeping, but she actually listened closely. She knew what Jim had in mind and wasn't sure if they could pull it off.

Jim continued, "The guesthouse has a Jacuzzi, so Marti can give me my whirlpool baths and massages, like at Shady Glen." Marti controlled a grin and hoped Jim also contained himself. She wanted to see Dr. Fran's reaction, so she let her lids flutter, then covered a phony yawn. She gazed blurrily at Fran, who eyed Jim, who watched Marti "awaken."

Dr. Fran looked at Jim with an expression of mild interest, but she didn't trick Marti. Marti knew that Fran hadn't created a multi-million-dollar business by being a fool about people. Jim wore a similar expression of bland innocence. This is going to be interesting, Marti thought. Jim was a person who responded aggressively to challenges. Observing the two controlling personalities in action would be an education in itself.

The situation provided Jim with multiple difficulties: seducing Marti while ensuring Fran and Rico knew nothing of their amorous activities. At this point, Marti hoped that Jim was sincerely fond of her and understood the significance of her job, because she wanted Jim as much as she'd ever wanted anything in her life. However, the presence of her boss, her father, and her brother on the Stone Cliff premises promised to dampen desire as well as narrow the romantic opportunities.

But she needed him with a drive that made everyone else unimportant. The feelings she had about this man dwarfed anything she'd ever experienced. Yeah, her heart fluttered when he walked into the room, but he wasn't merely a major hunk. He'd become her friend, caring for her when she needed someone to support her through her grief. She'd never felt so surrounded by love as the moment he held her under the birches after Donna Stockman's death.

Though he could be incredibly manipulative when it came to getting what he wanted, she had to admit he was right when he pointed out that each faced an equal emotional risk. I'll never know unless I try, she thought.

Midway through the long drive, they stopped at a gas station to refill the car and to stretch their legs. Although the limo was roomy, Marti and Fran both agreed that Jim needed to get out and walk around to avoid stiffening up.

As they got back into the limo, he complained of soreness. Fran gave him a muscle relaxant and water, but he said that he felt he might need to get into a whirlpool immediately upon arriving. He winked at Marti as he stated, "It's a bummer because it's gonna cut into my golf time."

"It's all right, Mr. Wellman," Fran said. "I expect to golf tomorrow morning also. You'll get plenty of golf."

They drove onto Highway 101. Watsonville, Marti's hometown, lay to the west. She stared westward and thought about her mother, tapping her fingernails on the padded armrest.

"Marti, I understand that today is the *Dia de los Muertos*," Fran said.

Marti stared at her. The Spanish sounded odd coming out of Dr. Fran's mouth. "The Day of the Dead? No, that's tomorrow. Today is All Souls Day."

"Do you want to visit your mother? We have time."

Tears pricked behind Marti's lids. "That's very kind, Dr. Fran. Um. I don't know. My mother didn't really hold with any of that stuff."

"What do you want to do, Marti?" Jim asked. "I think it's a good idea, if it'll make you feel better."

"Would tomorrow be more appropriate?" Fran wanted to know.

"It doesn't really matter. Different towns in Mexico have different customs," Marti said. "My mother was Romanian. She thought the whole thing was rather grisly."

"These rituals are really more for the living than the dead. It's up to you, Marti. We could also stop tomorrow, on the way home." Jim rubbed his leg, looking stiff and uncomfortable.

"The proper day is the second of November." Marti sensed that her patient was more than ready to end their journey.

"In that case, we'll continue on to Stone Cliff right now," Fran said.

They pulled into Stone Cliff, just south of Carmel, at about one o'clock. As their limo drove beneath the pillared porte cochére at the entrance of Stone Cliff, Marti saw that her father stood on the porch waiting for them. He waved with enthusiasm. Oh, boy, Marti moaned internally. Now it begins! When would she get used to her unpredictable father?

Rico wore classic golf attire: tweed wool knickers, brown and white golf oxfords, and an Argyle sweater. Marti was as embarrassed as the night her father had subjected her prom date to an interrogation worthy of Sherlock Holmes. Maybe she could crawl under the limo.

Rico stood with a couple Marti didn't recognize. The graying male had on tattersall golf pants and a Pebble Beach windbreaker. By his side was none other than Golfer Barbie, in a pink dotted outfit.

After the limo stopped, Rico eagerly opened the door for them. Marti gestured for Dr. Fran to exit first. Jim clambered out of the other side with the driver's help. As Marti left the vehicle, she heard Rico say, "Fran, here's one of your colleagues from the East Bay, Dr. Terrence Jacques."

Chapter Ten

Marti shut her surprised mouth before a fly flew in. Fortunately, she'd never told her father the name of the two-timing doctor in Berkeley. If her father knew it was Terrence who'd taken advantage of his daughter, Rico would probably beat the man to a pulp with his putter.

Fran graciously inclined her head. "I'm pleased to meet you."

Terrence burbled, "And I, you. Of course I have read of your theories in the *Journal of Occupational and Physical Therapy*. You have revolutionized the field."

Fran thanked him, then said, "You have the opportunity to meet someone who has made my success possible. May I introduce my Chief of Occupational and Physical Therapy at Shady Glen, Martina Solis." Fran turned to Marti.

Marti, standing like an automaton, found Terrence pumping her hand as though he wanted to draw water from a well. She snatched her hand away as he murmured commonplace greetings.

So this was what the lecherous Dr. Jacques had turned into—a dull little drone—not the villain Marti had blamed for stunting her emotional life for six years. She sensed Jim's protective presence behind her as she examined the good doctor. She grinned like a madwoman, realizing this man was nothing but a pipsqueak. Her contempt turned to anger. She'd let this feeble excuse for a human being mess up her head for way too long.

She contemplated the creep, seeing easy prey. "We've met, Doctor," Marti purred. "I interned at East Bay Community. Don't you recognize me? We had a very . . . special . . . relationship."

He stared at her and stuttered, "I'm—I'm sorry, there were so many interns . . ."

Marti shifted her glance to Mrs. Jacques' face. She, at least, had understood Marti's comment. Her mouth and eyes had hardened with anger, but no surprise showed in her expression. Marti chuckled gently. "Yes, I'm sure there were many. Many." Dr. Jacques' mouth dropped open. "Excuse me, please. I have to put my patient in a whirlpool as soon as possible."

She took Jim's arm and escorted him into Stone Cliff. Just before the doorman closed the big double doors behind them, she heard Rico explain that she accompanied Jim Wellman, the star football player. For once, she wouldn't condemn Rico for boasting. Success truly was the best revenge.

As soon as the doors closed, Jim turned to her. "Was that the infamous Dr. Jerk?"

"Yeah. And I didn't even recognize him!"

"You nailed him to the wall when you did. The look on his wife's face was priceless. She sure knows what was going on." He laughed. "Man, I'd hate to be in his golf shoes on their drive home."

"What's astounding is that I didn't even recognize him. All these years I've been blaming him for ruining my love life, and here I couldn't remember what the guy looks like. It's time for me to be over this."

"Well, duh." He walked over to the concierge desk and collapsed into a chair, stretching out his long legs. "Would you make sure that the chauffeur brings in my cane?" he asked the concierge.

"Certainly, sir. Whose cane is it?" the concierge asked.

"I'm Jim Wellman. Are you Mark? I called the other day."

"Oh yes, sir. I'll make sure that all your luggage is sent to the guesthouse right away." He picked up a phone.

"I thought I'd be eager to get to the links," Jim said to Marti. "But all I really want right now is that bath."

"We can do that. Where's the guesthouse?"

"I'm not sure, but I bet this guy can tell us." He struggled to his feet. "Steve, my man!" Jim greeted Marti's brother cordially before Steve hugged Marti.

"Nice duds, bro'," Marti said.

Steve wore immaculate gray trousers and a teal logo shirt. "Standard for Stone Cliff employees."

"Even the crease in the pants?" Marti asked.

Steve grinned. "Head groundskeeper is a management position, Marti. Gotta keep up with the big boys, and that means ironed pants and polished shoes—even if they are Reeboks."

"No more gardening?"

Regret crossed her brother's face. "No. But it's worth it."

Marti glanced at Jim. "Did I ever tell you about my brother Steve?" she asked. "When everyone else was flipping burgers at McDonald's, Steve went to the classiest golf resort in the western world and got a job. No paper routes or French fries for him."

Jim looked thoughtful. "A big place like this probably has a staff of full-time gardeners."

"Yeah, and I'm the head weed-whacker. But enough about me. You look tired." Steve examined Jim with obvious concern on his dark, tanned face. "Let me show you to the guesthouse so you can rest."

"Just what we want," Jim said. "I need that hot tub, bad. That drive was way too long, and this leg got real stiff."

Marti followed Steve and Jim as they walked through the extensive main building of the resort, passing a lounge and the restaurant. The gossipy males didn't stop talking, which surprised her. She had no idea that Jim and Steve had anything but a casual relationship. Had her brother set her up with his friend? She wouldn't put it past Steve to have steered Jim directly to her. Like father, like son, she thought. Steve had probably inherited her dad's busybody traits.

When the trio reached the back of the building, Marti quit worrying about the men in her life as she approached the huge windows at the resort's back wall. The view of the greens and the ocean beyond was magnificent. The lawns rolled and tumbled toward granite cliffs, which dropped jaggedly to the sea. Sand traps were naturally occurring dunes. The roughs, stands of juniper and pine, had been dramatically sculpted by the ocean breezes and winter storms.

Out on the patio with the talkative men, Marti turned her head to the sky to soak up the heavenly rays. Lucky that the unseasonably good weather had continued, allowing for golf. Soon the weather would turn stormy, and El Niño would pound the California coast. Sunny days would be few and far between, so Marti made the most of what nature gave.

Steve took them to a Spanish-style guesthouse a few yards from the main building, hidden by a row of Norfolk pines. Topped by a red tile roof, the guesthouse was a fully equipped one-bedroom cottage. The small entry led to a sitting room and adjoining kitchen, opening onto a patio with a small swimming pool, Jacuzzi, and deck enclosed by weathered redwood fencing.

A bellboy opened the front door as they arrived. Jim and Marti examined the luggage set in the tiled entry.

"This is Dr. Murdoch's." Marti pointed at a tapestry suitcase. "And these are her golf clubs. You should probably take them to her room," she said to the bellboy. "I'll take my gear to my room later. Hey, my portable massage table didn't make it in here. Could you find it right away?" The bellboy left with Fran's luggage.

Jim headed for the kitchen. "Any beer in this fridge?" he asked Steve. "I'd love a beer."

Steve blinked. "Let's find out. There should be."

Jim found a bottle of Anchor Steam. "Excellent," he said. "Now if your sister will get me into that hot tub, my life will be perfect."

"I'll see you later, then." Steve turned to the door. "Are you gonna be around here tomorrow?" he asked Marti.

"Yeah, we're staying over."

"I thought I'd bring Helene and the girls by," Steve said. "How 'bout if we all have breakfast together?"

"That sounds great." With a sneakered foot, Marti shoved her duffel bag to one side of the entry. "Say at eight o'clock?"

"You're invited, too," Steve said to Jim. "We wouldn't dream of leaving you out." Jim looked startled, but pleased.

"See ya," Marti said to her brother.

Steve left, and Marti looked at the beer in Jim's hand. "I don't know about that beer in the hot tub."

"Oh, one beer will be all right." He unbuttoned his shirt, then tossed it onto a chair.

She stepped outside to the hot tub. Switching on the jets, she swished her hand into the water to test its temperature. She turned the heat up a notch.

Jim came out, clad only in a towel. He dropped the towel on the deck, and, with her help, slid into the water. He sighed with pleasure as the warm water enveloped him. "Ahhh, much better."

"I wonder if it's okay for me to put some aromatherapy herbs in here."

"Should be all right," he said. "The filter will just catch them. Think they'll do any good?"

"I don't know. The holistic health people think aromatherapy herbs are the greatest, but there's no scientific data to prove it."

"Yoo-hoo! Anybody home?" a male voice called from the front door of the guesthouse.

Marti went to the door to find her father with Fran Murdoch. Fran had changed into golfing attire, and their caddies hefted two sets of clubs. A bellboy brought in Marti's massage table.

"How is Mr. Wellman?" Dr. Fran asked.

"Stiff and sore," Marti said. "I think the drive was too long for him. On the way home, we should probably take more breaks, let him walk around more frequently. He's in the tub now, and I'll give him a light massage before he heads out to play golf."

Fran frowned. "I'd recommend he start slowly. Tell him to try the putting green first and then hit some practice drives. Maybe he can go for nine holes tomorrow morning."

"Maybe tomorrow you can take a break on the drive home, visit the Santa Cruz district cemetery and see your mother," Rico said. "It is *La Dia de Los Muertos, mi hija.*"

Marti remembered the point Jim had made: the rituals were for the benefit of the living. "Yes, I probably will. I know it's important to you, Dad."

He looked pleased. "Are you having breakfast with us tomorrow?"

"Yes, we both are," Marti said. "Along with Steve, Helene, and the twins. It'll be fun."

After showing them out, Marti searched in her duffel for herbs and scented oil for Jim's massage. She found a small bag containing some dried leaves and twigs and took it out to the tub. She began sprinkling them in the water.

"Hey, those smell pretty good. Relaxing. You gonna chant some incantations?"

"Very funny."

"No, really, I think I'm falling into a trance."

Marti glared at Jim. "In that case, get out. I don't want you falling asleep in there. What about golf?"

"Golf, schmolf. I want my massage."

"Quit pouting and tell me how you feel."

"I'm all right. If you massage the legs, I should be ready to hit a few."

After a massage and a quick lunch, Jim and Marti headed out to the putting green with a caddy, who carried Jim's extensive collection of golf equipment. She couldn't figure out why he needed such an array of golf clubs. He had at least a dozen. Weren't there just two basic strokes, a drive and a putt? Why would he need any more than two or maybe four clubs? "Boys and their toys," she muttered.

"What?" he asked.

"Nothing important," she said. She noticed that for putting, Jim used only one skinny club. A putter, she guessed. He also wore gloves, which struck her as a ridiculous affectation. But who knew? Not her.

He wore khaki trousers and a splashy blue shirt with an embroidered shark logo, the colors of the shirt matching his vivid eyes. He looked as well groomed on the golf course as he had at their dinner date. Like everyone else at Stone Cliff, he wore silly-looking saddle shoes with small prongs on the bottom. As Jim and the caddy fussed with Jim's putter, his glove, and his special Titleist golf balls, Marti asked, "Did you get new golf shoes? These look shiny."

"Yeah, Shady Glen referred me to a shoemaker, and he made me an entire wardrobe of shoes. They have a lift or something to compensate for the difference in the length of my legs."

"The prongs are for traction?"

"Right. The grass on the course can be wet and slippery." He leaned over, grasping his putter with both hands.

Marti noticed that the slightly bent position he used to putt engendered no strain on his knees or ankles; in fact, it appeared to gently stretch the hamstring. As she watched other golfers in the distance on the links, Marti could see that driving the ball involved a complex twisting motion, which could stress the joints. She hoped Jim wouldn't reinjure himself. But Dr. Fran, a golfer herself, wouldn't have permitted her patient to golf unless she thought it was safe. So Marti relaxed and began to enjoy the day.

She'd been to Stone Cliff before but hadn't spent much time at the resort, but now she had the opportunity to appreciate its beauty. It was groomed to a tee—Steve obviously earned the outrageous salary Stone Cliff paid him.

It was a lovely late autumn afternoon. The sun struck sparks from the tops of the ocean's waves, visible in the distance. The scent of freshly mowed grass blended with salt spray and Jim's cologne to create an intoxicating fragrance. Marti took deep breaths of the bracing air.

Jim's first few putts were off a tad, and he compensated by changing his stance. He leaned on his putter after completing numerous competent shots. "I think I'm ready to try the driving range," he said.

Jim's caddy followed them over to the driving range,

which was in the lee of the main building, away from the sea. Marti was disappointed—she enjoyed watching the waves—but she figured that the practice range had to be sheltered from unpredictable ocean winds.

"Give me the persimmon-headed driver," Jim said to the caddy.

Persimmon? "Why not pear or orange?" she asked.

"Very funny." Jim swung the driver experimentally. He eyed the ball, which was set on a tee, and meticulously adjusted his stance. He was careful to stay a specific distance from the ball and to keep his feet a specific distance apart. He flexed his knees and gripped the shaft of the driver precisely before he swung it behind him. He twisted his body to the right, then put his shoulders into the swing back. He missed the ball completely. "Hmmm," he said.

The next time, he adjusted his stance, then went through the same procedure. The head of the club smacked the ball straight on. The small white ball shot down the fairway and hit the 250-yard marker with a loud whack.

He looked at her and smiled. "Haven't lost my touch."

The caddie, who had been standing nearby with his mouth open, said, "I should say not, sir!"

Jim pursed his lips. "Maybe I'll go into golfing next."

She grinned.

He tried a few more balls, hitting them down the range with increasing confidence. With no need to conceal her interest, Marti watched him closely. He was the reason she was present, wasn't he? She took the occasion to admire him with a touch of self-congratulation. He looked great, moved well.

His limp was imperceptible except to a trained eye. His films and other tests had told her that her early assessment was correct: one leg had healed shorter than the other. It had been partially remedied by the special footwear. The shortened femur wouldn't be a disability to anyone except a professional athlete, but it didn't seem to be affecting Jim's golf swing.

"Want to try?" he asked.

"Oh, no. I've never played golf before," she said.

"All the more reason to start now. Look, it's easy. I'll show you." He guided her to the tee.

She stood near it like a dork, not knowing what to do. She'd had the same feeling at age ten when no one would choose her for their volleyball team.

The caddie placed a ball atop the tee.

Jim positioned himself behind her. "See, you hold the grip of the club like this, with your thumbs kinda parallel to each other." He wrapped his arms around her, holding the club, and placed her hands around the shaft. He held her fingers in place as he demonstrated. "Then you lift and swing the club to the right and behind you. You have to get your whole body into it as you swing back."

He swung her hands and the club in a large arc, ending behind and to the right of their bodies. They missed the ball by a country mile.

"Aren't we supposed to actually hit the ball?" she asked.

"Yeah, but that was a practice swing," he said. "This time we'll get it good."

They repeated the same procedure. Marti was conscious of his arms around her, his body pressing against her back, his heat enveloping her. As he swung the club around, his slight erection brushed against her buttocks, and her own temperature heated up a degree or two. Gee, he must really love this game, she thought.

The club nailed the ball, which sailed down the fairway.

"See! You're a natural," Jim said. "Probably runs in the family."

The days had become shorter in November, and soon the driving range was in the shadow of the building. They walked over to the resort's outside bar, located on a patio facing the ocean. Jim ordered a beer for himself and a glass of Chardonnay for Marti. They watched the sun set into the Pacific Ocean while they relaxed. Clouds, gold and pink, decorated the darkening sky as evening fell.

"To you," he said, raising his glass. "To your handiwork."

"Oh, no," she said modestly. "Curing a patient is a collaborative undertaking."

"No, it was you. It sure wasn't Sunset Community."

"Why do you say that?"

"I've had my lawyers look into it. Apparently they screwed up and never told me. First they put the wrong pin in the femur. Their sterile procedures were faulty, and the bone became infected after the first surgery. I had to have an extra surgery because of their incompetence." He sounded grim. "My right leg ended up much shorter than my left, and I can never play pro football again. As you might have noticed while I was golfing, my balance and my back are way off.

"Worse, they took the information out of the chart."

"You can't be serious! Covering up a patient's condition by removing data from the chart is—is—" Appalled, Marti groped for words. "Well, it's completely unethical. How could they think they'd get away with that?"

"They won't. I'm suing. They trashed my career, Marti, and they'll pay." Jim's knuckles were white as he gripped his glass.

"You absolutely should sue them. Who knows how many other patients they messed up?"

"Exactly. They stole my life from me, but I'm not going to go away peacefully." He had the same determined glint in his eye Marti remembered from the first day they'd met, when she'd goaded him out of his wheelchair and made him walk.

"You shouldn't let them get away with it," she said. "No way."

"I'm glad you're behind me." Visibly calming, he sipped his beer. "Hey, what do you want to do about dinner?"

She shrugged. "How do you feel, physically?"

"Good, but maybe a little tired."

"Hmm. It's only five. Why don't you take a nap? We can eat dinner at seven or eight, when you're rested."

"That sounds about right. I'll make a reservation in the main restaurant for seven-thirty."

"Are we dressing for dinner?" Marti asked.

"We can hardly show up naked, considering that it's November." He smiled at her. "I brought a suit this time. I'm sure whatever you packed will be fine."

They walked slowly back to the guesthouse. After picking up her duffel, Marti used her free hand to squeeze Jim's shoulder. "Don't worry about Sunset Community. It sounds like a really clear case of medical malpractice. You'll stop them, and they'll never be able to hurt anyone else again."

Chapter Eleven

While Marti walked to her room, she pondered the conversation she'd just had. She remembered Jim's first day at Shady Glen, when she and Fran had examined his chart. They'd found only two x-rays in his grossly deficient file. Marti wondered whether Dr. Fran knew a lawsuit was impending, and if the case would affect Shady Glen.

She considered the possibility that Jim had residual effects from the malpractice he had experienced at Sunset Community, and decided to recommend another full set of films and tests on him.

At her room, she opened the door with her card key. Unzipping her duffel, she pulled out the dress she'd wear that night.

The ankle-length, long-sleeved black lace had a simple, round neckline. The embroidered Alençon lace was entirely see-through, but the black silk chemise worn beneath the lace overdress would save her from an arrest for indecent exposure. Both were outrageously slit to mid-thigh.

She removed black stockings, trimmed with elastic lace, and high peau de soie heels from the duffel. She hung the dress in the bathroom. The steam from her shower would remove the wrinkles from the chemise. The lace wasn't creased at all.

Grinning, she took off her Reeboks and stretched out on her bed for a nap. The clingy dress suggested more than it revealed. She also knew that if she bumped into Rico and Fran, she'd encounter no criticism. The black lace had been her prom gown, selected by her parents.

"Ah, Martina, what a lovely dress," Rico said as he met her later in the bar near the Stone Cliff restaurant. Marti smiled at her father and Dr. Fran.

"Yes, it is." Fran wore another evening suit, blue with creamy satin lapels. She looked every inch the distinguished doctor.

"Did he tell you it was my prom gown, and he picked it out?" Marti asked. "Of course he likes it."

"Yes, and I'm very proud that you still fit into it ten years later," Rico said. "I knew it was a good buy."

Without looking at the door, Marti sensed the moment Jim Wellman entered the bar. Heads turned and whispers of recognition wafted from the patrons. The hair at her nape prickled, while her heart did a now-familiar two-step. A blush heated her face as Jim, ignoring the rest of the room, headed straight for her.

He was perfectly groomed, in a navy chalk stripe suit that looked as though it had been molded to his superb shoulders. His red paisley tie was arranged in a Windsor knot. "Good evening, everybody. Will you be joining us here for dinner?" he asked Rico and Fran.

Marti raised her brows, surprised by his invitation. She'd thought that his plans didn't include her nosy father and her eagle-eyed boss.

"Very nice of you to ask," Rico said, "but we thought we'd go over to a great little seafood restaurant I know in Monterey, near the aquarium. Want to come?"

"No, thanks," Jim said. "We have reservations here. Would you like to take the limo? You can be a little more relaxed about drinking some wine if you have a driver."

"That's thoughtful of you," Fran said. "Rico?"

"We'd be delighted," Rico said. "That sounds fun."

Jim kept a straight face as he went to a quiet corner to phone the limo driver on his cell phone. He'd been pretty sure that Rico and Fran didn't want to hang around Stone Cliff any more than he and Marti wanted their company. But there was no harm in keeping tabs on them that evening.

He called the chauffeur and had the limo brought to the front of the resort. He also gave his cellular phone number to the driver, with directions to call as soon as Rico and Fran left Monterey for Stone Cliff.

Jim then escorted Marti to the resort's restaurant. The maitre d' seated them near a dramatic indoor fountain.

"I know you're fond of running water," Jim said. "Do you like the decor?"

"Oh, yes. I've always enjoyed Stone Cliff."

"This is going to be a very difficult dinner."

She frowned. "Why so?"

"What I want isn't on the menu."

She blushed charmingly. "Perhaps you can have some of the special later, if you're a good boy now and clean your plate."

"The black lace special?"

"Maybe. And some other things." She twisted a strand of hair around one finger.

The waiter arrived, and she said, "I'm not very hungry. I guess I'll order from the appetizer menu."

"May I suggest the chicken Caesar salad?"

"No, thank you. Nothing with garlic or anchovies tonight."

Jim smiled. Later, he saw that Marti only picked at her

meager order of stuffed Portobello mushrooms. "The chef here is supposed to be very good," he said.

She raised a brow. "I don't see you eating, either." She eyed his untouched pasta Alfredo.

"I'm just a little distracted." He sipped wine and regarded her over the top of his glass. She was stunning, but without a trace of self-consciousness or conceit. Her eyes sparkled with arousal and anticipation. Simply styled, her dark hair fell from a deep side part with a jeweled clip holding it back behind one ear. She wore no rings on her elegant fingers. *Her left hand would look nice with a diamond, or maybe an emerald.* He felt pleasantly mellow, yet expectant.

A jazz combo started up in the lounge. "Want to dance?" he asked.

"That would be great."

He stood and offered her his arm. The strains of "It Had to Be You" wafted from the band as he led her to the dance floor. They were one of only a few couples there when the music began, but the floor filled rapidly. He chuckled.

"Hmm?"

"You could choke on the pheromones out here."

"Yeah, and most of them are coming from you."

He smiled. "Don't underestimate yourself, sweetheart."

"Or our fellow dancers."

"Um-hmm."

Marti snuggled against his chest, and he hugged her tighter. He bent his head, inhaling her distinctive fragrance of Eternity and autumn leaves.

Jim finally spoke. He'd thought it would be hard, but it was easy, really. "I love you very much, you know."

She smiled, warming his soul. "I guess I do know that. Me, too. I've never known anyone like you." She tipped her head back to kiss his chin, then brushed her lips across his.

His grip tightened. "Me either. You're very, very special, and I'm never going to let you go."

After signing for the uneaten dinners, he walked her to the guesthouse in restless expectation. The night was dark. No moon illuminated the resort, and pearl gray mist cloaked everything.

"It's as though we're alone in our own foggy little world," he said.

"Listen to this." She stopped walking and tapped her heels on the stone path, which made an eerie clatter. She clapped her hands, and the noise reverberated.

"What's that?"

"There are no buildings around here, so the sound is echoing off the fog. Interesting, huh?"

"And here I thought I was setting up such a romantic scene for you. Smarty Marti strikes again," he muttered.

"Excuse me?"

"Nothing, honey," he said sweetly. "It's just that most people would notice the romantic setting, not the amazing phenomenon of sound waves bouncing off thick fog."

"Oh, yes. Very romantic. Fog and surf. I bow to your superior manipulation, O Devious One." She bowed to him from the waist. "You didn't have to go to all this trouble, you know," she said, in a softer voice.

"I didn't?" He opened the door of the guesthouse.

"Nope. It's the things you don't plan that I'm in love with. Your eyes. Your smile. Your kindness to others, like the way you worked with Andrea."

She stepped inside, and he followed, closing the door on the fog, shutting out the rest of the world.

"Yeah?" He took her elfin chin in his hand and smiled into her eyes before he kissed her.

"Yum," he said when he surfaced, his voice a husky growl.

"Better than the dinner nobody ate?"

"Much, much better." He bit her neck.

Surprised, she squealed. He licked the spot he'd savaged, then blew on it. A tremor ran through her.

"Oh yeah." He drew the lace up and slid his hands beneath it, rubbing her through the silk chemise. "Time to eat up Marti." Kissing her again, he palmed her breasts through the slip, making her quiver with delight. His big hands warmed her through the slick, cool silk, kindling her arousal. She arched her back, thrusting her breasts harder against him.

"Such lovely handfuls."

"They're really not big enough, are they?" She hadn't been naked with a man for years. What if he didn't like her body?

He laughed. "Baby, they're beautiful. Let me show you." He pulled up both the lace and the silk over her head, dropping them on the floor.

Standing before him, exposed, cool air whispered over her skin. She was sensually aware of her near-nudity while he was still fully clothed. The contrast heightened her vulnerability, and she shivered with want tinged by a little anxiety.

"You're perfect. If I didn't know how strong you are, I'd compare you to a doll." He delicately fingered a nipple. It hardened at his touch.

She closed her eyes. Relieved, her body shuddered as tension fled. Without judgment in his tone, nothing indicated he compared her to his former bedmates.

"You have beautiful breasts. They stand up all by themselves. And they fill my hands just right. Any bigger and you'd fall over onto your face, darlin'."

He rubbed her breasts with both hands and kissed her, nipping her mouth, her neck. Exquisite little flashes of pleasure flared through Marti's body. Like a giant jungle cat, he devoured her mouth more eagerly than the half-eaten dinner. His hand slid down her body and under her panties, caressing her until arousal and need tore a moan from her throat.

He tore off the wisp of lace and cupped her bottom, lifting her to rub her mound against his swollen rod, which tented the fabric of his trousers. Her flesh rippled with the pounding of her heart. "Too many clothes," she murmured.

She slid her hands underneath his jacket, around his back and up to his neck. She tugged the jacket off his shoulders, flinging it away as he cooperated by dropping his arms. She fumbled at his tie, clumsy with haste. He reached up and loosened it, smiling at her.

He took her face in his hands. His voice was deep and a little rough. "God, I want you so bad. I've dreamed of this moment a million times."

She smiled back, fully aroused, wantonly female. She kissed his mouth, looking into his blue eyes, now narrowed with need and longing. She pushed in her tongue to taste wine, and desire, and a flavor that belonged to Jim alone. She unbuttoned his shirt, taking her time. She teased each area of his chest she exposed, flicking his nipples into points, hoping the gentle torment would drive him insane.

He stroked her breasts as they kissed. Electric tingles ran through her as he excited her nipples to harder crests. He kneaded her backside and drew her hips closer to his, pushing one knee and then the other between her legs, spreading them apart.

Though still dressed, he'd stripped her naked but for her stockings, topped with black lace, and heels. The contrast made Marti crazy, and she couldn't, wouldn't, wait any longer. He seemed to share her urgency as he reached down and unzipped, continuing to kiss her mouth and massage her breast. His erection popped out of the slit in his boxers. She rubbed it against her mound as he groped in his pocket for a condom.

She was wet, open, and ready, but she gasped in surprise when he gripped her buttocks and lifted her onto him.

"Are you all right? I know I'm big for you—"

"I'm okay, I'm okay. Don't stop!" She grabbed his shoulders to steady herself, digging her fingers into his rippling muscles with mounting, frenzied desire.

"Okay, baby. What you want, I got."

He pressed her down onto his sex gently but firmly. Marti's senses were on fire as she realized that all Jim's body parts were hugely, gloriously proportional. She moaned with a mixture of pleasure and shock as his shaft thrust inside her; he pushed her to her limits, and she knew he wanted take her even higher.

"Open up for me, baby, let me in."

She exhaled, willing her taut muscles to relax. Surrendering to his control, she wrapped her stockinged legs around his waist to draw him inside her. Hooking his arms under her knees, he walked her backward until the wall, cool and hard, pressed against her back. He bucked into her, his muscular thighs rasping against her open, tender flesh. A burst of exquisite rapture flashed through her, like a comet at midnight.

She gasped for breath. Sharp, quick spasms of ecstasy shot through her body as she began to peak. He groaned as he came, flooding her in a violent rush.

He continued to hold her as she floated down from her orgasmic high. Compelled by a growing sense of oneness, she kissed him sweetly. He returned the caress, gently touching her tender lips with his.

"How about getting that massage oil while I undress?" he asked as he lowered her to the floor. Wobbly, she clung to him for a moment. He steadied her on shaky legs, and again brushed her lips with his. Love tinctured by a purely masculine amusement glowed in his eyes.

She went to find the oil. Standing at the bedroom door, Jim turned to watch Marti as she bent over to pick up her dress. She unconsciously exposed the wet cleft between her delicate buttocks, like a perfect cut peach.

She was beyond beautiful. He thought he'd faint from the sight of her. He turned back to the bedroom and smacked his forehead against the right doorpost. Rubbing his head ruefully, he scavenged through his belongings for some ibuprofen.

She returned with their clothes and the massage oil to hang her dress and his jacket in the closet. Jim, clad only in red paisley boxers, folded his trousers over a chair.

"Where's Minnie?"

He smiled. "I left Minnie at Shady Glen. Wasn't in the mood for a threesome."

"I'm surprised you left your lucky boxers."

"Maybe I was overconfident, but something told me I'd get lucky even without Minnie." He poked at the sore spot on his head. Was it swelling?

"I thought I heard a bump." She rubbed some oil between her palms. "Let me see that."

"It was nothing. I just got distracted for a moment and walked into something."

"You okay?"

"Oh, yeah. Better than okay."

She came toward him and everything was much better than okay. As he took her in his arms again, she slipped her oiled hands over his chest and around his back. He cupped her pretty little bottom, picking her up.

The king-sized bed had been turned down by the staff, and

a low light had been left on nearby. Marti's slender form was gently outlined by the soft glow as he laid her on the bed. She looked incredibly sexy, sprawled on the pink satin sheets naked but for stockings and heels. He removed them, tenderly nibbling each leg from the top of her thigh to the arch of each foot.

He ran his tongue over her, finding the delicious furrow between her legs he'd explored with his fingers the day before. He feasted on her sweet-salty flavor, running his tongue up and down her tasty folds.

She opened to him, spreading her legs to afford him access to her most private places. She twisted her hands into his hair and rotated her hips, moaning as she moved him to the areas that aroused her the most. With a flare of joy, he sensed when her desire increased to a swelling ache, demanding release. He used his thumbs to expose her bud, rubbing it with his tongue as she thrust her sex against his mouth.

She thrashed against the slick satin when she came, and he slid a finger inside her to feel her muscles clench in short, sharp bursts. Satisfaction thundered through him. He loved making her peak.

Her responsiveness astounded him. Her previous hesitation and shyness had disappeared, as though she'd made her decision and crossed over some invisible boundary known only to her. If she had any inhibitions, he couldn't find them. Everything he did seemed to excite her passion to heights he never knew a woman could attain.

He hoped he'd always been a considerate and caring lover, ensuring his partner's pleasure before taking his own. With Marti, he didn't have to worry about her fulfillment. He intuitively knew, without thought, what acts and positions would please them the most. He found himself making love to her in ways he had never experienced with any other woman, enjoying himself without restraint. A wild sense of elation flooded him when he realized that he'd finally met a woman who was his match in bed as well as out of it.

Both of them had been celibate so long, had stored up so much loving, that once was not enough. They made love, rested, made love again and again, finding new roads to pleasure. Neither censored the words of love which each murmured in their bliss.

During their fourth intimate encounter, Marti found herself clinging to the headboard and moaning, "It's too much. It's too much." Her flesh, sensitized by Jim's caresses, had turned to flames; her mouth, her sex, were burning hot, heavy, full.

Jim withdrew his fingers from her and gripped her hips, tugging her to him. He mounted her, taking her like a wolf takes his mate. He eased into her, letting their arousal rise slowly while savoring the tight fit. As she climaxed, he completely lost control, roaring as he came in her. He pulled her away from the headboard, turned her over, and again savaged her swollen mouth with his.

"Darling, it's not enough," he murmured into her ear. "I'll never, ever, have you enough." He wrapped her in his arms, and she hummed deep in her throat with a wondrous mixture of rapture and comfort.

His cell phone rang from somewhere in the closet, snapping them out of their erotic fog. He sighed, then got up to find it, finally locating it in his jacket pocket. While he listened, he returned to the bed and possessively explored her mound with his free hand.

"Yes, thank you," he said into the phone. He poked the "off" button and said to Marti, "Your dad and your boss are on their way back from Monterey."

"Oh. What time is it?"

"Almost one."

"Gee, that's pretty late for Dad. And for me." She lolled back onto his bed, smiling. "You certainly are a very stimulating man."

"Told you."

"You sure did."

"We're great together, you know. It's never been like this for me." He ran his finger through her sticky curls.

"Really? With all those hot Hollyweird girls you had, never like this?"

"Nope, never."

"Good. Me either."

"You gonna stay here or go back to the hotel?"

Marti shrugged. "I left my room with all the lights off and the 'Do Not Disturb' sign on my door. As far as anyone's concerned, I'm asleep." She grinned at him.

He grinned back. "Wanna try it in the tub?"

Chapter Twelve

Marti left the guesthouse and slipped back to her room at about five in the morning, sleepy but sated. She stepped into the shower, sluicing off the sticky traces of their activities. She smiled as she soaped her body, still pleasantly sensitive from their wild lovemaking.

Nothing she'd experienced had prepared her for a lover like Jim. Although she had a boyfriend in high school, and had thought she loved him, their adolescent fumblings in the back of his Mustang had really been child's play. In hindsight, she understood that her affair with Terrence Jacques had been characterized primarily by his selfishness as a human being and as a bedmate.

Neither male had remotely compared with Jim's tenderness and skill. He somehow knew better than she how her body would respond. He'd taught her things she'd never imagined about her own sexuality.

The future was still an unanswered question—*but isn't it always?* Liquid fire shot through her as she remembered Jim taking her the night before. She wasn't sure if she should believe all the sweet words they had exchanged while they'd made love. She'd meant what she said to him, but could she trust him to be telling her the truth?

Maybe it was time she did learn to trust. Trust herself, trust him, trust her feelings.

She slipped between the sheets to enjoy a solitary, short

nap and awakened with the phone ringing by her bed. She groped for the handset, finally getting it to her ear.

"Wake up, sleepyhead," Jim said, laughing. "It's time for me to meet the rest of the Solis family at breakfast, and I want you with me."

"Oh! Is it eight already? I feel like I just got into bed."

"Honey, you haven't been out of bed all night."

"You're making me blush again. The things you say, I have a red face all the time."

"Good. It's so attractive. I can hardly wait to tease you at breakfast."

"Now you be good. I'm not sure how our relationship is going to play with the boss."

"I'll be a good boy—for now. But eventually, they're gonna know."

"That can wait until you're discharged from Shady Glen. I mean it, Jim. This is important to me."

"All right. But it'll be all I can do not to kiss you hello and goodbye and every second in between."

"You'll just have to restrain yourself for right now."

"I'll think about it. See ya!"

She threw on her khakis and another polo, adding a pale yellow sweater against the morning chill before hurrying to breakfast. She had overslept and was way late. To make matters worse, she literally fell over a maid's cart as she left her room. The young lady blurted out a voluble stream of Spanish, and Marti took a few moments to assure herself that neither party had been hurt.

She finally found where her entire family, her boss, and her new boyfriend were seated. She gulped. Jim winked at her from across the table. He wore a Cheshire cat grin along with golfing garb. Marti narrowed her eyes at him, hoping her expression asked him to be discreet.

Fran, Rico, and Steve were also dressed for golf, though they lacked Jim's aura of smug satisfaction. Helene and the twins sported matching red and white gingham outfits: white leggings with checked baby-doll tops.

Marti beamed at the trio. "You are too cute for words," she cooed. The twins squealed at their Auntie Marti, stretching their arms up from their carriers to be held. She reached over and released Annalisa, the nearest twin, from her carrier. Emilia yelped for attention, and Rico deftly pulled her out of her seat.

Cradling Anna, Marti plopped down into the only empty chair at the table. Anna crawled over her chest and up her shoulder as Marti looked at the menu. "I'm starving."

"I'm hungry, too," Jim said. "I guess I got quite a workout yesterday."

Marti again narrowed her eyes at Jim as Steve asked, "You gonna try for eighteen holes today?"

"We'll be lucky if we get nine in before we have to leave, and that's probably enough. I feel good, but I don't want to push it after all the exercise yesterday." Jim gave Marti a blatantly sexual grin before sipping his coffee.

"I'm sure that you're the best judge of what you can, um, handle, Mr. Wellman," she said primly.

Jim choked on his drink while she hid her smile behind her cup. Helene, seated beside him, smacked his back. "You okay?" she asked him in her big, booming voice.

"Oh, yeah, I'm fine. Never better," he assured her.

The waiter arrived to take their orders.

"I'm gonna order something light." Jim put down the menu. "Just toast and coffee, please."

"No steak and eggs?" Marti asked. "I thought you were hungry."

He grinned. "I've learned the error of my grease-guzzling

ways. Besides, I don't want to waste time eating when I could be golfing."

"Good idea," Rico said. "Fran, when are you planning to leave?"

"About eleven," she said. "We need to be back by three to check on the patients before the end of the day."

"So, Rico, what are your plans?" Jim asked. "Are you staying here or coming back to Napa with us?"

Marti wondered if Jim would try to take events a step further. He always seemed to have his own agenda.

"I don't really know." Rico put down his water glass. "I have my car here, so I can't leave it and go in the limo with you. Fran, may I drive you back to Napa?"

"If it's not too much trouble. I'd enjoy that."

"Then it's settled," Jim said quickly. "Marti, you'll drive with me, and we'll all leave before noon."

Marti bit into her toast. She focused on chewing while she mused. What did Jim have in mind for the drive to Napa? She smiled.

"Marti, make sure that you don't rush the journey. Make more frequent stops than we did on the way here." Fran paused. "Feel free to visit the cemetery in Santa Cruz. Don't worry about getting to Napa late—I'll make sure your patients are checked out. We don't want Mr. Wellman stiffening up."

Marti swallowed her toast. "No, Mr. Wellman definitely should not become too stiff."

"If I do become stiff, I'm sure Ms. Solis will know what to do about it," Jim said, deadpan.

Marti bit her lip to keep from laughing out loud.

"Golfers, are we ready?" He stood.

The foursome left for the links, leaving Helene and Marti with the twins. Back in their carriers, the girls contentedly sucked on bottles. Helene's eyes widened as she examined Jim's taut behind as he walked out of the restaurant. "Marti, he's a dreamboat. How can you keep your hands off him?"

Marti hated to mislead her sister-in-law. She'd have to avoid the whole truth without lying. "He's a patient. I try not to think about it."

"I think he likes you."

Marti raised her eyebrows. "We'll see what happens when he leaves Shady Glen. Generally, they just go home and forget about me."

"You've dated patients before?"

"Not often. I don't think Dr. Fran likes me to have relationships with patients."

"She didn't seem uptight today about having breakfast with one," Helene said. "What's going on between her and Rico?"

"They're dating, and they seem very happy with each other. I don't know how serious it is."

"I'd say it's serious. Rico hasn't been around much lately. Usually he spends quite a lot of time with us in Monterey, but recently he's in Napa more."

Marti shrugged. "He's got a key to my house, and he comes and goes as he pleases. I felt weird about my dad dating my boss at first, but I guess it's okay. After all, Mom's been dead for over two years now." She leaned back in her chair, happy that the conversation had moved on to Rico's love life.

At that moment, Emilia threw her spoon across the room. It landed in the middle of a large, square table where two couples were eating breakfast, then skidded into someone's lap. Marti didn't know whether to hide under the table or to laugh out loud as Helene took Emilia over to the group to apologize. They went to the women's lounge to change the kids' diapers before loading the twins into their special double stroller for a leisurely walk around the resort.

The twins, on their best behavior despite the incident with the spoon, inspired Marti to wonder what her children would be like. Hers and Jim's. Dark-haired, certainly, with their father's charming smile and beautiful eyes. Would they have boys or girls? Jim would love to throw a football with his son, but she suspected that Mr. Macho Daddy would adore a baby daughter.

Marti envisioned a dark-haired little girl playing Barbies with Jim. Strangely, the child had Andrea's face and Shawna Wellman's eyes. Hmmm.

After Helene left, Marti returned to her room to shove her few belongings into her duffel. When eleven came around, she was in the lobby ready to leave. The rest of the party had also finished golfing and had packed, so everyone left Stone Cliff on time.

As she settled herself in the limo, Marti watched Fran and Rico leave for Napa in Rico's aged but classy Caddy. Fran seemed very comfortable in the leather front seat. Rico made sure she was seat-belted properly before getting into the driver's seat and starting the engine.

Marti chuckled gently.

Jim, beside her, asked, "What's funny?"

"Not funny exactly. Cute. Dad and Fran."

"They are pretty cute. Not as cute as you are, or those twins. Do twins run in your family?"

"I don't know. We have little contact with anyone from our families in Romania or Mexico."

"Yeah?" Jim leaned back into his seat and slid his arm around her. He cuddled her to him.

She basked in her sense of security, hoping it was real. She tipped her head back to kiss his chin. "How was golfing?"

"Great. I didn't realize how much I missed it until I played this morning."

"I bet you'll be discharged soon, and then you can golf to your heart's content. Did Dr. Fran say anything about it?"

"She was vague but upbeat. I think she wants to run some tests to be sure."

"I do too," Marti said. "I'm troubled by the problems you had at Sunset Community. I want to make sure you're one hundred percent okay."

"Didn't I seem okay last night?" He nuzzled her neck.

"You seemed more than okay." She grinned. "I just want to be sure."

"That's all right," he said comfortably. "Might as well."

"What are you going to do after you're discharged?" She was ashamed to hear the anxiety in her voice.

He turned to look her full in the face. "Honey, whatever I do, you're gonna be a part of it. I guess I'll go home. Will you come too?"

"Yeah, I'd like to visit."

"How about Thanksgiving or Christmas? I want the rest of my family to meet you."

"I don't know about that. I usually spend holidays with Dad. I'll have to find out how he feels about it."

"I understand that. I feel the same way about my family."

"So what else do you have going on?"

"The only other thing I have on my plate right now is that lawsuit. I want to pursue it full speed ahead. After I nail those creeps to the wall, I'll figure out what to do with the rest of my life.

"Mind you, I did get a great endorsement offer," he continued. "How'd you like to see your boyfriend on a box of cereal?"

Marti considered. "I really don't think orange is your color."

"It's not, but Wheaties won't change its traditional format because you and I think orange is garish." He hugged her tighter and tilted up her chin with one finger so he could kiss her. "Hey, have you ever done it in a limo?"

She felt herself blushing. "Actually, yeah, I have."

"Don't tell me. Please don't tell me you lost it in a limo on prom night."

She raised her hands in a gesture of mock surrender. "Guilty as charged. How did you know?"

"Just a lucky guess, California Girl." He chuckled.

"Hey, the turnoff is coming up." She lowered the glass separating them from the chauffeur and asked him to take them to the district cemetery in Santa Cruz.

Hand in hand, Jim and Marti walked up the hill to Gracia's grave. As Marti looked around the cemetery, she noticed the difference between the graves of the Latino dead and the others. Those who celebrated *La Dia de los Muertos* had decorated the gravesites. Two bunches of flowers adorned her mother's grave. Steve and Rico must have already visited, perhaps the day before.

Kneeling, Marti added the flowers she'd purchased at the cemetery office, and included a sugared doughnut she'd taken from the limo fridge. Blinking away stray tears from her eyes, she rose and smiled at Jim. "The departed appreciate sweets. At least they do in Mexico City. The kids eat candy skulls and leave them at the graves. Mom thought it was pretty bizarre."

He smiled and tucked her hand into the crook of his arm. "You seem to be much calmer about your mother than you were the other day."

"Yeah. It's weird, but I seem to have attained some peace."

"Death is just a doorway into another state of life, sweetie. No need to get all upset about it."

She looked at him, astonished. "That's a very Mexican philosophy."

He shrugged. "I've thought a lot about it, and studied philosophical theories of death when I was in college. Most cultures don't view death as the end."

The countryside slipped by as they talked, bantered, and periodically stopped for Jim to exercise. They arrived at Shady Glen at about four o'clock.

"I probably won't be seeing you for awhile," Marti said. "I have to spend tomorrow with other patients."

"I understand. After all, I've had your undivided attention for two whole days. But how about a short walk tomorrow afternoon, and maybe we can get together on Saturday night."

"It's a deal. And I want you to know, I meant everything I said to you last night." She gulped, aware she was taking one hell of a chance. What if he didn't feel the same way?

"Me too, sweetheart."

Relieved, she kissed him lightly, protected from prying eyes by the smoked glass of the limo.

The next morning Marti occupied herself with updating her patients' treatment plans. For Jim Wellman, she wrote: *Patient ready for discharge after final x-rays, blood work, and testing*. She wrote a private note to Dr. Fran indicating litigation was to be expected, but Shady Glen was not the target.

Marti arrived in Jim's suite to pick him up for his walk late in the afternoon. When she entered, he was on the carpeted floor, stretching as he watched Oprah.

"Ready?" she asked. "Or shall we find out about men who hate French fries and the women who love them?"

He groaned as he got up. "I'll watch anything to relieve the boredom of stretching exercises. Stretching's important, but it's so dull."

"Stretching *is* important. I wish every patient were as disciplined as you. I bet it's one reason you've done so well."

She preceded him out of the facility, leading him to the bench near the birches instead of to the creek, since there wasn't enough time for a long walk. A cool, misty dusk was falling, and she sensed rain in the damp air, redolent with the rich scents of wet autumn leaves and grasses.

Without his cane now, Jim moved slowly but steadily. "Busy day?"

"Oh, yeah. I took the time to update all the files. I've recommended your discharge after final testing. Now it's up to Dr. Fran. So, how was your day?"

"Not so hot. I talked to my lawyer about the case."

"And?"

Jim hesitated. "I don't know quite how to tell you this, Marti. He doesn't want us to see each other anymore."

Marti stopped walking and stared at him. Had she heard correctly? "Excuse me?"

"He feels it would damage the case if we're dating. You're a star witness. You were in charge of my therapy and my recovery here. You were the person who got me up and walking, you and no one else. Norm says that our legal position could be completely undermined if we're seeing each other."

"That's ridiculous. Facts are facts." *Is he dumping me?*

"But if you testify—and you'll have to—whatever you say will look like you're saying it to support me, and not because it's true."

She gasped, shocked. "I'm a professional. I would never lie about a patient. I would never even shade the truth. Why bother? What's true is what's true. You came, you were in a chair, I told you to get up, and you did. That's all there is to it." Marti fumbled her words as her voice rose in tandem with the panic threatening to engulf her. "Why is that so important that you have to dump me?"

"I'm not dumping you!"

"So what are you doing?" She stared at him, hoping he'd explain to her that she'd misunderstood.

"This is just until the end of this case."

He didn't explain, and she hadn't misunderstood. "The end of the case? That could be years! Let's not fool ourselves. You'll meet somebody else." She swallowed hard and fought to control herself against the rising tide of pain. "I can't believe, after what's happened between us, that you'd break up with me over a lawsuit. Isn't there any other way?"

"You said yourself that Sunset Community should be sued, that they'd probably messed up other patients and they should be stopped." He grabbed her arm. She jerked away. "Don't you see, I can stop them. I have the money and the resources to make them close their doors or clean up their act. Isn't that important?"

Marti tried not to whine or wail. "Yes, it's important. But I'm important too. My feelings are important, at least they are to me."

"They're important to me, too. It's just for a while, and then we can be together again."

"Are you saying we can't see each other, talk to each other—what? What exactly do you mean? And for how long?"

"Norm says we can't do anything that any other therapist and patient wouldn't do till the case is settled or after the trial."

"You're leaving next week. Does that mean we won't be seeing each other while this lawsuit is going on?"

"I guess so. I mean, he says that if I even call you, that'll show up in my phone records."

She tried to read the expression in his fathomless blue eyes, flat as glass. "We can't even talk? For months? For years? What kind of relationship could survive that?" She felt as though her mind had shorted out. All her fears about loving Jim—a celebrity athlete with a reputation as a womanizer—had exploded into horrible reality. "I can't believe you're doing this. Don't I mean anything to you?" She was shocked to hear herself screaming. She never screamed.

"Aw, come on, Marti, you mean everything to me. I love you! But we both know these people have to be stopped! Norm said that they might even suggest that I'm dating you just to make sure you testify in my favor. Do you want people saying things like that about us?"

Her heart froze. "Is that true, Jim?"

"Oh, come on! What kind of man do you think I am?"

"I don't know. Right now, you're not thinking about us at all! You're just thinking about getting even because they messed up your precious career!" She fought for air, managing to suck in a breath as she realized that nothing she could do or say was going to change Jim's mind. He'd made his choice, and now they both had to live with it.

Only pride kept her voice even. "I accept your decision, especially since I can't do anything about it. Excuse me, but I don't want to be with you right now. Or ever." She turned and ran back to the facility, stumbling over her feet. She knew that Jim, still impaired by his injury, couldn't catch someone who jogged daily.

Her eyes glazed by tears, she floundered toward the staff lounge, wanting only to grab her keys and her purse and get away. As she staggered through the door, she saw vague forms through the mist impeding her vision. Nauseated and hot, she found her way into the lavatory and threw up into the nearest sink.

A few moments later, a cool hand caressed her forehead, brushing her hair out of her face. Dr. Fran said, "Marti, you're ill."

Leaning her elbows on the white porcelain sink, Marti rinsed her mouth. She hiccupped and vainly tried to control her breath. Her stomach lurched. "I think I need to go home."

"Will you be able to drive?" Fran asked.

Marti straightened and breathed deeply. "Yeah, I'll be okay for that."

She searched for tissues in her purse as she scrabbled for her car keys. Desperate to get away from Wellman, she bolted out of Shady Glen. She never wanted to see him again.

What kind of a love was so shallow that something as trivial as a legal case could shatter it? Marti didn't believe the story that Jim told her. She knew that the focus of the litigation would be the treatment at Sunset Community, not the therapy at Shady Glen. He's just using this as an excuse, she reflected bitterly, blinking tears of rage out of her eyes. This is perfect for him. He's had his little fling, he leaves, his life goes on. Well, so will mine!

After reaching her cottage, Marti dragged herself out of the car. Jolly pranced up to greet her, always happy to see her come home. She knelt in the grass beside him and hugged her dog around his neck. "Whatever else happens, you're my sweetie, aren't you?" she murmured into his furry throat. She stood up and took the tennis ball he offered. She didn't really feel like playing, but Jolly seemed so eager that she didn't have the heart to refuse. Strangely enough, she felt better after five minutes of catch with her pet. She ignored the ringing phone, assuming it was Wellman.

She entered her cottage and tore the phone cord out of the wall, destroying the plastic jack in her haste. She ran herself a hot bath and lay in it, considering the situation.

Just thinking about Jim's rejection made her feel sick inside, especially since it had come on the heels of the most incredible night of her life. She'd been caught totally off-guard, and regretted it. She was shocked at her own stupidity. The guy was a card-carrying lady killer, the Casanova of football, and she'd known it, but silly Marti hadn't been able to resist playing with fire.

She'd played, and now she had the third-degree burns on her blistered heart to show for it. The first time in years she opened herself to a man, she got trashed again.

Marti simply gave up on the idea of loving any man, ever. She didn't know if she could face this pain another time. As she contemplated a lonely future, tears began to pour down her cheeks. Her body was racked by sobs that came from deep inside and felt like they'd tear her apart. Was she destined to live alone and unloved forever?

How did other couples manage to get together and stay together? She'd been so sure about Jim. She had waited over a month before opening up to him, a month during which they had seen each other every day, had grown to know each other, and, she had thought, to truly appreciate and love each other. Maybe his next career should be in acting, she thought angrily. He could get a star on Hollywood Boulevard.

She gritted her teeth, clenched her fists, and turned her mind to the immediate future.

Chapter Thirteen

Even though he hadn't slept at all while at Stone Cliff, Jim still couldn't rest the evening he returned to Shady Glen. The first heavy rain of the winter pelted the windows and roof. Shawna called him at midnight with bad news and, even more painfully, he was haunted by the fight with Marti.

Why couldn't Marti trust him? At least he'd see her soon, and have the opportunity to explain, maybe work it out.

The next morning, he stretched in his suite while he waited for Marti to take him to therapy. He expected a stormy scene—hell, she was a woman, wasn't she?—but he could handle that.

She'd refused to answer the telephone at all last night, but he forgave her, he decided, as he sipped some of Shady Glen's excellent decaf French roast. She just needed time to cool off and consider the situation rationally. Surely by now she understood how important she was to his happiness and how much he cared about her. He just needed to get her alone. He knew she couldn't stay mad at him for long.

He was unpleasantly surprised when Katrin and Eileen arrived at nine o'clock.

"Where's Marti?"

"Oh, Marti went home sick yesterday. Didn't you hear? She might have the flu or something." Katrin picked up his cane, which he kept hooked over a chair at the dinette.

"Yeah? She seemed fine to me."

"No, she was very sick to her stomach. Have you had your flu shot, Mr. Wellman?" Eileen Stuart asked.

"Er, no."

"We'll arrange for one at once. Are you still using this?" Katrin held out the cane.

"No. I guess I can take a taxi to the hospital for that shot," he said, his mind working overtime.

"That's a good idea," Eileen said. "Dr. Fran doesn't dispense them, but Napa Hospital can fix you up."

"If Marti's sick, I should take care of that now." He shooed the therapists to the door, then dressed quickly. He'd go to the hospital, all right, but not before he went to Marti's cottage and talked to her. This little problem had to be dealt with right away.

He didn't believe the story about Marti's supposed illness. She was acting true to form, jumping to conclusions, then hiding out and avoiding him. He grumbled inwardly. What the hell did he need to do to prove himself to this touchy woman?

When he arrived at her home, he found another unpleasant surprise. No car, no dog, and no Marti. The bird had flown the coop. The frown on his face remained through his visit to Napa Valley Hospital and after, when he directed his cabby to take him to Edward's Place. Late on a rainy weekday morning, the café was deserted except for Edward and Zelda. The couple bustled around, polishing the copper and brass flowerpots, which lent color and life to their café.

Edward greeted Jim as a friend, showing him to the espresso bar. "Hallo, there, Mr. Wellman! How's Napa's favorite quarterback?"

"Pretty good, thanks. No crutches, no cane. I'm glad, since I needed my hands free to use an umbrella."

"Yes, winter's finally come in, and with a vengeance."

Zelda joined Edward, a coffeepot in her hand and new piercings in her eyebrows. "We'd heard from Marti how well you're doing."

"So, where is Marti?" Jim asked, going for the touchdown.

"Oh, didn't you hear? She went out of town," Zelda said. "Cuppa coffee?"

He nodded, irritated by the conflicting news. And why should he have heard anything? Did the entire world know of his involvement with Marti Solis? He shut down his annoying train of thought when he remembered that it was Marti who'd insisted upon discretion. He'd advertise their romance in every paper on the west coast if it would help.

"So when did she leave? I just saw her yesterday afternoon, and she didn't say anything about it."

Zelda poured coffee for Jim. "Well, you know Marti. She's a very private person. Cream and sugar?"

"Please. When's she coming back?"

"We aren't sure." Edward wiped a nearby table as Zelda put a pitcher and a bowl near Jim. "She went with her dog somewhere up on the north coast, I think. She wasn't very clear when she stopped by this morning."

"Hmmm." Jim glowered as he stirred sugar and cream into his coffee.

"Anything wrong?"

He didn't know if he wanted to discuss the situation. He didn't know Edward well, and he felt sure Marti wouldn't like him to gossip about her behind her back. He was as vague as he guessed she'd been.

"Um, actually, I'm leaving in less than a week, and I wanted to thank her. I'm afraid I might have said something yesterday to upset her." He sipped his coffee.

"Why don't you stay around until she returns?"

"I have to go home. My sister called and said that the creek and the pond overflowed their banks, so I have to check out what needs to be done. I don't want my garage to flood." He put down his cup, then searched in his wallet for a five.

Edward waved the cash away. "On the house. Just don't forget us if you ever pass through Napa again."

"Oh, I'll be sure to stop by," Jim assured him.

"Good luck, Mr. Wellman."

Because he'd been a favorite of the staff and the other patients, everyone turned out to see Jim off when he was discharged the following Wednesday morning. Their friendliness and good wishes made him miss Marti even more.

At ten o'clock, Shawna arrived in Jim's Toyota 4-Runner to pick up her brother and his gear, and to drive with him to his estate near Colfax. As they headed east on Interstate 80, his mood matched the gray, rainy sky.

Shawna turned the volume down on the radio. "So, where was Marti today?"

His lips tightened. "The rumor is that she's on vacation."

"But you don't believe that."

"Shawn, don't pry."

"What did you do to her?"

His foot pushed harder on the accelerator. "Why are you so sure it's my fault?"

"Because I know you," his sister remarked unkindly. "Not every woman is like the bimbos you generally hang out with."

"Shawn, shut up."

"Don't get mad at me. You're the one who blew it."

"Hey, I'm not to blame."

"So, what happened?"

"I'm not going to discuss Marti with you." The 4-Runner picked up even more speed.

"Who are you going to discuss her with? Carl? He'll tell me if you do."

Jim changed the subject. "So what's going on with you and Carl?"

"Nothing," Shawna said primly. "He just broke up with Glenda, remember? What about you and Marti?"

They were now rocketing down the road at ninety miles per hour. Blue and yellow lights flashed, and he winced as he checked his rearview mirror. "Uh-oh," he groaned as he pulled over.

A California Highway Patrol officer stalked over to the driver's side window of the 4-Runner and asked for Jim's driver's license. He reached into the back pocket of his jeans for his wallet. "Yes, Officer," he said glumly.

Shawna, tucked into the passenger seat, started to laugh. "Looks like this is your karmic penalty. So what did you do to Marti?"

The officer eyed the pair of them, then looked at Jim more closely. "Hey, you're Jim Wellman!"

He calmed, happily presuming that the officer was a fan, and that she'd let him off with a warning. The officer examined his license. Her head bobbed up and down as she compared the photograph on the license with the reality. He leaned back into his seat and gave the CHiP his thousand-watt smile.

"Officer, I was just released from rehab, and this is the first time I've been behind the wheel for nearly a year. I'd appreciate it if you'd let me off with a warning this time. I promise it'll never happen again. Control yourself, Shawn," he added at his snickering sister.

"Imagine that, Jim Wellman," the officer murmured. Her voice sharpened. "This license has expired!"

Shawna guffawed.

"What?" Jim grabbed the license back and glared at Shawna. "Hey, how come you didn't tell me when the DMV sent an application for renewal?"

She wiped her streaming eyes. "You were in a wheelchair at the time. I didn't think you'd need it." She leaned past Jim toward the driver's side window. "Officer, all of this is really my fault. If you let my brother off this time, I'll drive him home and make sure the license is taken care of tomorrow."

The officer looked mollified. "All right, but be more careful in the future." As Shawna left her side of the car to go to the driver's seat, the CHiP asked, "May I have your autograph?"

"Sure, as long as it isn't on a citation." He located some paper and scribbled *Best wishes to you, Jim Wellman,* and handed it to the officer. He got into the passenger seat and adjusted it for his height as the CHiP clumped back to her patrol car in her high black boots.

Shawna started the 4-Runner and accelerated to sixty-five miles per hour. She adjusted the cruise control and sat back in her seat. "Are you going to tell me or not?" she demanded.

He sighed, well aware that she would pester him like the Chinese water torture unless or until he told her. He wasn't going to tell his baby sister about his one glorious night with Marti, but gave Shawna the essentials. He concluded, "And she reacted worse than I expected. She thinks it's all my fault!"

"Isn't it?"

"No, it's not my fault that Norm Whitehead says that seeing Marti would mess up the case."

"Screw Norm and his opinions."

Jim looked at his sister, astonished. Shawna could be mouthy but was never crude, and she rarely used expletives.

An English major, she believed that cursing was the refuge of illiterates.

"Marti's the best thing that ever happened to your love life," she said. "Think about it, Jim. You've never been married, and all your relationships have been shallow and superficial. You told me yourself that Marti has the sweetest soul of any woman you ever met. Are you gonna trade that soul for cold, hard cash?"

"I don't care about the money I could make from the lawsuit," he said. "But if the hospital hadn't messed me up, my bone wouldn't have become infected. I might still have a career. As it is, I have nothing in my future. Nothing. Don't you understand? They took everything away from me that really matters."

"Gee, thanks, bro'."

"Aw, come on, Shawn, you know what I mean. I have no life left. And who knows how many other patients they've done this to? Marti said herself that they should be stopped."

"And I'm sure you threw her words right back at her when you talked about it."

"That's an unfair way of putting it."

"But I bet it's true, and I bet that's when she really got upset."

Jim paused, then said, "I think you're right. Actually, the whole conversation was so bad that it's hard for me to remember exactly what was said."

"Get her back, Jim. Give yourself a chance to be happy. Whatever you have to do, do it."

Marti spent a week in the seaside town of Jenner without human company except for brief, intermittent contacts with cashiers and food servers. Dressed against the gray

November weather in sweaters and jeans, she ran and played catch with her dog on the beach. Every dawn and dusk found Marti and Jolly at an outdoor café near the mouth of the Russian River where it emptied into the Pacific Ocean. She contemplated the constant flow of the river, and the rushing tide as it surged and receded. She found harmony in the endless horizon, and peace in the morning mist.

Her soul cleansed, she returned to her Napa cottage on the evening of Sunday, November twelfth. She grimaced at an arrangement of dead flowers that desecrated her porch. Ignoring its card, she took it to the big garbage can she kept in her garage and dumped it. She figured the flowers were from Jim Wellman, and she was going to do whatever it took to make Wellman a part of her past, no matter how much it hurt.

After unlocking her door, she slipped on a pile of mail in her entry where it had landed when the mailman had pushed it through the slot. She unpacked her car and fed Jolly, then took the mail over to the farmhouse table and sorted through it.

Three letters from Wellman. Marti tossed them into a kitchen drawer without opening them. She smiled to herself, proud of her restraint. She flipped through the rest of the mail. She discarded the advertising fliers and stacked the few bills that had come in. Before she'd left for Jenner, she turned off her answering machine, so there were no telephone messages to worry about. Satisfied, she settled down for a quiet evening at home.

The rest of the month was uneventful. That was okay. Marti had more than enough excitement recently, enough to last her an eternity. Thanksgiving was quiet at Shady Glen, and the next day, she made her usual stop at her friends' café after her morning run.

"Hey, girl!" Zelda came out from behind the counter, wiping her hands on a dishtowel. "Did you bring Jolly?"

"Of course. You know nothing can keep him home when I jog." Marti pushed back the hood of her sweatshirt.

"Not even the rain?" Zelda glanced out the window, where a drizzle spattered the glass.

Marti shook her head. "Nope. Retrievers love water. It's their element."

"Put him under the overhang and I'll get him a little something." Zelda found the dog a day-old roll while Marti ordered Jolly to down-stay beneath an outside awning, then sat at the empty counter. The shop was quiet, and she guessed most people were home with their families.

The empty café gave them a chance to chat. As Edward poured Marti coffee, he asked, "So what brings you here, Marti? I thought you Americans made a big to-do about this Thanksgiving holiday. Don't you usually go to your father's place?"

"Not this year. Remember, I took that long vacation at the beginning of the month. I had to trade my Thanksgiving and Christmas vacations for those ten days." Marti sipped her brew.

"Croissant?"

"Sure. The holidays are no big deal, though. They're always quiet at Shady Glen. Sometimes their families even pick up patients for Thanksgiving and Christmas and take them home for a few days. Shady Glen's as dead as roadkill over the holidays."

"You won't have Christmas with the family? Would you like to be our guest this year?" Edward used tongs to place a croissant on a plate, then served Marti her breakfast.

"Thanks, but I'll be working Christmas Eve and Day. Dad's gonna come here for the Shady Glen Christmas party, though."

"That's good." Zelda joined them at the counter. "We hate to think of you alone for the holidays."

Marti shrugged her shoulders. Loneliness had become routine after Jim had dumped her. *Better get used to it, sweetheart!* she'd told herself repeatedly during her empty evenings, figuring she'd be without a man for a very long time.

"Dad thought I deserved a celebration since I'd be working over Christmas, so he's bringing the family gifts to the Shady Glen party. It'll be fun. We decorate the whole place with a half-dozen trees and at least a hundred poinsettias. You should come by and check it out."

"Sounds like the staff goes to a lot of trouble," Zelda said.

"Yeah, but it's worth it. The patients really love to get dressed up. We have a special dinner, and there's a gift for everyone."

"Dr. Murdoch does all that?" Edward raised his brows. "I never saw her as the Christmassy type."

Marti smiled. "She says the presents are from Santa, but I've always suspected the Saint Nick of Shady Glen is a white-haired doctor, not a white-bearded elf."

Edward reached into a stack of magazines. "We thought you might want to see this." He handed Marti the latest issue of *People* magazine, which featured its list of the twenty-five most intriguing people of the year.

With a start, Marti noticed that Jim Wellman's was one of the faces splashed on the cover. She wanted to look at it in spite of herself. She reached for the magazine, then jerked her hand back.

She'd done well in her project to kick Wellman out of her life, carefully avoiding anything that had to do with him. She hadn't even watched football for weeks. Why spoil her perfect track record now? So what if she thought about Jim, ached for him, every morning, noon, and night? She still ignored his phone messages, threw aside his letters, and let his flowers rot rather than take them into her house.

She'd even come home one evening from work to see a 4-Runner with the license plate #1QTRBK in front of her cottage. Guessing it was Jim's, she'd gone to a movie even though she was still dressed in her scrubs. When she returned at nine o'clock, the car had disappeared, but another bunch of roses waited on the porch. She envisioned acres and acres of hapless blossoms destined to meet purposeless deaths.

Ten million roses wouldn't change her mind. Jim had shown his true colors when he'd decided his lawsuit was more important than their relationship. She understood he was angry—with good reason—over his lost career, but sacrificing their love wouldn't make his shortened leg grow that extra inch. He was number one in my life, she wailed silently. Don't I deserve as much?

Zelda noticed her inner turmoil—no wonder, since Marti's traitorous hands were shaking. "Get out of here, Ed." Zelda gave her husband a friendly shove. "This is private girl stuff."

Edward pulled a can of Brasso from beneath the counter and headed toward the metal flowerpots, a rag in his hand. Zelda came out from behind the counter, then sat down. She pushed the magazine at Marti.

"Well, are you going to look at it, or hide?"

Marti bit her lower lip and flipped through the pages. The two-page spread on Jim had a small photograph of his Wheaties box in the upper left corner. The box was dominated by a three-quarter color face shot which made her heart clench and her eyes start to tear.

After a few deep breaths, she collected herself and looked at the rest of the article. There was also a smaller photo of Jim in his Cougars uniform, about to throw a pass, with a football in his upraised right hand.

The second page consisted of a picture of Jim, thigh-deep in water. The caption stated he was repairing the wooden weir of the pond located on his Colfax property. As she looked at the photo, Marti's heart ached yet again. Even in waders, with a bulky waterproof anorak covering most of his body, Jim looked hot, even better than she remembered.

The text indicated Jim was living quietly with his sister in Colfax. Other than occasional stints as a TV sports commentator, his sole project at the moment was his lawsuit against several surgeons, the Cougars' team doctor, and Sunset Community Hospital.

Marti's jaw clenched. She'd hoped that the case hadn't assumed mammoth proportions in his life. But as long as the lawsuit dominated center stage, there wouldn't be any room for her.

She finally broke the silence. "This is weird."

"Why? He looks normal to me."

"I thought he'd get back into the celebrity lifestyle right away. I wonder what's stopping him. Maybe it's that court case. He seems willing to sacrifice a great deal for it." *Including me.*

"Perhaps he's not completely healed."

"Oh, no. He wouldn't have been discharged if he weren't one hundred percent well. Dr. Fran is very careful." Marti tossed the magazine aside. "But it doesn't matter. He's just not my problem anymore."

Zelda glared at her. "You're evading."

Marti shoved her hands into her hair, which was already messy from her run. "Zel, please. This is hard enough, okay?"

"You're holding too much in."

"I don't know what else to do. Jim and I talked it all out, he made his decision, and that's it. Nothing I said seemed to make any difference to him."

"He stopped by here a few days ago. He seemed anxious to see you."

Marti shrugged. "That's just Mr. Macho Quarterback reacting. He needs to always feel wanted, I guess. But the fact is, I just can't trust the guy." She shook her head slowly as her eyes filled with more tears that she refused to shed. "It's over."

Chapter Fourteen

Four days before Christmas, Marti went home early to change out of her customary white scrubs and arrived back at Shady Glen clad in her party clothes: black wool trousers and a green satin blouse. She helped Andrea, who had graduated to crutches, don her red velvet dress, white lace tights, and black patent Mary Janes. Marti brushed out Andrea's fair hair and pinned it into a topknot on her head, secured with a big white bow.

"Look at how pretty you are," Marti said, leading Andrea over to a cheval mirror. Marti knelt beside her. The girl's eyes shone as she regarded herself, but her small face clouded as she met Marti's eyes in the mirror.

"Marti," Andrea asked, "what's wrong?"

"Darling, nothing's wrong. How could anything be wrong when I'm with you?"

"You seem sad lately."

Marti blinked, surprised. She had buried her feelings for nearly two months and assumed that no one at work had noticed.

"I'm not sad, darling. Everything's fine."

"You don't smile or laugh very much anymore. You used to laugh all the time."

Marti floundered for an explanation that a young child could understand. "Well, honey, there just isn't much for me to laugh at right now. But that doesn't mean that anything is wrong. Everything is going along just as it ought to, nice and peaceful. So, don't you worry about me. Let's go to the party!"

Marti took Andrea to the common room, where they joined the steady stream of patients, assisted by staff, who were making their way to the party. Christmas carols played softly in the lavishly decorated room, which featured a giant tree, silver snowflakes, and poinsettias. Out of respect for patients and staff of the Jewish faith, a lighted menorah shone in one window, and potato latkes were also part of the holiday menu. Outside, darkness had fallen, and the evening mist pressed against the windows. Inside, it was merry and bright.

After settling Andrea on one of the couches with a plate of food ("No, you may not have five Christmas cookies!"), Marti circulated among the patients and staff, directing traffic around the loaded buffet table and ensuring that each patient's specific dietary needs were met. Those who were wheelchair-bound used lap desks and flip-away armrests as dinner trays in conjunction with their chairs.

The Shady Glen cooks, assisted by Marti's father, had outdone themselves. Marti nibbled at vegetable crudités with fat-free dip, which were followed by roast turkey with all the traditional side dishes and trimmings. Rico had prepared dozens of tamales, traditional Mexican Christmas fare. Christmas cookies and coffee cakes were served for dessert.

After dinner, it was time for gifts to be opened, a long process due to the number of patients and staff. During the gift giving, people continued to circulate, munching on desserts and drinking decaf coffee or herb tea. Staff quietly began to clean up, removing dinner items and used plates from the room.

"Marti," Fran called softly, "Santa's brought something just for you."

Marti chuckled. Fran's gifts were always fun. Last year she had given Marti scrubs in a loud Hawaiian print after Marti had expressed boredom with the usual whites. That present had effectively stifled her complaints.

Fran handed Marti a small wrapped box, then gave gifts to Tommy and Katrin. Each employee opened his or her box, which contained a cut crystal snowflake, with a hole pierced in the top so it could be used as a Christmas ornament. "They're beautiful. Thank you so much, Fran," Marti said.

Fran raised her eyebrows. "They're from Santa," she corrected. "He has plenty of them at the North Pole."

"Uh-huh," Tommy said. "Right. Well, Doctor, I'll trust you to thank Santa for me, but just in case, thank you."

Marti watched as Katrin raised her ornament to the light and looked at the rainbows through it, then at her husband's face. Katrin smiled at Mark. A stabbing pain lanced through Marti's heart, and she turned away from the touching sight. *Why not me? What's wrong with me?*

Rico put his arm around her and said, "Let's open the family gifts."

He led her over to the tree, where two presents were wrapped in a distinctive blue and gold paper, printed with stars.

"Nice wrap job, Dad. Where'd you find the paper?"

"In Santa Cruz. I wanted something unusual, so they wouldn't get mixed up with everyone else's gifts."

Marti groped under the tree and handed her father a beribboned box. "For you, Dad. Merry Christmas."

Her father opened his gift and found a sheepskin cover for his Cadillac's steering wheel. *"Gracias, querida."* He gave her a hug and a kiss.

She tore open the paper on the first of her two gifts, which turned out to be a pair of pearl earrings from Steve and Helene. "Oh, these are great," she said. The second present, from Rico, was a Nordstrom gift certificate.

"I didn't know what you need, so you can go to the after-Christmas sales and buy whatever you want," he said. "I gave the same thing to Fran. I guess I don't have much imagination when it comes to gifts."

"Thanks, Dad. This is just right."

"Marti," Katrin called from across the tree. "There are other presents for us."

"What? Who are they from?"

"I think they're from Jim Wellman. There's one for every person who took care of him while he was here."

Marti's stomach twisted as she glanced at several boxes. There were presents for Eileen Stuart, Tommy Kline, Katrin Young, Fran Murdoch, and for herself. There was even a gift for Andrea.

Andrea squealed as she opened hers—a Peter Pan costume, complete with green boots and a Peter Pan hat. Eileen and Tommy received shirts with the Stone Cliff logo. Katrin's gift was a teddy bear, wearing a Cougars T-shirt. Fran's gift was a pearl drop on a gold chain.

Marti hesitated. Everyone else had opened their gifts, and they were waiting for her. *Oh, God, this is so embarrassing. How could he?*

She slowly removed the gold and silver paper and found a long black velveteen box. The logo on the box read: East-West Traders, Vancouver. She opened the box to reveal a bracelet, constructed of nine identical jade frogs attached to each other by gold links. Each of the one-half inch frogs was beautifully carved, the detail exquisite.

"Oh boy, little frogs, jeez." The frogs were a clear reference to their walk to the creek and the lovelorn bullfrog they had encountered there. *What's that sneaky quarterback up to now?* she wondered. The gift was layered with meaning, she was sure.

"Oh my God, Marti! It's incredible!" Katrin yelped. "May I see?"

Marti grimaced. She handed the box to Katrin, wondering all the while what everyone would think.

While her nosy colleagues oohed and aahed over the jade frogs, Marti opened the card which accompanied the gift. It contained a haiku written in calligraphy on hand-made rice paper.

jade, less beautiful
than are your eyes and cool heart
lonely lost always

Lonely lost always—is he saying he's lost loneliness always, or does he mean he's lost and lonely always? Her head spun.

The gift was deliberately provocative. It was also very costly, judging from the excellence of the carvings and the pure perfection of the apple-green jade. He'd gone to a lot of trouble to get it for her. Because it had been presented so publicly, she couldn't return it without creating questions and gossip. She already heard a buzz of comment from the other Shady Glen employees as she contemplated the bracelet and the poem.

On top of that, she had to communicate with him to thank him for it. Marti frowned. She knew Jim was manipulative to a fault. What had he said? *I'm apt to get what I want.* But what did he want?

Her brooding was interrupted when Rico put his arm around her and said, "A very nice gift, very appropriate."

"I don't know," she said. "It seems very expensive. And, if

I'm going to be a witness in that lawsuit I heard about, I don't think he should be buying any of us gifts."

"Pshaw. He's properly grateful for the good work all of you did for him." Rico took the bracelet from Katrin and slipped it around his daughter's left wrist. After fumbling with the elaborate catch, he attached the safety chain. "Lovely, very special. Be sure to write him a nice thank-you note, sweetheart."

The next day, Marti did. She became appalled at herself after an hour of indecision. She seemed unable to write a simple note to Jim without ruining several sheets of her creamy, textured stationery. Finally, she simply gave up on sounding clever. She sure wasn't going to write what was in her heart, which was: *Jim, I miss you like I miss the chicken pox!*

Or: *Jim, I miss you with each beat of my aching heart . . .*

Or: *Jim, you big jerk, how could you do this to us!*

So, she wrote:

December 23

Dear Mr. Wellman:

Thank you for the lovely bracelet. The gifts you sent to all of us were a very thoughtful gesture and were greatly appreciated.

All of us at Shady Glen hope you are healthy and happy, and we wish you well.

Happy holidays,
Martina Solis

She sealed the note into a matching envelope and left it for the mail carrier. It would be picked up that very same day, but because Christmas was on Monday, Jim wouldn't get it until Tuesday. Soon enough.

Despite herself, Marti wondered what kind of Christmas

he'd have. Jim had wanted her to visit Colfax over the holidays, which meant that his family probably gathered at his home for Christmas. Located in the Sierra's evergreen forests, Colfax was beautiful in the winter, especially if snow fell.

"A white Christmas!" Shawna exclaimed with satisfaction. From inside the warmth of the living room, Jim, his best friend, and his sister surveyed the snow-covered lawn, which sloped down to the icy pond. "Just what I wanted!"

Jim raised his brows. "We'll see if you're still happy with the snow tomorrow when we have to dig out the driveway."

Shawna giggled as Carl led her to a sofa near the fire, which crackled merrily in the big stone hearth. Jim watched as his sister and his friend laughed and flirted by the Christmas tree, which towered near the fireplace in his stone, wood, and glass home deep in the forest. A flash of envy jabbed through his heart, as sharp as the scalpels that had ruined his leg and torn apart his career. *Why not me? What's wrong with me?*

He turned away from the joyous scene in his living room and stared out the window at the falling snow.

A presence at his side made him start. "What's wrong, son?"

He slipped his arm around his mother's still-slim waist. Karen Wellman hadn't had many opportunities to gain weight while running after three active children and working two jobs. Later, when her sons had become successful, she'd started to enjoy the benefits of their wealth. A personal trainer was only one of the goodies Jim and Jack had been able to provide their mom.

Karen brushed Jim's hair off his forehead with a gentle hand. "That wasn't a rhetorical question, dear."

He smiled. "Sorry. I was thinking."

"Don't work too hard. It's Christmas. It's a time to be happy, not to brood. And you've been very broody lately."

"I know." He gazed at the fluffy white puffs floating down outside the window without really seeing them. "I miss a friend, that's all."

"That girl Shawna told me about—what was her name—Marti?"

"Yeah. I really blew it bad, Mom."

"So go get her back. You've never had trouble getting a woman before."

"This one's different."

"Good. You need different."

The harsh note in his mother's voice surprised Jim. "I thought you liked Glenda."

"I liked Glenda, and Rachel, and Wanda, and Trudi, and Margo, and all the rest of them in the same way I like reading *Style* magazine. Amusing but hardly essential."

"I miss Marti. You'd like her. She's more like *Newsweek*. She's got substance."

His mother smiled. "So what are you doing to get this substantial woman back into your life?"

He waved his hands helplessly. "I've done everything I could think of! Phoned, sent letters and flowers—I've even gone out to Napa to try to see her. I can't catch up with her at work—she'd blow a fuse—but I've stopped by her house a couple of times. Somehow, she's never there. Once I stayed in Napa all night. I guess she was out of town or something.

"I don't know what else to do, Mom." His voice cracked, embarrassing the heck out of him, but he'd never bothered to keep his feelings to himself, and didn't try now.

"Does she love you?"

"Well, she said so, and she's a very truthful person. I think she's avoiding me because I hurt her so much. I can't really blame her, 'cause I've been such a jerk."

"Why?"

"I knew she was . . . well . . . not shy, but cautious, like those deer out there." He gestured to a pair of does who picked their way through the snow toward one of the piles of fodder he and Shawna had put out for them. After every few steps they lifted their graceful heads, scanning the terrain for any dangers that might lurk in the surrounding forest. In contrast to their wariness, blue jays brawled loudly at a nearby bird feeder.

"Spooked her, huh?"

"Yeah, really bad. Norm Whitehead told me to stop seeing Marti until the case is over, and, like a fool, I told her."

Karen winced. "Well, you know what they say. Nothing good comes easy. And you've had it pretty easy till this year."

"I know. I've been lucky. But right now, I feel as though my luck's run out."

"You'll think of something. You're very resourceful, son. It's one of your best qualities."

On Tuesday, the rest of his family went skiing. Jim didn't know if he was allowed to ski and wasn't going to take a chance. Instead he drove the 4-Runner into the town of Colfax to pick up mail from his post office box and to go to the grocery store. He ripped open the cream-colored envelope that bore Marti's return address, but the cool little thank-you note inside made his blood boil.

What the hell was with her? *Happy holidays from Martina Solis?* He'd thought she was an iceberg when they met, but now he knew the truth. The virgin queen facade hid his wild, sweet lover, and he'd never rest until he smashed to smithereens the shell encasing the woman he adored.

★ ★ ★ ★ ★

On the morning of January second, Dr. Fran called Marti into her office. When she arrived, a young man wearing an ill-fitting suit handed her a paper, saying solemnly, "You are hereby served with process."

Chapter Fifteen

"A deposition subpoena?" Marti stared at it, drawing a blank. "I've never been subpoenaed before. What does this mean?"

"I've been served one also," Dr. Fran said. "Marti, this is Mr. Graham, from James Wellman's law firm. He's here to brief us on what we can expect on the eighteenth."

"The eighteenth and the nineteenth, actually," Graham said.

"Oh, my God." Marti's chest tightened. "Do I have to go to court?"

"Oh, no. This is—this is a question-and-answer session in our office. But we expect the depositions to be extensive, since there are numerous lawyers and parties involved."

She sat down. "What do I need to do?" Her nervous fingers crumpled the document.

"I'm providing Mr. Graham with a copy of Mr. Wellman's file for his attorney's evaluation," Dr. Fran said. "My understanding is that you should review Mr. Wellman's records. The attorneys will ask you questions, and all you need to do is tell the truth."

"We'll put the two of you up at the local Holiday Inn," he said. "We'll also take care of your transportation. A car will come for you on the morning of the eighteenth."

Marti took a deep, calming breath. Her throat muscles still felt oddly tight. "Then it's all arranged. Will Mr. Wellman be there?"

Mr. Graham crinkled his forehead. "I don't know. I've never actually talked to the client. Mr. Whitehead, the managing partner, takes personal care of Mr. Wellman. I hope he'll be present," he added with a touch of boyish enthusiasm. "I'd like to get his autograph."

The morning of January eighteenth dawned cold and foggy. At eight o'clock, stiff with dread, Marti waited with Dr. Fran in the lobby of Shady Glen for the arranged limo.

She didn't know what to expect, but her imagination and "Court TV" had supplied some frightening images. Her darkest fantasies featured a room full of pinstriped attorneys firing questions at her, all trying to show she had done something wrong. She knew that the lawyers representing the defendants—the surgeons and the hospital—would try to blame Shady Glen for Jim's permanent disabilities, to deflect attention from their own negligence.

Marti sat in the limo as Dr. Fran organized herself for the drive. If Marti had been in a better mood, she'd have been tickled by yet another of her boss's quirks. Dr. Fran somehow made every space she inhabited her own. Part of that dominating personality, Marti mused. It was like watching a hermit crab take over an especially appealing shell.

Dr. Fran pushed the button that raised the barrier between the driver and the passengers. She took off the jacket of her tailored, gray flannel suit, and laid it on the seat next to her, revealing a pink silk blouse. She flipped open her briefcase, withdrew her BlackBerry, and poked buttons, examining a screen that read: JANUARY 18. Apparently satisfied by what she saw, she clicked off the BlackBerry and tossed it back into her briefcase. Then she ran one hand through her short, silvery hair, and leaned forward, facing the rear seat where Marti huddled.

Unexpectedly, Dr. Fran took Marti's cold hands in both of hers, squeezing them gently. "I know you're tense about the deposition. Let me assure you that, first of all, I'm sure that I'll be the one they'll spend the most time questioning. I've done this before. It's not hard. Just pretend you're talking to anyone, and simply tell the truth."

Letting out her breath in a long sigh, Marti pulled one hand away and rubbed her throbbing temple. She'd barely slept for several nights. She thought she looked terrible and felt even worse. Clever of her boss to have divined that Marti needed reassurance, but what Dr. Fran didn't know was that Marti was less scared about the deposition than she was about encountering Jim.

Worse was the possibility Zelda had suggested: that Jim wouldn't show up at the deposition, and Marti would never see him again. His efforts to communicate with her had abruptly stopped after she'd sent him her formal little note. He'd told her oncc that there was no use pursuing something that wouldn't work out. Maybe he'd placed her in the category of lost causes.

She'd thought that she wanted him to leave her alone, but strangely enough, when he ceased trying to contact her, she missed the small proofs that he might still care for her—even if it was only a little bit. She didn't want to think she'd been used and dumped.

She was confused. She was overwrought. She was afraid she'd burst into tears if anyone even looked at her cross-eyed.

"Secondly," Dr. Fran continued, "I want to again compliment you about your performance with this patient. Marti, you did a great job. There was a distinct possibility that Mr. Wellman would never walk again without a cane."

"I know, but I didn't tell him. He seemed so discouraged a few days after he got to us that I never let on."

"You did the right thing. Your treatment was impeccable, as usual."

"I really didn't do anything. I just told him to stand up and walk. That's all."

Dr. Fran smiled. "Some therapists have a knack, and you are one of the lucky few. You have excellent instincts. You know when to push and when to hold back. Respect your intuition with this deposition in the same way you do with patients, and everything will be fine." Dr. Fran released Marti's hand, then rummaged through the limo's refrigerator. "One of the advantages of Mr. Wellman's wealth is that we travel first class," she remarked. "Juice?"

"Is there hot coffee?"

"No, but we can stop for some." Fran rapped on the window separating them from the driver.

They stopped for coffee. Her immediate needs satisfied, Marti stared out the window at the pallid winter scenery while contemplating Dr. Fran's words. Marti knew Dr. Fran well enough to realize that she rarely did or said anything without a reason. Her boss expected a stellar performance at this deposition. Even so, Marti felt better. She chuckled.

"What?"

"I guess I'll be going out there and winning one for the Gipper."

Dr. Fran laughed. "Maybe we should have created special Shady Glen T-shirts just for the occasion."

"Yeah, and a Shady Glen cheer. Rah, rah, sis-boom-bah, Shady Glen, yay!" Marti giggled.

"That's the spirit! Marti, treat this new experience like any other. It's an opportunity for learning more about life, more about people. When I'm in a new, frightening situation, I always ask myself, 'What can I learn today?' And in a deposition, you have the chance to teach and educate others.

Believe me, your knowledge base about rehabilitation medicine will exceed that of anyone else in the room. They won't be able to snow you or trick you. There's nothing to fear in this experience, and a great deal to be gained."

They arrived precisely on time at ten o'clock, and proceeded up the elevator to the tenth floor offices of the large law firm that Jim employed. A receptionist escorted them into a conference room.

The room was empty except for one attorney, who introduced himself as Norman Whitehead. The paunchy lawyer, who wore a navy jacket and gray pants, had a full head of white hair. *An aptly named gentleman!* thought Marti.

She reddened as she felt Whitehead's interested glance sweep her. He was one of the few people in the world who was aware of her affair with Jim. *He's probably wondering what Wellman saw in plain little me. I certainly don't have much in common with those centerfold chicks Wellman usually hangs out with.*

Whitehead invited them to be seated and offered them coffee. Marti, who'd already drunk several cups in the limo, declined, requesting ice water instead. She had the jitters from too much caffeine. Or was it nerves? She clasped her hands in her lap to conceal their shaking.

Whitehead said, "The deposition will begin as soon as the last attorneys show up. Everyone is here except for Garrett Conkling's lawyer, and as a courtesy to him, we'll wait until about ten-thirty. If everyone isn't present, we'll start then anyway.

"I just want to let you know that we appreciate your attendance at such short notice. As you may not be aware, my client, Mr. Wellman, is pushing this litigation forward at a very fast pace, and—"

Dr. Fran interrupted. "I thought that the notice of deposition was within statutory requirements."

Whitehead appeared startled at her knowledge. "Yes, it was, but normally we give more notification than the statute requires. I understand that the client has personal reasons for rushing the proceedings." He again eyed Marti.

She tensed, pressing her lips together in a thin line. She heard a door open behind her. She scented Jim's distinctive tang and felt her treacherous body respond to his nearness. As she blushed even more hotly, her heart jumped into her throat. Her belly squirmed and twisted. With an effort, she kept her back straight and her voice even as she asked, "How soon can we leave?"

Whitehead hooted. "Young lady, you just got here. I suggest you enjoy the ride."

What a patronizing jerk! "Who's going first?"

"We'll start with Dr. Murdoch. It may be that after her testimony, we won't need you at all."

Marti's reaction mirrored Dr. Fran's as both women stiffened. "Do you mean to imply," her boss asked, "that it's possible that Ms. Solis will not be deposed at all?" Controlled fury edged Fran's words.

"Yes, that's true."

"I don't mean to offend you, sir, but Ms. Solis is a crucial member of the Shady Glen team. She is my head therapist. Your deposition subpoena left my facility understaffed, and now you are telling me that Marti probably won't need to testify?" The doctor's voice, normally commanding, was louder and angrier than Marti had ever heard it in five years of working at Shady Glen.

"We'll be sure to compensate you with witness fees for the lost personnel," Whitehead said.

"Witness fees don't cut the mustard," Dr. Fran snapped.

"My facility is shorthanded and no amount of money can replace my chief of therapy."

Jim moved into Marti's line of sight. "Good morning, everybody. Norm, may I speak with you?"

Whitehead reacted immediately. Money talks, thought Marti. The two males retreated to an isolated corner of the conference room. They returned shortly, and this time, both men seated themselves at the table.

"We've changed our plans," Whitehead said. "Ms. Solis, you'll be deposed first. Then we'll question Dr. Murdoch. We'll ask you, Ms. Solis, to remain in attendance through tomorrow in case there are follow-up questions in light of Dr. Murdoch's testimony."

Dr. Fran nodded, but her expression didn't soften.

Marti glowered at Jim. Why did he want to put her through a deposition if it wasn't necessary?

A buzzer sounded, and Whitehead picked up a nearby phone. "Everyone's here, and seated in conference room two. So let's proceed. Dr. Murdoch, you're free until lunch. You can wait in the reception area, or even leave the premises, as long as you're available at noon."

Marti guessed that conference room two must double as a library; it was windowless and lined with law books. As in her nightmares, the room was jammed full of dark-suited attorneys. She sat in the center of one side of a large, oval table, feeling miserably conspicuous. She wanted to hide. How did celebrities tolerate the spotlight? The gulf that separated her from Jim felt enormous, an abyss as wide and deep as the Grand Canyon. They were different, so different. How could she have ever believed they'd have a chance?

Six attorneys surrounded the conference table—one for each litigant—plus their paralegals. Jim Wellman sat on the other side of the big teak table, but not directly in front of

Marti. She could see out of the corner of her eye that he wore the same navy suit he'd worn at dinner in Stone Cliff. The reminder of that particular evening made her feel even more dejected. His burgundy tie bore the team logo, small cougars printed in gold, an ironic selection since the team doctor was one of the defendants. Jim looked grim and determined.

A court reporter was tucked in a corner next to a video camera. Marti guessed that both the camera and the stenographer would record the proceedings.

Whitehead opened the deposition by distributing copies of Jim's records from Shady Glen before introducing Marti to the assemblage of attorneys. She nodded after each lawyer was introduced to her. She decided to address the attorneys as "sir" or "ma'am," certain that there wasn't a chance in heaven or earth that she'd remember everyone's names. Their faces were just a blur as her stomach churned and her heart wrenched in her chest.

The attorneys silently flipped through the records as Marti sat and sweated. She glanced over at Jim Wellman, who openly stared at her. She flushed and looked away.

Jim's heartbeat thudded in his ears as he gulped water from the tumbler near his elbow. He couldn't drag his eyes away from Marti. Though she looked lovely, she wasn't the vibrant woman he remembered. Before she'd been slender, but now she was thin. Her high cheekbones were more pronounced, and her fine eyes were huge in her pale face. He knew there had been no excess fat on her exquisite body. *From where could she have dropped weight?* he wondered. She never had any to lose! And it was his fault. He'd blown it badly with this fragile, vulnerable girl. He'd never forgive himself if he couldn't make everything right again.

Her pallor accentuated the tiny lines around her hazel eyes

and full lips. Her mouth and eyelids drooped. She sat quietly, dressed in the same old-fashioned outfit he'd stripped off her on Halloween. A stab of longing lanced through his flesh as he remembered the scent of her skin and the texture of her nipple as it had hardened in his mouth.

He supposed that the green outfit with the long skirt was perfect for the occasion, especially with the peek-a-boo lace blouse covered by a tight jacket. Marti kept the jacket buttoned all the way to the top as though she felt cold. Her dark hair was tied at her nape with a black velvet bow.

Lace swept her wrists, so Jim couldn't tell if she wore the bracelet he'd given her. He felt superstitiously sure that if the jade frogs adorned her wrist, he'd get her back. He was also wearing his Minnie Mouse boxers for luck. So how could he lose?

After Marti took an oath to tell the truth, Norm opened the questioning by asking her to identify herself for the record. She did so, then detailed her professional qualifications. Jim was impressed. He'd known that his Marti was smart, but hadn't previously been aware that she'd been a national merit award winner, and had attended university on full academic scholarships for both her bachelor's and her master's degrees.

After briefly outlining her work history, Marti, led by Whitehead, slid into a discussion of Jim's case.

"Mr. Wellman came to us on September twenty-eighth of last year," she said, enunciating clearly for the court reporter. "My understanding is that he had suffered multiple injuries the previous February, including a fractured left ankle. However, his major involvement was a midcervical adduction fracture of the right femur."

"Whoa," the court reporter interrupted. "Can you spell mid—whatever—fracture?"

Marti smiled as she spelled out the technical term for the severe break he'd suffered, but Jim was miffed. How come no one had ever told him what kind of fracture he'd sustained? "Hey, what does that mean?" He nudged his attorney with an elbow.

Whitehead repeated Jim's question for the record.

Marti answered, "In lay terms, a midcervical adduction fracture is a break in the middle of the neck of the femur, which is the big bone in the thigh. The femur narrows as it approaches the pelvis, then widens into a knob. The cervical portion of the bone is that narrow area. An adduction fracture is a midline break."

"Please describe the plaintiff's therapeutic course."

She raised her brows. "I've never heard that phrase, 'therapeutic course,' but I'll assume you want me to talk about Mr. Wellman's treatment and recovery while he was at Shady Glen. Okay." She took a breath. "There was no therapy the first day, as he arrived late in the afternoon. I did not see Mr. Wellman at that time. His records reflect he was placed in a therapeutic whirlpool bath, given a light massage, and put to bed upon his arrival.

"I met with Mr. Wellman the next day. He was attended by myself, Katrin Young, and Thomas Kline. Mr. Wellman was taken out of the wheelchair and placed on horizontal therapy bars to test the strength of his legs. Mr. Wellman was immediately responsive to therapy. He requested crutches and was handling them competently within a few days."

Jim suppressed a grin as he remembered the battle he'd fought with Marti and Fran over the crutches. He tried to catch Marti's eye and wondered if she was thinking about the same incident.

Instead, she took a sip of water. "Mr. Wellman continued to improve at a rapid rate. His daily routine consisted of physical and occupational therapy in the mornings, followed by a whirlpool bath and a massage. After lunch he took a walk, which was generally followed by another therapeutic bath, or hydrotherapy. Mr. Wellman was discharged from Shady Glen on November eighth."

Whitehead asked about the contents of Jim's chart.

"Shortly after his arrival at Shady Glen, both Dr. Murdoch and I checked Mr. Wellman's chart. It was striking for its lack of information." Her tone was dry and objective. "That problem was immediately remedied, as he was sent to Napa Valley Hospital on September thirtieth for full x-rays and blood work."

"What did you hope to discover?"

"It was necessary for us to have current information on Mr. Wellman's condition. While the patient appeared healthy, and had been cleared for therapy by Dr. Conkling, we needed to ascertain the condition of his bones and joints, and whether infection had set in. Testing showed that Mr. Wellman was fit to proceed with a full therapeutic regimen."

"Is it your expert opinion that Mr. Wellman was in a wheelchair for too long?"

"Yes."

"Please describe Mr. Wellman's chart when it was received at Shady Glen."

"As I stated, it was remarkable for its lack of information. There were only two x-rays, and they were undated and useless." Marti reached into a copy of the chart, which was by her left elbow, and extracted the films. "As you can see, one of the x-rays shows the right femur with a cancellous bone screw inserted. That's c-a-n-c-e-l-l-o-u-s. The x-rays obtained from Napa Valley showed an angled blade plate fixating the bone. Both are controversial treatments."

"Did you or anyone else at Shady Glen contact Sunset Community Hospital to get the rest of his chart?"

She paused. "I did not. I don't know what anyone else did or didn't do. No additional records from any source other than Napa Valley Hospital and Shady Glen were placed in the file."

"Why didn't you check with Sunset Community?"

"First of all, it is customary for the patient's entire chart to follow the patient. Secondly, we've had similar problems with Sunset Community before. We know from experience that contacting Sunset Community is likely to be a frustrating waste of time."

With satisfaction, Jim saw the hospital's lawyer squirm. Still, the woman didn't say anything. He frowned. He sensed that she had something up her sleeve and made a mental note to ask Norm during lunch to worm it out of her.

Marti continued, "We simply tested Mr. Wellman to get the baseline information we needed. Also, I believe that Dr. Murdoch may have made some telephone calls to Mr. Wellman's doctors."

The deposition seemed to drag on for hours, and Marti was exhausted long before noon. Although they ate at an expensive restaurant, lunch was an uncomfortable affair. She sat rigidly in her chair and picked at her food as she watched the interaction between Jim and the paralegal, Mr. Graham. She wasn't sure which of them made her more nauseated: the admiring young paralegal, or the gracious celebrity pandering to his fan.

Whitehead kept telling her she was doing well in a smarmy unctuous way that told her volumes about his character in general and his attitudes toward women in particular. Dr. Fran was the only one who ate and acted normally.

"Mr. Wellman, how have you been?" Dr. Fran asked.

"Hangin' in there," Jim said tersely. "With this case occupying my time, I haven't done much else lately." He looked over at Marti. She'd be damned if she'd meet his eyes. She dropped her gaze, stirred her soup, and fiddled with her napkin instead.

Jim turned to his lawyer. "Norm, I have a feeling that the attorney from the hospital is hiding something. What kind of tricks can she pull this afternoon?"

Whitehead shrugged. "She can do quite a bit, since you rushed the process and didn't allow me to demand documents before the deposition. She can pull anything out of her bag of tricks that she's got, and throw it at either of the witnesses." He leaned back in his chair and smirked at Marti. "On the other hand, Ms. Solis has been very impressive this morning. Very impressive," he repeated, staring at Marti's lips.

She ignored him, preferring to save her energy for the afternoon session. Only one of the six attorneys involved in the case had questioned her, and she anticipated a tiring session after lunch.

At one-thirty, the other lawyers deposed Marti. First came the lawyer for Garrett Conkling, the Cougars' team doctor. He quickly established that she had never met Dr. Conkling and didn't know what Conkling's role had been in Jim's case. The questions of the attorneys for the other surgeons were similar. Relieved, she concluded they thought she was small fry and not worth their time.

Next, the attorney for Sunset Community Hospital started in on Marti. Ms. Bowdoin was in her early fifties with frosted hair. She looked like a barracuda, as she had long thin hands, a thin mouth, and was dressed in a pearl-gray suit.

"Ms. Solis, you are aware that plaintiff Wellman is alleging negligence on the part of the defendants, are you not?"

"Yes, ma'am."

"You worked with Mr. Wellman every day for over a month, isn't that correct?"

"I didn't work with Mr. Wellman on weekends, ma'am," Marti kept her voice low and even.

Ms. Bowdoin stood and paced across the room. "How do you feel about Mr. Wellman?"

"I feel great about Mr. Wellman!"

Heads turned at her vehemence. The attorney looked at Marti with upraised eyebrows. "Why, what do you mean, Ms. Solis?"

Marti looked over at Jim. He was set and unsmiling. "I got this man up out of a wheelchair and walking, and I'm damn proud of my work!"

The barracuda turned tail. Evidently the attorney had been expecting some sort of declaration of love. She went on to the next part of her examination.

"When did you notice that plaintiff's legs were of two different lengths?"

"Almost immediately."

The barracuda attacked. "Why isn't this noted in Mr. Wellman's chart?"

"It is," Marti replied. "I distinctly remember making the notation shortly after Mr. Wellman came to Shady Glen."

Bowdoin's lip curled. "Find it." She tossed a photocopy of Jim's chart across the polished table to Marti.

Marti flipped through the familiar pages. She located and retrieved her notes from October second, and held them out to the attorney. As she did so, the lace trim at her sleeve fell away, exposing the jade bracelet on her wrist. Out of the corner of her eye, she saw Jim smile and lean back in his chair. *What's he so smug about?*

"I don't see where you discuss his legs," Bowdoin said, her voice flat.

"Do you have a highlighter pen?" Marti asked her.

The woman dug in her briefcase.

Marti circled her scribble: *Pt.l/l>rt.appx.3.0cm.*

"What does that mean?" Bowdoin wanted to know.

"It says that the patient's left leg is longer than the right by about three centimeters."

The lawyer's lips curled again. "Can anyone read these, ah, unusual abbreviations other than yourself?"

"The people I work with can read them," Marti said. "We did not anticipate litigation. Nor did we expect that Mr. Wellman would be treated by anyone other than ourselves in the near future at the time those notes were written. They were strictly for in-house use."

Outsmarted, Bowdoin tried another tack. "What, if anything, did you do to alleviate this condition?"

"Nothing."

"Nothing?"

"His chart indicates the patient had been in traction for an extended period of time at Sunset Community. Further efforts to lengthen the leg were, in our collective opinion, useless and might even damage the joints. The patient himself stretched frequently, and mild stretching during massage took place, but the radiograms showed the disability to be permanent. This is not an unusual consequence of a femoral fracture. However, the multiple surgeries, plus the apparent compromise of the sterile field during the first surgery—which caused infection of the bone—may have contributed to the disability."

"What about this golfing excursion with you and Mr. Wellman?"

Marti frowned. She didn't know how to answer. Norm Whitehead jumped in. "Object to the form of the question as vague and unintelligible."

"I'll rephrase," Bowdoin said. "Is it correct that you and Mr. Wellman went golfing on or about November first of last year?"

"No, it's not correct," Marti said. "I do not play golf. Dr. Murdoch and Mr. Wellman went golfing at the Stone Cliff Golf Resort in Pacific Grove. I went along to provide therapy for Mr. Wellman as needed."

"Isn't that a trifle unusual?" The attorney's thin upper lip curled yet again. What an irritating habit, Marti thought.

"It was somewhat out of the ordinary, but Mr. Wellman was an unusual patient. He's a celebrity. We were anxious to ensure his speedy recovery and satisfaction with our facility."

"What was the therapeutic purpose of taking Mr. Wellman golfing a distance away from Shady Glen?"

"Shortly after he came to Shady Glen, we noticed that Mr. Wellman was showing signs of clinical depression," Marti said. "I became aware that Mr. Wellman enjoyed golf, but had not been golfing since before his injury. We felt that Mr. Wellman needed something to look forward to. He had been expressing sadness and hopelessness about his future, stating that he had lost his career and his friends.

"We felt he needed some concrete encouragement if he were to heal. Early in October, I told him that if he continued to improve at a fast rate, he could golf at his club, Stone Cliff, in a month or so. Dr. Murdoch felt it best that he be accompanied and monitored by both of us."

"Is it unusual for both you and Dr. Murdoch to be absent from the facility at the same time?"

"Yes, it is, but it does happen. Today is another example," Marti stated pointedly.

"Where were the three of you accommodated on this little golfing junket?"

"Mr. Wellman rented a guesthouse on the Stone Cliff grounds for himself, and Dr. Murdoch and I had rooms in the main resort hotel."

"Did you sleep in your room?"

"Yes, I did, and I'm incredibly offended by that question," Marti snapped, her temper rising. "What I do privately is no concern of yours!"

"Let me show you a picture." Opening her briefcase, Bowdoin took out a manila envelope that contained a stack of photos. She passed one to Marti.

The barracuda had darted in for the kill.

Chapter Sixteen

Anticipating a sneaky play, Marti took her time studying the picture while Bowdoin passed out copies to everyone seated at the table. Though Marti kept her emotions under control, she heard a whoosh, as if someone at the table had drawn in a surprised breath.

The dim photo, which looked as though it had been taken without a flash, showed Marti and Jim dancing at Stone Cliff. The blurry side view showed their profiles, including her distinctive sharp chin. She assumed that some celebrity watcher had snapped it.

When she felt she was ready, Marti looked up. "Nice photo. May I have a copy?"

Caught off guard, Bowdoin stuttered, "I—I guess you may." She recovered her poise. "Let me ask you again—did you sleep in your room that night, or did you sleep with Mr. Wellman? You obviously danced with him."

Marti said serenely, "I can assure you that I did not sleep with Mr. Wellman." *We did a lot of stuff, but sleeping wasn't on the agenda.* "I slept in my room. If you don't believe me, you can ask the maid."

"The maid?"

"Yes. I tripped over the maid's cart as I left my room for breakfast. I apologized to her, and we had a conversation. Her name is Raquel Solis Escamilla, and she came from the same village in Pueblo, Mexico, that my father left forty years ago. I'm sure she'll remember me."

After a pause, Bowdoin said, "I don't have any more questions for this witness at this time. I understand that she'll be available tomorrow for further questioning if necessary."

The barracuda was routed.

Marti settled back into her chair weary, but with a sense of accomplishment. She'd felt the same way when she'd run her first and only marathon. The experience had been grueling, but worthwhile. She knew she had performed well in a trying situation.

Whitehead nodded. "Let's take a break and start with Dr. Murdoch in ten minutes."

The lawyers headed out the door, and Marti put her head in her hands, letting herself sink into her exhaustion. She sensed a presence beside her and looked up.

"Oh, it's you," she said tartly to Jim. "What more can I possibly do for you now? Or, should I say, what more can you possibly do to me?"

"Let me take you home," Jim said. "You're all tuckered out. It's nearly four. They won't want you for the rest of the day."

"Are you a wacko, or is this another trick? I thought you dumped me because you didn't want to be seen with me."

"That's not true. Come with me and let me explain."

"I really don't want to talk with you, Jim. Really and truly."

"That's all right. We don't have to talk. It's just a ride, okay?" He dropped down onto one knee beside her. "I know I've treated you badly. At least let me do this for you."

She sighed and rubbed her forehead. Dammit, she wanted to run her hands through his shiny, dark hair, so temptingly close as he knelt by her side. *Will I ever learn?*

Her brain told her firmly that she didn't want to go anywhere with Jim, but the rest of her was too tired to argue. Besides, she wanted to get to her hotel A.S.A.P. So she followed Jim out of the building to a Toyota 4-Runner that was parked in a back lot.

"Do you have my overnight bag?" she asked.

"Yep, all taken care of." He looked over at her, smiling slightly. "You know I sweat the details."

She bit back her answering smile. "Yes, that's true."

He unlocked the passenger door of the truck and, as she gathered her long skirt in her right hand, overtly watched her climb into the truck and arrange the folds of green wool around herself. His intent gaze had the same effect it always did, making her hot and bothered. That bothered her even more. She tamped down her feelings as she settled herself into the passenger seat and buckled her safety belt.

He got into the truck and drove out of the parking lot, turning eastward. She assumed the hotel was in that direction, and closed her eyes. Not only was she exhausted, but a nap would be a good way to avoid talking.

Groggy, Marti awakened from her snooze. Why on earth had Jim driven onto a highway? Surely the hotel wasn't far from the law office! Looking at the dashboard, she stiffened. The cruise control was set at precisely sixty-five miles per hour, overkill unless Jim's destination was more than a couple of off-ramps away.

"Where are we going?" she asked, even though she suspected the answer.

"Home."

"Hey, you can't just hijack me this way. Take me to my hotel. Now."

"I told you I was taking you home, and you didn't argue with me."

"My home's in Napa."

"Well, mine's in Colfax, and that's where we're going."

"Why?" She wailed in sheer frustration. "Look, I've had a horrible day. I had to get up early and ride in a car for two hours. Mean, nasty people have been asking me irritating, stupid questions all day long. I hate your lawyer. He's a pompous jerk. I hate Sunset's lawyer. She's a vicious witch.

"All I want is to be left alone. I don't want to be kidnapped and taken on some mysterious journey. All I want is to take off my clothes and get into a bathtub and not be bothered by the rest of the world."

He laughed. "Honey, I'm taking you to a place where no one will ever bother you. No one's gonna know you're there, except your boss, if we choose to tell her. You know, we can just say that I'm taking you out to dinner, and you'll be dropped at the hotel later. As you told the vicious witch, what you do privately is no one else's business."

"You'll bother me." She knew she sounded like a sulky child, but she couldn't help it.

"Yes, I probably will." He sounded unruffled. "I told you, I like to bother you. Tease you, flirt with you, love you."

"I can't believe you have the gall to still say that."

"Babe, I'll never stop saying it. I'll say it as long as it takes to convince you, and longer."

She bit her lip and stared out the window.

"Marti, you're stuck in this situation. You might as well enjoy the ride."

She turned back to him angrily. "You say something like that every time you con me into doing something I don't want to do."

"You said you'd visit my home with me."

"When did I say that?"

Jim clutched the steering wheel so hard that his knuckles

whitened. She hoped his tension wouldn't affect his driving. They were approaching the mountains and the roads could be icy.

"The day I screwed us up," he said.

She took a deep breath. "At last you admit it was a mistake."

"I knew it was a mistake as the damn words were coming out of my mouth!"

"Then why did you do it?"

"Norm said—I don't know. I don't know!"

For the first time in her memory, he seemed at a loss. Then he said, "It wasn't what I wanted. I guess I didn't think you'd react so badly. I assumed we wouldn't see each other for a while, and then everything would be all right again."

"You were wrong," she managed to whisper as tears gathered in her eyes. "Nothing's been right for me since that day. Nothing's right now."

"We can make it right." Jim sounded certain.

But she wasn't. "Can we? After what's happened between us, how can I trust you?"

A muscle twitched in his jaw before he answered. "That's up to you. I can't change what's already happened, but as far as I'm concerned, there's only one woman for me, and that's you. At least let me show you the kind of life you'll have if you stay with me."

She jerked upright. "I don't care if we'll live in a palace. You can't buy love and trust."

"I'm not trying to buy you. Quit being so damned touchy. That's not my point. I just think you'll like living in Colfax. It's as pretty as Napa. Prettier, really, and more peaceful."

She relaxed a bit. "It *is* nice up here." Evergreens lined the highway, their boughs sprinkled with a light snowfall. "Will you promise to take me back when I ask?"

He released a breath as though relieved. "I promise, but you have to give me half a chance. At least stay for dinner." Frost crunched beneath the tires of the 4-Runner as Jim turned off the highway and drove through a small town.

She considered. What harm could dinner do? Besides, she was already in Colfax, so she might as well stay for a little while. She rolled down the window and took a deep breath. The cold, pure air was scented with pine. "Well, okay. But no funny stuff, you know what I mean?"

"Fine. You want funny stuff, you'll have to ask." He shot her a considering glance through narrowed blue eyes. "Beg, even."

She raised her brows. "Dream on, dude."

Grinning, he halted at a stop sign, letting an aged Jeep International pass through an intersection in front of the 4-Runner. The jeep honked, and he stuck his hand out of his window to wave. "The local postmistress," he said. "A very important person."

As Jim drove through the town, Marti became impressed by the number of pedestrians and motorists who honked or waved at him or at each other. "Colfax seems to be a friendly place."

"It is, but without being intrusive. I've never felt hounded here."

He turned northward out of Colfax, following a road which led up a hill, driving for ten minutes along twisting, turning country lanes until he stopped. "Here it is."

She couldn't see anything in the forest that resembled a house. "Where?"

He pressed a button set in his dashboard. A rustic redwood gate, set into a stone wall, swung inward, revealing a cobbled drive. Another touch of the button closed the gate behind them. He drove down a lane lined with stands of valley oak, ponderosa pine, Douglas fir, and manzanita, all speckled with melting snow, pale in the twilight. After the roadway curved through the woods, the house emerged from the wilderness. Marti's breath caught in her throat. Jim didn't live in just another house; his home was as unique as he was.

The place was big but, more importantly, it exuded a rustic comfort. Constructed of wood, stone, and glass, it didn't dominate the landscape but blended perfectly with the forest. A grazing deer, startled, bounded away from the 4-Runner as the car approached. She gasped with surprised delight.

He parked the 4-Runner in a garage around the side of the house and ran to open Marti's door before she could get it herself. He helped her out, then walked her around to the front of the house. "We can get in through the garage, of course, but I want to take you in through the entry. It's much nicer."

Holding her arm, he escorted her along a path constructed of granite stepping stones, interspersed with greenery on which the light snowfall had partially melted. She stopped and sniffed. "Jim, what do you have planted between these rocks?"

He smiled. "Creeping thyme. It's very tough and can stand up to both the snow and foot traffic. Smells good when you step on it, too."

"I didn't realize you're a gardener, as well."

"What do you think I do during the off-season? I'm up here pulling weeds. This place needs major upkeep."

"You can't hire someone for that?"

"Yeah, I get help, but there's always something to do in a place this size."

The double front doors were silvery weathered redwood, with large oval inserts of stained glass. One depicted a pine tree next to a lake, and the other, flowers and butterflies. They were different from each other while being complementary. He opened the door and ushered Marti inside.

"Unlocked?"

"People don't lock their doors around here." He closed the big double doors behind her. They shut quietly.

Floored with polished granite slabs, the entry hall was lavishly decorated with tropical plants and Asian art. The large living room in front of her was dominated by a huge stone fireplace.

"We can take off our wet shoes here," he said. "Did you pack a pair of slippers?"

"Slippers? No. I didn't think I'd need them at the hotel," she said pointedly.

"You can borrow a pair of my socks. Come this way." He led her through a pair of open double doors on the left side of the entry and padded down a carpeted hall, carrying his black leather loafers. She followed, her boots in hand.

They entered a bedroom, and she realized with a start where she was. Judging by the scent, this had to be Jim's room. The bedroom was enormous, at least as big as her entire cottage. She again experienced the sense of intimidation she'd first felt when Jim began pursuing her. Even though they were in the same room, the gap between them still yawned, threatening to swallow all her hopes and dreams.

The carpet was soft gray, thick and deep. The bedroom was appointed with tasteful, modern teak furniture. A nook off the main bedroom appeared to be a glassed-in sun porch, floored again with polished granite. Myriad tropical plants flourished there, and she spotted a redwood tub from which steam rose.

She'd never known anyone who had a hot tub in his bedroom.

A fire crackled in the fireplace, which was opposite a king-sized bed topped with a fluffy feather comforter. The Chinese print duvet cover, blue and white, matched Jim's eyes. A vision of the two of them snuggling in that bed jumped into her imagination. She blushed and looked away, then unbuttoned her jacket, suddenly feeling overheated.

An older woman wearing black pants and a starched white shirt was unpacking Marti's suitcase, placing the contents into a cedar-lined closet. "Ruth, hello," Jim greeted her. "Ah, you found Marti's things. Good. Marti, this is Ruth. She comes every day from Nevada City to clean up after Shawna and me."

"As though you're so much trouble." Smiling, Ruth extended a hand. "Marti, hello." Marti shook it. Ruth's grip was firm and dry.

"Ruth, we won't be needing anything else today." Jim slipped off his jacket.

Ruth grabbed it and hung it up. "Thank you, sir." She disappeared, carrying their shoes.

"I want her to get home before the roads become too icy," he said. "Ordinarily she would have left even earlier, but I wanted everything to be just right for you."

"You planned this?" she asked, frost edging every syllable. "You fiend, you rat, you—you—sneaky quarterback!"

He sat on his bed and grinned up at her, his cobalt eyes glinting as he blatantly enjoyed her discomfiture. "Is that supposed to be an insult? All good quarterbacks are sneaky."

Damn, but he's smug! Marti's mouth tightened.

He went on, "I've told you, sweetheart, I'm apt to get what I want. And what I want is you."

Despite her better judgment, a sensual, hot jolt of anticipation leapt through her body. She repressed it with difficulty but sat down on the bed next to him. "Jim, we need to talk."

"Yes, we do." He slipped his arm around her.

She stiffened. "Don't do that. Please, don't do that."

"Why not? Don't pretend that we don't love each other."

The quiet truth in his words hit her like a hammer striking an anvil. She swallowed past the lump in her throat and picked her words with care. "That might be true, but so what?"

He looked outraged. "So what? What do you mean, 'So what?' I love you, Marti! And I know you love me!"

"Listen to me." She tugged on his sleeve, looking into his face. "The day you dumped me, I resolved to make a clean break of it." As she lost her composure, tears filled her eyes and her voice choked. "It was terrible. It was like cutting off an arm, or a foot. I don't know if I can go back."

"Aw, sweetie—" He tucked her into his lap.

She jerked away. "Quit grabbing at me. Sex won't solve anything."

"I'm not! You're upset and I'm just trying to comfort you. Damn it, I'm tired of being unfairly judged by you. This has got to stop!" He jumped up and glared down at her.

"What are you talking about?"

Jim jabbed an accusing finger at her to punctuate his tirade. "I'm talking about the fact that you have, since the first day we met, constantly treated me as though I'm a slimy letch who's out to use every chick he meets. I see that attitude all the time. People treat me as though I'm . . . well . . . I guess they believe the crap my publicist puts out.

"Yeah, there have been a lot of women, but I've always played fair. Besides, I thought we'd grown beyond the surface stuff."

"I have not been unfair to you! I worked my butt off on your case!" Feeling small and intimidated, she jumped to her feet and went toe to toe with him. "You're arrogant, condescending, and manipulative!"

"Yeah, so what?" He faced her, arms akimbo. "You expect Mr. Perfect? Forget it! You have to let the people you love mess up without shoving them out of your life!"

She gasped. "I don't do that! I'm a very fair person!"

"Girl, you do a cut-and-run routine whenever the going gets tough or you get scared. Don't you understand? You'll never be happy unless you face your problems, not avoid them."

"My happiness has nothing to do with you!" She knew she'd lied as soon as the angry words left her mouth.

He saw right through her. "Baloney. Our happiness has everything to do with each other. I'm your man, honey, and I'll never let you go."

"I won't be manipulated. You're trying to manipulate me right now!"

"You bet, I'll manipulate you. I'm gonna manipulate you right into marriage, if you'll let me!"

"Marriage? Marriage? Are you insane? You broke up with me!"

"I never, ever broke up with you!" He shook a finger in her face.

She smacked it away. "Excuse me?"

"I merely told you that Norm Whitehead didn't want us to date for a while. You jumped to the conclusion that we were breaking up. I didn't want to leave you, sweetheart, and if you'd given me some time, I would have figured out a way to make everyone happy—you, Norm, and me."

She stared at him, trying to remember that awful day.

His voice calmed. "I've been over and over it in my mind. I remember telling you that Norm didn't want us to date, and why. I remember saying it was just for a little while. You decided that could be years." He paused. "You say that you love me—and I know you do!—but you have no faith or trust in me. You never did. You always misjudged me, jumped to conclusions before you had all the facts. I'm not perfect, and I may have hurt you, but God knows I didn't mean to. But you've never really been fair to me."

"That's not true!" Even as she protested, she had to admit to herself that Jim was right. She'd mentally nicknamed him "the patient from hell" after only their first meeting, labeled him a problem, and described him as arrogant and manipulative. She'd never completely trusted him with her heart, and yet, she'd expected him to trust and believe in her.

Even if he was arrogant and manipulative, did it matter? In her haste to pigeonhole Jim, she'd overlooked his best qualities. His kindness. His determination. His loyalty to those he loved, including herself.

He was right. She'd never truly opened to him or trusted him. Could she do it now? Should she?

"You said we couldn't even talk on the phone. What was I supposed to think?" She tried to hold back her tears, but, to her shame, her voice cracked and wobbled.

"You're right!" He flung out his arms in a gesture of helplessness. "You're right. I let Norm Whitehead do my thinking for me instead of thinking for myself. It was a totally stupid thing to say. On the other hand, maybe you should have trusted me to deal with the problem. Don't I always find a way to get what I want?"

"That's true," Marti said slowly. "You certainly seem to be able to turn any situation to your advantage. But, sweetie, you told *People* magazine that this case was the most important thing in your life. How do you think that made me feel?"

"Aw, honey, you should know by now that the magazines don't print the whole story. Yeah, it was the only project I had going, but that's only because you weren't with me. We're number one. Nothing can change that."

"But it really could be years until this case is resolved."

"Babe, I'm never letting you go again. The lawsuit will just have to stumble along in whatever way it does." He closed the gap between them and hugged her.

She pushed him away. "No touching yet. Not until we've gotten everything resolved."

He arched his brows. "You mean I have a chance?"

She sighed with exasperation. "Of course you have a chance. Several chances. I love you, you lunkhead! I missed you more than I can say."

He slipped his arm around her again, but this time she didn't shove him away. "No more than I missed you, sweetheart. I hated going through the holidays without you. Everyone was here, but without you, I felt emptier than a football stadium in springtime."

She framed his face with both hands, looking deeply into his eyes. "Speaking of football, I know you really miss your job. I know you're angry, very angry at the hospital and the surgeons for destroying your career. If we're back together, it could mess up your case. Can you accept that?" She searched his expression, hoping for some clue to his true feelings.

His gaze turned impenetrable. "No problem."

"Stop that!" she snapped, jerking her hands away.

"What?"

"Don't you give me that look. That cold blue-glass stare you get when you're shutting me out. Don't you dare shut me out, not ever, do you hear?"

Thank God, he didn't fail her. His eyes warmed as he touched her face. "I'm sorry, baby. I know I pull away when something really bothers me. That's just how I am.

But Marti, honey, I'm not stupid. Yeah, I'm hurting because I'll never play pro ball again. But I'm not gonna throw you away or trash the rest of my life because of this one setback."

He took her into his arms and kissed her forehead. "I'm not worried about the case. You did a great job today, sweetheart. You fielded every question perfectly. You told the truth. You didn't freak out or even blush when the, uh, vicious witch showed you that picture. Hey, I was pretty shocked when she whipped out that photo."

"Yeah, I heard you gasp. I almost told you to shut up."

They both laughed, their rapport regained. The knockdown, drag-out fight had cleared the air.

He met her eyes and hugged her closer. He caressed her face with both hands, whispering, "Marti, Marti, Marti, how could you think I'd give you up? You're the best thing that's ever happened to me."

She laughed gently. "Better than the Heisman?"

"Oh, yeah."

"Better than two Super Bowls?"

He stopped and frowned. "Now that's a hard choice."

Her mouth dropped open in mock dismay, and she grabbed for a pillow. She managed to whack him a good one over the head before he wrestled it away and retaliated. She snatched his tie and yanked. He took the opportunity to pull her close again, taking her lips in a deep probing kiss which seemed to pierce to the very heart of her, thrilling her down to her toes. Reveling in his scent and feel, she caressed him and entwined her fingers through his hair as they rolled around on his bed.

"Well, you askin' for that funny business yet?" He grinned at her.

"Yeah. In fact, I'm begging." Smiling back, she playfully

batted her eyelashes. God, she'd missed him. She'd never again feel complete without him in her arms. "Do something for me, sweetie."

"Anything."

Chapter Seventeen

Marti didn't know from where her wild impulse came. She only knew she was hungrier for him than ever. She said, "Strip for me. I want to watch you."

For a moment, the room was utterly silent, except for the crackling of the fire and their own heavy breathing. Jim looked shocked before he gave her a long, sexy smile. "Martina Solis, you're outrageous," he murmured. "You want it, you got it."

He walked away from her and stood, deliberately displaying himself as she sprawled on his bed. He loosened his tie and pulled it off. He stalked toward her, tall and gorgeous and entirely predatory, intent upon his goal. After passing the tie behind her neck, he used it to bring her close for another wet, sensual, tantalizing kiss.

As she began to respond, he turned away from her. "No, baby. You get to watch, and wait."

He unbuttoned his white dress shirt slowly, exposing his chest inch by inch. He pulled the shirt away from his body in one quick, dramatic snap of starched cotton.

She went weak with desire. He looked better than ever. Life in the mountains had made his rugged body more slim and defined. She ached to run her hands over his washboard stomach, kiss the whorl of hair spinning over his chest.

As he slipped off his trousers, he revealed cute red printed boxers.

Marti grinned. "Hello, Minnie," she said.

"Guess I did right by wearing the lucky boxers, hmm?"

He walked toward her. His bedroom eyes made her feel both hot and limp at the same time. His erection tented the silk.

He bent over her, fumbling with her small pearl buttons, ensnared in tiny loops. "Sweet Lord, this blouse!"

Her smile stretched wider. "What about it?"

"It's a love-hate thing. You look so sexy in it that I want to rip it right off you."

"Don't you dare. It's vintage lace."

"I'll be careful with each tiny little button. Almost as careful as I'll be with you."

While he removed her blouse, she pulled off her skirt, and lay revealed in more lace: her bustier and panties. The air, only partially warmed by the fire, felt good on her overheated body.

He flipped her over so she was on top of him. She couldn't restrain a moan as he squeezed her buttocks. He moved his hands higher and unhooked her constricting bustier. He stripped it off her, tonguing her breasts as they escaped the cups. Sharp, jagged bursts of pleasure raced through her body and she pressed against him, pushing her sensitive nipples closer to the source of the ecstasy. He drew one firm tip entirely into his mouth in a long sucking bite that made her whimper with need. He gave the other breast the same treatment as he caressed her bottom. She rubbed herself against his shaft, delighting in his readiness.

He turned her over again and looked down at her. "Your breasts are so wonderful. Are you larger than I remember?"

She smiled faintly, still lost in bliss. "I don't think I'm growing anymore."

He nibbled at one nipple, plucking it with his lips. "You

look like strawberries on top of whipped cream . . . even if you don't like strawberries."

"That's okay. I'll take it as a compliment." She rolled off him and stretched. "So how about that hot tub?" Marti stroked his erection as her memory cast back to their midnight encounter in the Jacuzzi at Stone Cliff.

Jim frowned. "Is a hot tub all right for someone in your condition?"

"Excuse me?"

"When were you going to tell me about the baby?" he asked.

"What?"

"You're pregnant."

"What?"

"Aw, come on, Marti. Stop acting surprised. It's all over you."

"I really don't know what you're talking about."

"I got you pregnant that night at Stone Cliff," Jim stated baldly. "I heard you went home sick the next day. You're thin, obviously haven't been able to keep much down. Morning sickness." He patted her hand. "Don't worry, honey. The nausea should pass in a few more weeks. Your breasts are unusually large and sensitive, which is another symptom."

She sat down next to him and shook her head in total disbelief. "Jim, I'm not pregnant."

"Honey, it's all right. Sometimes condoms fail. Whatever choice you make about this baby, I'll support you. But I want you to know, if it were up to me, I'd never let either of you go away again." He tightened his arm around her.

"Darling, being back with you is heaven, but you need to understand. I'm not pregnant. I'm sorry, since you so obviously want me to have your child, and I'm very flattered. But I'm not pregnant."

He stared at her, his brow wrinkled. "When was your last period?"

"About three weeks ago. I'm not pregnant. My breasts are sensitive because I'm premenstrual. You can cut the chivalry, babe. I'm not pregnant."

"Hmm." He kept his arm around her, looking disappointed before he perked up, flashing that thousand-watt smile at her. "Let's make a baby."

She pushed away. "What are you talking about?" she practically shouted. "Are you out of your mind?"

He continued with the little-boy grin. "Don't you like children?"

"Yes, I like children. That's beside the point."

"Well, what is your point?"

"Sweetie, please understand. It's important that you want me for myself, not for some dream-baby you've conjured up."

"Aw, come on. I love you! It's the most natural thing in the world for me to want a child with you."

The phone beside Jim's bed chimed gently. "Mind if I take this, sweetheart? It might be the lawyer." After she nodded, he reached over to grab the handset without letting go of her. "Well, hel-lo, Norm. What's going on?"

A long pause, and then, "Really. Well, that's good."

A shorter pause. "Oh, no way. No way. Tell them fifty and full disclosure, or I'll take them for more."

Jim clicked the handset off and grinned at Marti. "Precisely as predicted. They're wheeling and dealing because you and Fran Murdoch knocked them dead."

"We knocked them dead?"

"Oh, yeah. I watched while you testified. You were busy waving x-rays around and pointing at my chart. I checked out their reactions. You should have seen their faces. And Norm said Fran was great, even better than you. She skewered the surgeons and Sunset Community. Said they should all lose their licenses." He chuckled.

"What kind of offers are they making?"

"In the fifty million range. They have to decide who's gonna pay what. Plus, they don't want me to talk about the case to the press. Fat chance!"

He turned to her. "It seems as though this case is going to settle. But you know, baby, I want you back to stay, whatever happens. You've got to understand that." He lightly ran his fingers up her spine.

"I do want to be with you," she said, almost shyly. "But what about my home and my job?"

"Keep them if you want," he said. "I have complete freedom, and so will you. If you'd prefer to continue living and working in Napa, you can sure do that. I like your cottage. But, honey, we can be wherever we want, doing whatever we choose to do." He paused. "I'd like you to try living here for a while, see how you like it. Will Fran give you a leave of absence?"

"I don't know. She did tell me once that I'm a talented therapist and that I'd always have a job. At the time, I wasn't sure if she meant I'd always have a job with her. I can ask. But I'm not the only factor. What do you want?"

Jim shrugged. "Actually, I want to write."

"Excuse me?"

"I said, write."

"Really?"

"Yeah, really. I can do that anywhere, but I like it here. By the way, what did you do with the poetry I sent you?"

"You mean, the haiku you sent with my bracelet?" Marti waved her left wrist.

"Yeah, and all the other stuff."

"What other stuff?"

He looked irritated. "I sent you a new poem just about every week since I left Shady Glen. Please don't tell me you threw them away."

"No, I don't think so. I put everything into a drawer in the kitchen. I didn't care to read them at the time."

"Some of my best work is in your kitchen drawer. I was gonna start a literary magazine up here. *Poesie*, or *Colfax Literary Times*, or something."

"That sounds great, honey," she said, hoping she didn't sound too insincere. She figured that he'd be throwing his money away, but that was his business, not hers.

The phone chimed again. He clicked the "on" button and put it to his ear. "Norm! What's up?"

As he listened, he carried to handset over to the hot tub and climbed in. "Well, I guess I'll take forty-eight, just to get it over with."

She took off her bracelet and placed it on a small teak table beside Jim's bed as he continued his conversation. "Are they really?" he asked.

She slid gratefully into the steaming water.

"Set up the *E!* interview anytime," he said. "Nah, let's do it in the spring, when the wildflowers are blooming up here. Oh, where's Fran Murdoch?"

Another pause. "All right. Tell her I'll have Marti there tomorrow at ten o'clock." Jim thumbed the "off" button and beamed at Marti. "All settled. It's over."

She breathed a sigh of pure relief. "What terms?"

"We get forty-eight mill, full rights to the story."

"Wow." She blinked. She was glad he'd said "we," even though he had no reason to include her. "So now what?"

"Whatever." His shrug made the otherwise calm surface of the water wrinkle into waves. "Let's spend the night here, and I'll get you down tomorrow morning to talk with Fran."

His fingers tippety-tapped on her thigh, steadily approaching her mound.

She fought to maintain control over her body, her heart, and her feelings as his index finger began a slow, steady stroke. "I c-can't leave her in the lurch."

"Should I pack a bag and come with you to Napa?" His look reminded her of Jolly begging for a snack.

Relaxing, she waved a wet arm. "*Mi casa es su casa,* sweetie." It was comforting to know he'd compromise. Comforting to realize he'd give as well as take.

Pure joy to be back with the man fate had picked just for her.

Nine months later

On a sunny October morning, Marti awoke in Jim's sumptuous bedroom at about ten, feeling more and more like a beached whale. The bedroom was deserted, so he was already up. Lately he'd been working hard on the second issue of his quarterly literary journal, *Poetiks*. He was probably in his study.

Breathing deeply, she swung her legs over the side of the bed. One of the big windows allowed a cool, pine-scented breeze to filter into the room. In the corner, Jolly thumped his tail against the carpet, saying "good morning!" in his doggy way.

She hiccupped and rubbed her tummy. The initial stages of her pregnancy, which had begun in January, had been marked by periods of monumental morning sickness. And as far as the baby was concerned, the morning lasted all day and all night. About the third month, her appetite returned, and she had rapidly swelled to cetacean proportions.

She stood with difficulty, and began searching for a garment, any garment, large enough to cover her gravid body.

Fortunately, their wedding ceremony had taken place in April, while she was still slender. She smiled at the memory. They'd married at home in Colfax, on a lawn that sloped down to the pond. Drifts of daffodils, narcissi, crocus, and tulips had decorated the property, which Jim had planted in years past. Both families were present at the intimate party, which took place on a sunny Sunday morning.

The twins, who showed a remarkable ability to throw unwanted objects, had been fine flower girls. Helene had wheeled them along the grassy aisle in a white carriage decorated with green and yellow streamers. The twins tossed rose petals out of their baskets without any real knowledge of the part they played in the ritual. They also threw out the baskets, narrowly missing Jim's mother.

Shawna and Jack followed them as the maid of honor and the best man. All the females, including the twins, had worn dresses in a soft green and yellow flower print, with big bouffant skirts and white trim. The men, including the groom, had worn white linen; Jim and Marti had decided that both the bride and the groom would wear white.

Escorted by her father, Marti had glided out of Jim's house and over to the site of the ceremony. Swathed in layers of white silk georgette, she'd felt like a cloud floating by Rico's side. She'd carried a small bouquet of lilies of the valley, plucked early that morning from the dell.

She'd reached Jim, and smiled mistily up at him. He'd looked gorgeous in his white linen suit, with a yellow rose tucked in his lapel. A lavish wedding breakfast followed the brief ceremony, after which the bride and the groom traveled by private jet to Morocco.

They'd explored North Africa for a month, seeing everything from the souks of Marrakech to the pyramids at Gizeh. May found them back in Colfax, with Marti eating everything in sight. Summertime turned into one long, unbroken food-fest.

Although she'd worked part-time at a local hospital, her job hadn't interrupted her feeding frenzy. Now, she could hardly wait for this baby to be born. Not only had the last two months been utter misery, sheer living hell, but she was afraid she'd eat until she exploded.

"Ouch!" She yelped as Grace Solis Wellman announced her presence by kicking Marti underneath the ribs from the inside. She unsuccessfully massaged the area from the outside. She bet there was a huge bruise on the underside of her ribs where little Grace's left foot seemed to be permanently wedged.

In fairness to Grace, the baby was also ready. Her head had dropped into position. Marti expected to alert her doctor and her midwife at any time.

She managed to pull a thin chambray shift over her head, and padded, barefoot, down the hall and into the morning room. Jolly followed, toenails clicking on the slate tiles.

"Good morning, sleepyhead," her husband said from behind the newspaper. He put the paper down and stared at her belly.

"Hi, sweetie." Marti headed for the refrigerator.

Shawna wandered in to plunk herself down at the big pine table. Two identical pairs of cobalt blue eyes examined Marti's stomach.

"Think it's today?" Shawna asked.

"Maybe," said her brother. "Any contractions?"

"Yeah, but just Braxton-Hicks, I think." Marti found a watermelon and handed it to Jim's housekeeper, Ruth, to slice.

"I bet it's today," Shawna said. "In fact, I'm sure."

"Why are you so sure?" Marti asked. She frowned with annoyance at the sensation of moisture trickling down her legs. She'd turned into a sweat ball at about her sixth month and boy, was she tired of perspiring constantly.

Shawna chuckled. "Don't look now, hon, but you're wet."

Marti looked down and gasped. This was more than sweat. "Oh my God! My water broke!"

Pandemonium erupted as three voices began yelling at once:

"Call the midwife! Where's her number?"

"Marti, lie down now!"

"Where's the towels and stuff we're supposed to have?"

Ruth rapped with a spoon on the polished granite counter. "Everyone calm down!"

Silence. "Everything's going to be fine," she said. "Martina, please go into the second guest bedroom. We're set up for you, plastic sheets, towels, everything. Jim, take her there. I'll call the doctor and the midwife. Shawna, can you pick them up if it's necessary?"

Weeks later, Marti sat on the sofa in the living room, nursing Grace before her afternoon nap. As she held the baby up to her shoulder for a burp, her husband and Carl Worthing ambled into the room.

Grace let out a loud *blat* and the adults laughed. She looked around with her mild blue eyes, seeming to wonder why the big people thought she was so funny.

"I'll take her." Carl reached down. Kissing Grace's downy head, he tucked her in the crook of his arm as securely as he'd ever cradled a football. The NFL's biggest, baddest receiver carried the baby to the window and began to point out the sights to Grace. "Do you see the tree, honey?" he murmured. "Can you say 'tree'?"

Marti and Jim exchanged a smile. Jim sat down and kissed her forehead. "How are you feeling, sweetheart?"

She stretched her arms up above her head. "Pretty good, maybe a little restless."

"I know how to get some of that restlessness out," he said softly. "Still sore?"

She looked at her husband, whose cobalt eyes held a familiar lustful glint. He continued, "Any chance you'll welcome an ol' broken-down quarterback into your bed, pretty groupie?"

She grinned. "I don't know about playing quarterback and groupie, sweetie. Maybe something a little less strenuous, like knight and virgin. It'll be kinda like the first time for me."

"Me, too." He caressed her shoulder.

Shawna entered the room and made a beeline for her niece, joining Carl over by the window. Grace gurgled.

"I feel like I'm an appendage," Marti remarked. "Did you see how Shawna ignored me completely? Since I moved in here, I've gone from being Jim Wellman's wife to Gracie Wellman's mother. Where's Marti?"

He grinned at her. "Aw, come on. That's not really a problem for you. Smarty Marti can always handle everything."

"Excuse me?"

"That's what I used to call you." He smirked.

"Luckily for you, not to my face. Your massages would have been far less pleasant."

"I knew better than that."

"To me, you were the patient from hell. A controlling know-it-all, with that insidious charm—"

He grinned. "I haven't changed all that much, have I?"

"You've mellowed."

"Well, so have you. Parenthood will do that."

"Most first parents become more anxious, not less."

"Not Smarty Marti."

She narrowed her eyes at him. "I hope this smarty thing doesn't become a habit."

He kissed her again. "You're my habit, sweetheart. And you always will be."

About the Author

After surviving a brutal career as a trial attorney, Sue Swift turned her talents to writing novels and has sold six books in as many years. A best-selling, award-winning author, she and her husband shuttle between their homes in northern California and Maui, Hawaii. Her hobbies are ice hockey, kempo karate, and snorkeling.

Her Web site is located at http://www.sue-swift.com, and she can be contacted at sue@sue-swift.com or at P.O. Box 241, Citrus Heights, CA 95611-0241.